High Stakes

FREYA BARKER

High Stakes

ISBN: 9781988733746

Cover Design: Freya Barker
Editing: Karen Hrdlicka
Proofing: Joanne Thompson
Cover Image: Jean Woodfin—JW Photography
Cover Model: Theodore Brown

When her sister, Pippa, goes missing, Nella Freling tells her boss she's taking time off from her job as a research librarian, hops in her sensible van, and heads south of the border to Montana. However, local police don't seem too concerned about a missing woman living in her motorhome. So Nella will have to look for Pippa by herself, unless she can convince a highly recommended tracker to help her, but sadly the rude and angry cowboy won't even listen to her at first.

But Nella can be persuasive.

The first time High Mountain Tracker, Fletch Boone, laid eyes on Nella, her ass was stuck in his grocery cart. The next time was at the ranch; she was wearing mud, head to toe. But when he catches sight of her a third time, hanging off a cliff, he can't turn his back again. What Nella lacks in survival skills she makes up for in sheer determination. Unfortunately, neither of those is enough protection when bullets start flying.

Fletch has no choice but to jump in before the woman gets herself killed.

And that would be a damn shame.

One

NELLA

"How can I help you?"

The woman behind the desk has a friendly smile, but her eyes are cautious.

"I have a reservation. Antonella Freling."

I picked the Sandman Motel because I can park right in front of my unit, which I prefer.

"Ah, yes. I have you here. Four nights?"

"Yes."

"You requested the end unit with a kitchenette?"

"That's correct."

I'm not here to see the sights or waste money and time on eating out. Much cheaper and faster to pick up some groceries and fend for myself. I keep a small cooler in my van for drinks and something to eat in case I'm out all day.

She slides a form across the desk and I quickly fill it out before handing it back to her.

"I'll need a credit card, please."

I look around the small front office and shudder at the pictures of proud hunters with their prize kills. My dislike must've shown on my face.

"Not here for hunting, I gather?" she inquires, a little smirk on her face.

"No. Not a fan," I admit.

I'm the biggest hypocrite on two legs because I won't say no to a good steak from a poor anonymous cow, who never had a chance to start with, but I can't bring myself to try game meat from an animal at least able to live its life free. Somebody offers me venison and all I can envision is Bambi with those big brown eyes.

My meat comes shrink-wrapped in plastic so I can keep my emotional detachment. I tried a vegetarian lifestyle for a little over a year but found it a challenge living in a small mountain town in British Columbia, Canada. My first juicy burger after that episode was a purely orgasmic experience.

She smiles, a sparkle in her eyes. "We cater to a lot of hunters, but they won't be coming in until next week when the season opens. Until the fifteenth only bowhunting is allowed and there aren't that many of those. Mostly locals anyway."

I mock-wipe my brow and smile back as she hands me the key card.

"Unit twenty-three is yours."

"Thank you. Oh, where can I find the closest grocery store?"

"Just down the road. It'll be on your right-hand side as you get into town. Rosauers, you can't miss it. If you need anything else, my name is Martha."

"Thanks so much, Martha."

I'm almost out the door when I think of the more important question.

"The police station, is it easy to find?"

After shooting me a curious look, she gives me directions. The station is only a few minutes from the grocery store, so I'll head there first and pick up supplies after.

My unit is nothing special. A generic motel room with an art-by-numbers painting on the wall over two double beds, a dresser holding a TV, a functional—and thankfully clean—bathroom, and beside it a tiny kitchenette with microwave, hotplate, coffee maker, and a bar-size fridge. It'll do.

I spend twenty minutes putting my stuff away, toiletries lined up on the small vanity in the bathroom, some things in the dresser, and the rest of my clothes on hangers in the narrow closet. It does little to give the room more personality. I don't own much aside from work clothes and those are all rather drab in grays, blacks, and some muted tans. No color other than the single pair of jeans I own.

Hiding my light under a bushel, that's what Pippa always tells me. She's my opposite in every way: colorful, exuberant, and adventurous. I'm a strictly inside-the-lines person, while she breaks every conventional rule she can.

I went to the University of British Columbia studying library and information sciences, while she went to trade school to become a mechanic.

As different as we are—coming from the same nest—we've always been close. Especially after our parents died in a house fire eighteen years ago. We're all the other has, which is why I can't simply sit around and wait to hear something. I need to find her.

The Libby Police Station is a nondescript red brick building and I snag a parking spot when a vehicle backs out.

"Yes?" The not so friendly officer behind the desk looks at me like I'm here to confess a crime.

I automatically feel guilty, even though I'm pretty sure I haven't broken any rules in the past few decades.

"Is Officer Franklin available? I spoke with him on the phone the day before yesterday. My name is Antonella Freling."

"He's on patrol. What is it regarding?"

"I filed a missing person report on my sister, Fillippa Freling, with him."

He types the name into her computer.

"Right. I have it here. It says she drives a motorhome?"

"Yes."

"And you haven't heard from her since August twenty-sixth."

"Correct. I was hoping perhaps you'd found out something more?"

"Doesn't look like it. We'll continue to keep an eye out for the vehicle."

His tone is dismissive, much like Officer Franklin had been when I filed the report. I don't know why I thought a visit here would have a different result. Maybe a bit more urgency, but it doesn't look like that'll be the case.

I get it, my sister is a bit of a nomad, roaming the continent, often staying off the grid but she would always let me know where she'd be and for how long. Exactly what she did this time. Except she was coming home, she said she'd be there on Monday. Only two-and-a-half hours to get from Libby to Cranbrook, British Columbia, it's not like she had a long way to go.

I know my sister. If she had run into any trouble causing a delay, or even in the unlikely event something changed her mind about visiting, she would've let me know.

Unfortunately, my gut feeling Pippa is in trouble doesn't go very far with law enforcement. I can't really blame them, from what I understand quite a few people go missing in these mountains, exposed to the elements, so they're not going to waste resources on a woman who travels in her home. Not unless I have something more concrete to give them, which is why I'm here.

My boss wasn't happy with the short notice I'd be taking time off, but that can't be helped.

My bread and butter is research so I'm not entirely unprepared. I know what to look for, I have every camping app downloaded on my phone, and I have the name of someone who might be able to help me.

If only he'd call me back, I've already left a couple of messages. If I haven't heard anything by tomorrow, I'll chase him down.

I'll do what I have to do, to find Pippa.

Fletch

"Who the fuck do you think you are?"

I don't bother answering.

The punk is squirming, but I have my knee in the middle of his back with my full weight on it. I pull a few zip ties from my pack and strap his wrists together.

Then I sit him up, right next to the young bear he shot with his goddamn hunting rifle. I prop the rifle up against the bear as well. Next, I pull out my phone and take a bunch of pictures while the kid is swearing at me. Every time he tries to get up, I kick his feet back out from under him.

It's easy for me to tune him out, I've had lots of practice. My hearing has gotten very selective after years of living in virtual silence. The only thing that penetrated it was the rifle shot earlier. Startled me so bad I fucking dove right for the dirt. It took me a few seconds to register what I heard, then I was on my feet and aiming straight for the excited laughing I heard down the trail.

Fucking poachers. No more than kids. Unfortunately, the second guy took off running while I was taking this one to the ground.

It takes me half an hour to get the kid and the bear back down to the trailhead where my truck is the only one parked now. Catching my breath, I take my phone out. Only one bar, but enough to dial out.

"Sheriff's Office."

"Ewing, Fletch Boone here. I'm up by the Granite Ridge Trailhead parking lot. Got a dead bear with a bullet hole, the rifle that shot it, and the punk who fired it. Second kid got away. You wanna come pick this one up?"

Guess it was a slow day because less than half an hour later his cruiser rolls onto the parking lot, followed by a pickup. The kid loudly complains about his rights as Ewing hoists him to his feet and tucks him in the back of his vehicle. The deputy stepping from the pickup is already poking at the bear.

"Trust me, he's dead," I tell him dryly.

"Want it?" Ewing asks as he walks up.

He peeks in the back of my truck where I left my bow and the rest of my gear.

"Me? No. Still have plenty of bear from last season. Got a tag for a bighorn this year."

"Bighorn? No shit? Those are hard to come by."

"Especially for bowhunting," I add. "Tried every year for the past six and this is the first tag I got my hands on."

I only hunt with a bow.

Don't like guns. I may wear one, but I don't like it. It would have to be an extreme circumstance before I pull my weapon, let alone fire it. Instantly my mind goes back to the spring, when my boss had the barrel of a gun pressed to the back of his head. That counted as an extreme circumstance, but even knowing it would've been Jonas's life otherwise doesn't stop the sour burn in my gut. It was James who pulled the trigger, but we all carried that kill.

"It's a fresh kill, shouldn't be wasted," the sheriff points out before asking me, "Mind if I drop it off at Pete's?"

Pete owns a butcher shop and processes game for folks who don't like doing that dirty job or don't have room for it. Most hunters I know clean their own like I do.

"Have at it. And by the way, the second kid that got away? He's driving a rusted, blue Chevy pickup, my guess would be 1985 or thereabouts. Rear bumper is tied down with wire. Shouldn't be hard to find."

"Sounds like Willy Stubblefeld," the deputy suggests.

"Yeah. We'll go have a chat with Willy after I drop this other punk off. Don't know him, do you?"

"Never seen him," I answer.

It takes all three of us to hoist the bear in the back of the deputy's pickup.

"If there were any bighorns around, they're probably gone by now," Ewing observes. "May wanna check south of Cedar Creek. Talked to a guy the other day who spotted a couple of sheep up there."

"Thanks."

I've got a few other spots I want to try first, but if I'm running out of time, I know a couple of logging roads that'll get me close to that creek.

"See ya later, Boone, 'preciate the assistance."

I wait until they're driving off before packing up my

own gear, but the moment I get behind the wheel, my phone rings.

"Yup."

"Fletch, it's Ama. Are you anywhere near town?"

"I'll be driving through in about five minutes. Why?"

"Would you mind picking up some coffee? I would, but I'm in the middle of dinner prep and—"

"Sure," I cut her off.

I need to get some stuff myself anyway. I've been putting it off because I hate fucking grocery stores. Always too many people getting in my way. I like to go in, grab what I need, and get the hell out of there.

"Ah, you're a lifesaver. Thanks. No coffee in the morning would've made for a grumpy bunch tomorrow."

"True."

She's right about that. All of us count on that big pot she always has ready to get us going.

"You stopping by for lasagna?" she asks as I start the truck.

More often than not I eat at my own cabin, instead of at the house with the other guys. I don't mind my own company, I'm used to it, and I happen to enjoy cooking, which I know the others do not.

Having said that, Ama's lasagna is legendary and I have to drop off the coffee anyway. She usually has dinner ready at five, before she heads home, which means I'll still have the whole night to myself.

"You bet," I respond, knowing it'll please her. "See you soon."

Ama is not only the wife of my teammate, James, but the den mother, manager, and housekeeper, for the entire crew at High Meadow Ranch. Jonas Harvey—my boss—

owns it, but Ama runs it. She even tackles the office work for High Mountain Trackers.

Jonas Harvey was the commander of our special ops combat tracker unit. He was the first to be aged out and bought High Meadow ranch, building its name as a respected horse breeding facility. Then, one by one, he brought our former unit together to form High Mountain Trackers.

I was the last to join, running my own small tracking venture just outside of Fernie, British Columbia. I liked being on my own. My cabin in the mountains was secluded and I kept my interactions with other people to a minimum.

But Jonas had been relentless in his pursuit to find me and, finally, convince me. Not with promises of money—which wouldn't have meant much to me—but by offering me the only family I've ever known; my team.

A lot of our downtime is spent running the ranch, but these days we're hired more frequently to track down and rescue missing individuals. Some of them go missing accidentally, but in a few cases their disappearance had been intentional. A few months ago, we assisted law enforcement in tracking down a couple of escaped domestic terrorists responsible for a pair of deadly bomb blasts outside state buildings.

Over the summer we've had our share of missing hikers, not just around Libby, but all over Montana's northwest. I like the work, it's unpredictable, can be challenging, is mostly gratifying, and definitely feeds my craving for adventure. In addition to that, I get to take a couple of days off every fall during bowhunting season.

I grunt when I see the busy parking lot at the grocery store full.

Great.

For a second, I contemplate stopping at the smaller Libby Empire Foods, but Ama prefers the coffee at Rosauers. Besides, I'm pretty sure the parking lot at the other store won't be much better. It's Saturday afternoon, everybody is out and about.

I find a spot around the side of the building and manage to snag a cart on my way in the doors. Afraid I'm going to forget otherwise; I aim for the coffee first. The din inside the store grates on my nerves so I tune out, keeping my eyes focused on the shelf halfway down the aisle.

I don't even notice the woman hanging onto the shelves at first. Not until I accidentally brush my cart against her legs and she startles, landing with her ass in my cart.

"What the fuck?" slips out before I can check it.

Staring up at me are big eyes, that weird color some-where between brown and green.

"No need to swear," she says in a clipped tone as she struggles to get out of her precarious position. "Especially since it was you who knocked me off."

"I barely touched you and I wasn't the one climbing the damn shelves," I grumble.

This is why I avoid people.

The woman's lips press tightly together as I grab her under her arms in an attempt to dislodge her from my cart. There is some grunting involved before I can set her on her feet. Standing in front of me she barely makes it to my chin.

I size her up in two seconds flat. *Middle-aged spinster.* She has a few silver streaks in her hair, is wearing ill-fitting clothes and serviceable black shoes, and has a pair of glasses on a chain around her neck. In addition, the contents of the half-full basket on the floor are as drab as the woman in front of me.

"I had no choice, they're too high," she huffs, shaking

her shoulder-length waves from her face. "And my brand is up there."

She points at a single, red can of coffee sitting well back from the edge of the top shelf before smoothing her hands down the front of her plain, white blouse.

I reach up, grab the can, and drop it in the basket by her feet.

Without another word I move past her, tossing Ama's coffee in my cart as I aim for the produce section.

Fifteen minutes later when I push my cart out the doors, I just catch a glimpse of her behind the wheel of an older Dodge Caravan.

She's so close to the steering wheel, her nose almost touches the damn windshield.

Two

Nella

"I'm sorry. I don't recognize her."

The woman gives me an apologetic smile before returning to her computer.

I tuck Pippa's photo back in my purse. It's one of the last pictures she sent me a few weeks ago. A selfie in front of her rig with a beautiful mountain view behind her.

"Thank you for your time," I mumble, walking out the door.

This was the third RV park I've tried today without any luck. I figured if I could find the park she stayed at last, perhaps she spoke to someone there about where she was heading. She mentioned the name to me in our last conversation, but for the life of me all I can remember is the name had something to do with trees. So I've narrowed my list. This was the Paul Bunyan Campground.

I do recall her telling me she was off to boondock near Scenery Mountain for a few days before coming home, but that's a pretty vague concept considering the vast area that would include. Boondocking is just another term for dry-camping and means camping off the grid, which makes it harder when you're trying to find someone. It would be of great help if I could pin that down to a general area on the map, which is why I'd love to find someone she's spoken to recently.

Scratching another RV park of my list, I check my map for the next closest one. Libby Creek Campground. It doesn't sound like it has anything to do with trees, and from what I could glean online, it has dispersed, primitive camp-sites but Pippa would probably like that. It's only a mile or so down the road, I may as well check it out.

Ten minutes later, I'm pretty sure this wasn't the best idea. I had an inkling when a few hundred feet in I noticed the road turn into no more than a pair of muddy ruts. I should've turned around there, but instead decided I'd come this far, I may as well see it through.

Well...I'm not going anywhere soon. Not with my front wheels buried up to the rim in mud. I've tried to rock my way out of the giant pothole, but all I've done so far is spray mud everywhere. And of course there's no one in sight.

I feel like crying, but that's not going to get me out of this pickle, so instead I try to channel my sister to find a solution. What would Pippa do?

How ironic; I'm supposed to be looking for her—an experienced outdoors woman—when I don't even know how to deal with a little mud. Good intentions alone will get me nowhere and for the first time I'm starting to doubt my blind determination.

In the end it isn't so difficult after all. Once I stop feeling sorry for myself and start thinking, it doesn't take me too long to come up with a plan. Gathering a stack of branches approximately the same thickness, I line them up behind each of the front wheels. I hardly notice my clothes are now as covered in mud as the van is when I get behind the wheel.

Starting the engine, I put the vehicle in reverse and ease my foot off the brake, praying the wheels will grip onto the branches. The moment I feel the traction, I get a bit too excited when I hit the gas. I wince at the crunch as my rear light is taken out by the trunk of a tree, but at least I'm no longer stuck in the mud.

Unfortunately, I'm wasting too much time. Time my sister may not have.

The moment I feel the hard dirt under my wheels, I stop the van and pull out my phone. Time to call in the big guns. Or gun. I have the number saved.

"High Meadow Ranch."

The same friendly female voice answers again.

"Yes, hello. It's Antonella Freling and I'm terribly sorry to bother you again, but I really do need to speak to Fletcher Boone."

"He still hasn't called you back?"

"I'm afraid not."

"Well, I'm looking out the window at him right now. Why don't I go grab him? He's on his way out."

Rather than running the chance he'll dismiss my call again, I have a better idea. The ranch is only a couple of miles farther down the US-2, maybe I should drop in. He can hardly ignore me if I'm standing right in front of him.

"Actually, I'm not far. Is there any way you can keep him there for a few minutes?"

The woman on the other side chuckles.

"You bet. I'll make sure he sticks around."

I white-knuckle it all the way to the turnoff to the ranch, going as fast as the speed limit will allow.

The ranch is to the left of the drive, a rustic two-story building with a porch stretching the width of the house. On the other side is a fenced enclosure where I spot someone working a horse. Beyond it are two barns, one large one with its doors wide open, and a smaller one set farther back. Outside the enclosure two men in cowboy hats are leaning on the fence, their focus on the horse.

It's a beautiful animal, even as someone who avoids any animals taller than my knees, I can see that. Horses intimidate me, they always have, which is why I'm suddenly hesitant to get out of my vehicle.

Both cowboys turn their heads at once and my hand reaches for the gearshift, primed to back right out of here. I almost jump out of my skin when I hear a tap on the window beside my head.

A beautiful, dark-haired woman peeks in the window, smiling wide.

"Are you coming out or what?"

Oh dear, that doesn't make for a great first impression.

I quickly brush uselessly at the splatters of mud clinging to my shirt, before grabbing for my purse and opening the door.

"You must be Antonella," the woman says, holding out her hand. "My name is Ama."

"Pleased to meet you," I mumble politely as I shake her hand.

"You're persistent," Ama says with an easy grin. "I'll give you that."

Then she turns her head toward the small group. "Fletch! You've got a visitor."

I follow her line of sight and get a good look at the taller of the two men in the light-colored hat when he turns this way.

Oh, no. I should've left while I could.

Fletch

It can't be.

Yet apparently it is; the woman from the grocery store. Even without the van, I would've recognized her. Fuck if I know why.

I wouldn't recognize the barber in town I see every six weeks if I bumped into him on the street, so why is this unremarkable woman—after about two minutes of interaction, ever—so memorable? It's clear from the look on her face she remembers me too.

That fucking van looks like someone threw buckets of mud at it, and as I get closer, I notice she's covered in it too.

"What the hell are you doing here?"

Bo, the nosy bastard, starts chuckling right behind me.

"Way to charm the ladies, brother."

I ignore him and instead focus on the woman, who is pressing those generous lips into a thin line as I approach.

"Uh, Fletch?" Ama interrupts. "Remember those four messages I handed you? This is the woman who left them. Meet Antonella Freling."

Holy shit. She even has a name to fit the profile.

Bo ducks his head around me and holds out his hand.

"Name's Beauregard Rivera, ma'am."

"Fuck off, Bo."

She startles at my bark and immediately pulls her hand back.

"Can you try and be civil?" Ama scolds.

I grab the woman's elbow and march her a few steps away from those two.

"What do you want from me?"

I have to give it to her, she may have all the appearances of a doormat, but the way she twists her arm free and shoves her chin defiantly in the air shows fire.

"Absolutely nothing. You may be good at what you do, but I dare say you are the most unpleasant individual I've ever encountered. I've changed my mind."

With that she walks back to Ama.

"I'm terribly sorry I've wasted your time. I won't bother you again."

Then with a nod to Bo but ignoring me, she reaches for her door handle.

"That van is not the best vehicle to go off-roading in," Bo comments dryly.

She freezes for a second before swinging around to him.

"Thank you. That's good to know, but for your information, I got stuck in the mud while looking for my sister. She's missing. Your friend's contact information was given to me as someone who might be able to help, but my information was clearly incorrect. Like I said, I won't bother you again. Have a good day."

With that she turns back to her vehicle, yanks the door open, and slips behind the wheel. As she backs up to turn around, she darts a quick glance my way and I catch a suspicious shine in her eyes.

Her sister's missing? Well, *shit*.

"I swear, Fletcher Boone, if I didn't know under that foul mood of yours there's a good heart, I'd lay you out myself," Ama declares before stomping off to the house.

"Can't argue with her there, brother. That was pretty brutal, even for you."

Then Bo turns his back as well and returns to the corral, where Dan is working with one of the young horses.

Ignoring the niggle of guilt, I try to go about my day while staying out of everyone's way, but I keep seeing that woman's tearful eyes.

I may have been a bit of an asshole. Fine, a huge asshole. Already in a bad mood because, while I should've been up in the mountains trying to bag my bighorn, I'm here with Bo holding down the fort while the others are out on a job.

A fifteen-year-old never came home last night. The last place he was seen was at a party in a clearing off one of the hundreds of logging roads not far from the Kootenay River. A preferred spot for underage drinking, especially on the weekends. Wouldn't be the first time someone with a little too much alcohol in their system wandered off and got lost.

They rode out this morning, leaving Bo and me with the running of the ranch. Jonas's old man, Thomas, usually chips in, but he's not feeling well today.

We're busy, but thoughts of Antonella Freling eventually drive me inside where I find Ama in the kitchen.

"Sorry."

She turns when she hears my voice.

"Not me you should be apologizing to. I called Tiva—"

Ama's sister is an evidence technician with the Libby Police Department.

"—and she says a report was filed on Thursday for a Fillippa Freling, who was last heard of August twenty-sixth."

She recounts the details from the report but there isn't a whole lot to go on. A physical description, the license plate and make of the motorhome, and the last known conversation the missing woman had with her sister.

That still doesn't explain why Antonella came looking

for me, but I guess she would be the best person to explain that.

"Do you still have her number?"

Ama rolls her eyes at me and disappears into the office, coming back with her message pad. She points at the carbon copy left on the pad and I enter the number in my phone.

Then I walk outside and lean against the porch railing, hitting dial. Five rings and then the call goes to voicemail.

"You've reached Antonella Freling. Please leave a message and I'll return your call as soon as I can."

I fucking hate leaving messages so I hang up instead. I'll try again later.

Later comes when I'm back in my cabin after eating another meal at the big house. The team returned around dinnertime and after squaring away their horses for the night, Jonas waved me inside.

They'd found the kid wandering around in circles; dehydrated and confused. Stupid kids, drinking more than their bodies can handle. It doesn't take much to get alcohol poisoning, and without food and water to dilute the alcohol content in the blood, it can have serious, even life-threatening effects.

This kid was lucky, but we had a case a few years ago where a seventeen-year-old wasn't so fortunate. When we found him his heart rate was so low, we didn't think he was alive at first. That boy lived for two more months in a coma and hooked up to machines. What a waste.

I flick on a few lights when I walk in and drop down on my threadbare couch. It doesn't look like much but it's comfortable, molded to my ass over the years. Toeing off my boots, I lift my feet on the coffee table and pull out my phone.

Five rings and the same message, but this time when I hang up, my phone rings right away. It's her.

"Boone," I answer.

Dead silence on the other side.

"Antonella?"

Jesus, that name is a mouthful. Doesn't exactly roll off the tongue.

"Uhh…yes. I'm sorry I missed you earlier, I'm a bit surprised you called."

Heck, lady, so am I.

"Guess I'm curious to know how you got my name."

I wince, I should probably have led with an apology for being an asshole, but it's too late now.

"Of course," she responds primly. "Jeanine—a friend from my book club—suggested I contact you."

I wrack my brain trying to remember if I know anyone by that name, but I'm drawing a blank. Not a surprise, since I don't socialize much and I'd been with only a few women while in British Columbia. I have a hard time remembering what they even looked like, but I'm pretty damn sure they weren't in any book clubs.

"The name doesn't ring a bell."

"Oh, it's Jeanine Hicks, her husband is a park ranger. She mentioned you'd worked with him?"

"Yeah."

I have no trouble remembering Phil Hicks. I'd helped him out a few times locating missing campers. One of the very few people who knew how to find my remote cabin and possibly the closest I had to a friend while living up there. He'd even crashed there a couple of times when the late hour and inclement weather made it dangerous to return to the station.

A veteran, like me, he was someone I could be myself

around, much like my team here. Still, we'd lost touch six years ago when I moved here. Guess neither of us is the kind of person to check in from time to time, but it's good to know he hasn't forgotten me either.

"Well, if that's all," she says suddenly in a curt tone, jarring me back to the present. "It's been a long day."

Before I have a chance to say anything else, the line has gone dead. Goddammit, I never even got around to asking about her sister, she'd been too eager to get off the phone.

So be it.

I push the conversation from my mind, drop my phone on the coffee table, and pick up the remote for some news before I hit the sack.

Getting up early to try and bag me a bighorn tomorrow.

Three

NELLA

"Four hundred twenty-seven dollars and sixty-three cents, please."

I wince at the price tag as I pull out my credit card, and remind myself this is for Pippa.

It's not that I'm without means, but I have my share of the inheritance and a good chunk of savings tied up in investments. I'm simply used to living a frugal life on a precise budget. Which means no lavish vacations, fancy hotels, or reckless shopping.

However, as the friendly camper at the Timberlane Campground so kindly pointed out, I would need appropriate gear if I intended to head into the mountains.

Yesterday was wasted, hitting up another couple of RV resorts and campgrounds near town. Talking to a manager if I could find one, or otherwise any campers I came across. Pippa's picture I printed out was already getting grungy from all the different hands it passed through.

I'd connected with local police again, who didn't have anything new to report.

Then today I got the break I'd been hoping for. A nice lady the motel breakfast bar this morning mentioned the Timberlane Campground about half an hour north of town on Pipe Creek Road. She mentioned staying there with a trailer a few times when her husband was still alive. She's in town to visit a daughter who lives here, but opts for the motel these days.

I headed out right after breakfast and ended up spending a large chunk of the day there. Unfortunately, I had to wait until noon to speak to Chuck Yates, the manager, but he was extremely helpful.

Yes, Pippa had stayed here for three nights and left August twenty-sixth, however, Chuck wasn't sure where she was heading. He hadn't seen her leave, but pointed me in the direction of a trailer parked in the site across from her.

Betsy Waters had been in that same spot for the past three weeks and not only remembered my sister, but recalled a conversation they had around boondocking on Scenery Mountain. She helped me mark up my map with the possible dispersed camping spots she discussed with Pippa and offered to help me look.

Given that the woman is at least in her seventies and firmly in the claws of arthritis—judging by the misshapen joints in her hands—I thought it prudent to kindly decline. She did, however, point out I would need sturdier clothes to be clambering through the wilderness.

Hence my costly visit to the Libby Sports Center, where I was able to find everything from hiking boots to bear spray. I added in a sleeping bag, a blow-up air mattress, a small bottle-top propane burner, and the cheapest camping cookware I could find. This was after seeing a poster advertising van camping. Sure, the van in the picture was modified, but I'm sure I can make it work if I take out the back seat.

It's already past dinnertime and my stomach is rumbling when I lug my bags to the van and drive back to the motel. The plan had been to extend my reservation, but I figure I can save a bit of money and time if I simply camp up on the mountain.

The open sign is still on the office door so I stop out front and dart inside. Martha looks up from the computer.

"Checking out early?" she asks.

"I'm not leaving until tomorrow morning, but if I could settle up now, that would be wonderful."

"No problem." She pulls up my bill and prints it out. "Ready to head home?"

"Not quite yet," I tell her, realizing I never mentioned the reason for my visit to Libby. "My sister went missing. She was last seen in this area a week and a half ago."

Martha's face instantly shows concern.

"Oh dear, that's dreadful. I'm sorry, I had no idea. Did she live here?"

"No, just visiting. She was traveling in her motorhome and stopped here on her way home. She never made it."

"Oh dear," she mutters again. "And I've heard some horrible stories of women traveling alone."

I can feel the blood draining from my face. I've heard those stories as well but have managed to keep my mind from going in that direction. At least until now.

Martha clues in she may have said something insensitive and claps her hand over her mouth.

"I shouldn't have said that. I'm so sorry, that was terribly insensitive of me."

I force a smile. "Not to worry. In any event, I still have a few leads I'd like to follow up on."

"You're welcome to stay longer," she responds. "The room is available until this coming Saturday."

"I appreciate it, but I'm heading into the mountains and will be sleeping in my van. I just need to find a place to store the rear bench to make room."

Martha's face lights up, maybe eager to help because of her earlier faux pas.

"You're welcome to store it in my shed. My son keeps a few tools in there but other than that it's empty and dry. In fact, he can probably take it out for you. Those things can be heavy."

I've seen a friendly young man around, maybe early twenties, coming from the residence behind the office early in the morning.

"I wouldn't want to impose on you, or him," I quickly add.

"Nonsense. He's just finishing up dinner, let me get him now. That way you can leave at your leisure in the morning."

She wasn't going to take no for an answer and twenty minutes later my bench is safely stored in the shed on the side of the property, and Wyatt—Martha's son—is blowing up my air mattress with his compressor. A lot faster than filling it by mouth, which is what I'd intended to do.

Wyatt had kindly offered a bucket for my *nightly needs*, as he put it, and told me to grab any toilet paper rolls from my room. I hadn't even thought about that, and as it turned out, about a lot of other standard things. By the time I thanked Wyatt and bid him goodnight, I had another comprehensive list of things I might need. First thing tomorrow morning I'll have to make a few stops in town before heading up to Scenery Mountain.

By the time I have everything packed away in the van, it's after nine and I don't have energy left to cook. I wolf down a quick peanut butter sandwich before hopping in the shower. It may be a while before I have that luxury again.

Clean but exhausted I roll into bed, yet sleep doesn't come easy.

My mind is bouncing in all directions. Imagining horrible outcomes for my sister, second-guessing my plans to head out there without any experience, and an unreasonable anger toward the police and Fletcher Boone for not taking me seriously.

I'm not sure how, but it's clear I'll have to find Pippa myself. One way or another.

I had no idea how tough it would be going up some of these logging roads. Of course I'd learned my lesson getting stuck in the mud earlier in the week so at times I was going slower than molasses, but then I'd suddenly encounter a steep incline and would have to floor it to get up.

My nerves are getting a workout.

So far, I've found only two of the five spots Betsy Waters marked on my map. One was a narrow cutout along a creek with beautiful views, but it had been occupied by a young couple with two dogs and a tent trailer who had been in that spot for almost two weeks already. I showed them Pippa's picture, but neither of them recognized her or the camper.

No one was in the second spot on the map. A large open space at the end of the dirt road. I presume it was used to load and turn around logging trucks. There were still a few large logs lying beside a pile of gravel. A discarded bucket, a few empty water bottles, and an old oil drum were left behind as well.

I took my time there, looking around the clearing first for any signs of recent occupation before I decided to out my propane burner to boil some water for tea and had something easy for lunch. Then I stuffed a few things in my new pack, clipped my bear spray to my belt just in case, and explored some of the surrounding woods.

I found nothing. Not that that's saying a lot, I'll readily admit I'm not exactly qualified, but I have a healthy dose of common sense and I'm not stupid. Still, I wish I at least had a second pair of eyes.

Maybe I'll try Mr. Boone one more time.

But when I grab my phone, I notice I have no reception.

Wonderful.

Already the light is waning when I make my way up yet another logging road. I'm going to have to find a spot to park soon, because as nerve-wracking as it is to drive these narrow trails in the daytime, I don't even want to contemplate trying this in the dark.

From the satellite views I looked at over breakfast, there are a total of four clear-cut areas on this road. I've already passed two and hope to make my way to the farthest one today. But when I pass the third clearing on my right, I catch sight of something and stop the van to get a better look.

Standing on the running board I'm able to see over the roof. Grazing on the far side of the open space up against the tree line is a small herd of about a dozen bighorn sheep.

Not the first time I've seen them, we have plenty up in the Canadian Rockies as well, but the only time I encounter them there is when they venture close to civilization. Out here I'm on their turf, and suddenly the sight of them strikes me with awe.

I allow myself a moment to take them in before the fading sunlight pushes me on. But as I get back behind the wheel, I feel I have a bit more insight into what draws my sister to these remote locations.

I don't have to go far, maybe two minutes, before the trail comes to an end and the trees once again open up. About three or four feet of new growth covers most of the clearing here except for the rock shield right in front of me. Roughly the size of a tennis court, I imagine it was used as a staging area for loggers.

Disappointment has my stomach churning—no motorhome. But then I notice what looks like a firepit made with rocks and a small pile of firewood stacked by its side; my heart starts racing in my chest.

I drive over and get out of the van. The firepit holds ashes and a half-burned log. Someone was here recently and my gut tells me it was Pippa, but where is she now?

Dammit, Pippa, where the hell did you go?

Already the trees look dark and foreboding and I know it won't take long for the last strands of daylight to disappear. First order of business is to get a fire going. I've never built one before, but I've seen plenty of pictures.

It takes me half an hour, but I finally get it going. Sitting in the folding chair I had the foresight to buy, eating the canned chili I heated on my propane burner, and staring into the flames, I feel oddly accomplished. Pippa would be proud of me, stepping out of my comfort zone.

Thinking of her makes tears burn my eyes and forces my mind into a different direction. Unfortunately, it picks the dark, brooding man I spoke with a few nights ago. Guilt immediately follows because I didn't try hard enough for my sister, who always warned me pride would be my downfall.

It startled me when I realized it had been him trying to get a hold of me. I'd been disappointed when all he'd been interested in was who passed on his name. Maybe I should've begged for his help, but didn't want more disappointment so I ended the phone call before he could.

A rustling sound comes from my right and I snap my head around. The orange glow from the dwindling fire only serves to intensify the black shadows in the tree line beyond. A tendril of fear slithers down my spine as I strain to hear.

There. Another rustle.

Something is moving through the trees.

My hand moves to my belt for the bear spray, but comes up empty. I left it inside the van when I was opening the can of chili.

Shit.

The loud crack of a branch has me jump to my feet, and make a run for the van, my dinner still in my hand.

Fletch

"No luck?"

I glare as Sully walks toward me.

Today was a bust again.

I'd been tracking a small herd yesterday but lost daylight and this morning they were gone. When I moved to another spot on top of a ridge I spotted eight or nine rams feeding at the bottom, but they were mostly small. They took off before I could get close enough to really look them over.

I wasn't able to get anything large enough in my spotting scope to waste an arrow on. Don't like the idea of taking down a young one—they don't have enough meat on them yet—but at this rate, I may have to. It would really fucking suck if I didn't have anything to show for that prized tag.

"Thinking of taking up fishing," I grumble, drawing a chuckle from Sully who claps me on the shoulder.

"You've got a week left yet. You'll get one. Of course, you can always let me tag along. I could put the drone up and spot you a good ram from the air in no time."

"Fuck off," I growl.

Sully isn't in the least intimidated and laughs as he continues to his cottage, still limping some from an injury he sustained in the spring.

Bastard. He knows damn well I don't like cutting corners. You can also draw game to a spot by feeding them, or lob a damn grenade into a herd and call it a kill, but that's cheating. Only way I like to hunt is fair, one-on-one. Except, so far, the bighorn are getting the best of me.

Maybe tomorrow I'll check out the area Ewing mentioned the other day. South of Cedar Creek up on Scenery Mountain. I haven't been up there much—my usual hunting grounds are a bit farther north—but maybe it's time for a change.

I may know just the spot.

Four

"Did you ever get in touch with the woman?"

Fuck. Two minutes later and I would've been gone.

I turn to face Ama, who snuck up on me.

"I did. She blew me off."

It's not a complete lie, she was the one to hang up, but I hadn't really tried that hard. The truth is she's been on my mind and yesterday when I tried a few times to get in touch with her, I got bumped straight to voicemail.

Ama rolls her eyes.

"I saw Tiva last night. She says no one is actively looking for the sister. The general consensus is she changed her mind about going home and left the area."

"Who's to say that's not the case?" I note.

"Antonella Freling," Ama fires back. "And the fact her sister's voicemail appears to be full and no one answers. Tiva has been trying."

"We're in the mountains, she could be out of range."

It sounds weak, even to my own ears.

"An experienced camper going to the trouble of carrying a satellite phone with her?" Ama points out with a healthy dose of sarcasm.

And now neither of the sisters can be reached. Dammit.

I rub my face with my hands. She's never going to let it go.

"What do you want me to do?"

"Find Antonella. She has to be staying somewhere. Can't be too hard to find that van around town."

She's right. Don't think there are too many folks here driving a van. Mostly pickups or SUVs, something with a decent suspension and, more often than not, four-wheel drive.

"Fine. I'll have a look around town."

Ama looks way too pleased with herself as she heads for the main house.

I'll have a quick look around, see if I can spot her van parked at any of the hotels in town before I head up the mountain.

Forty-five minutes of my day wasted driving around six damn parking lots. I even tried calling her phone number a few times, but with the same result as yesterday.

I'm sitting in the parking lot of the last place, the Sandman Motel, trying to figure out my next move. Hotels won't give out personal information on their guests unless you're law enforcement, but Martha Crandall runs the Sandman. I know her son, Wyatt. He helped out at the ranch one summer a couple of years ago.

The small bell attached to the top of the door announces me. Martha is sitting behind her computer, but her face lights up when she sees me.

"I remember you. You're from the High Meadow Ranch."

I tip my hat. "Fletch Boone, ma'am."

"Well, what can I do for you, Mr. Boone?"

"I'm looking for Antonella Freling. I believe she may be staying here, but I don't see her van and she's not answering her phone."

I try for a smile. I'm a bit rusty, I don't use it much, but it seems to do the trick on Martha.

"She's probably out of range," she volunteers. "Left here yesterday, aiming to head up the mountain to look for her sister."

"And she didn't come back last night?"

"Wasn't supposed to. She was aiming to spend the night up there, save herself the time driving back and forth, I reckon. My boy, Wyatt, helped her get the van ready. She mentioned something about Scenery Mountain."

Five minutes later I hit the turnoff, cursing the stupid woman. It doesn't take a genius to figure out she has zero experience camping, or she wouldn't be driving that damn van or wearing those ridiculous shoes. Yet she heads out here entirely unprepared, putting herself in harm's way. Now we have two fucking women missing.

To add insult to injury, I spot a few bighorn on a ridge to my right as I make my way up the mountain.

Bighorn, but no van. Not in any of the clearings I've passed this far. There is a network of logging roads up here and she could've taken any one of these. I stop at a split in the dirt road, with one branch heading farther north, and the other directly west.

Getting out of the truck, I look for tire tracks. Most folks venturing up here would be driving a four-wheel-drive vehicle and the truck tires would have a wider, heavier tread.

The woman I'm looking for is driving a van not built for off-road travel and it shouldn't be too hard to find the fresher, narrower tread.

It takes me a couple of minutes to find the tracks heading west.

I shake my head when I think of her coming up this road with some pretty narrow drop-offs and steep inclines. The woman has more guts than sense. Apparently, she made it all the way up though, because I find her van on a rock plateau at the end of the trail and park behind her.

No sign of Antonella Freling though.

A camping chair is left by the firepit and I'm surprised to see some firewood stacked on the other side. I'm having a hard time envisioning the prim and proper woman wielding an axe. The ashes are warm, but not hot. She had a fire last night, but not this morning.

Peeking into the back of her van, I spot an air mattress, a sleeping bag neatly straightened, a cooler, a few jugs of water, and a propane burner. At least she isn't entirely unprepared.

I try the door, but the van is locked. My stomach clenches at the thought of her stumbling through the wilderness in her gray slacks and sensible shoes.

Christ.

I flip off my hat and scratch my head as I scan the clearing and the tree line. Where would she have gone?

My eyes are drawn to an opening in the trees on the far edge of the rock shield. It looks like there's a bit of a drop-off. When I start walking in that direction, I spot a splash of something on the ground. I crouch and rub my finger over it. Still damp. Then I sniff my finger. *Coffee.*

I straighten up and notice what appears to be another open area beyond the break in the trees. I can see part of a rock face reaching up. The early morning sun would've lit up that pale rock like a beacon.

I'm willing to bet she took her coffee to watch the sunrise.

~

Nella

I decided sometime last night after my heart started beating a normal rhythm again, my visitor was probably nothing more than one of those bighorns I'd seen earlier. Still not a creature I'd want to have a close encounter with in the dark, but honestly, a squirrel probably would've freaked me out.

I never finished my dinner before bone-deep fatigue knocked me out, so I woke up surprisingly well-rested but hungry as a horse. Cold chili is not something I'd recommend, but it served to tide me over until water for my coffee was boiling.

By the time I'm ready for a second cup, I'm hungry again and the sun is starting to peek over the horizon. I slap together a peanut butter and jam sandwich, wrap it in a napkin, and grab my travel mug.

I'm pretty sure no one is up here to steal my van, but I lock it anyway. Force of habit. Then I head toward the break in the trees I spotted, hoping for a pretty view to enjoy my second breakfast of the day.

The scenery is stunning. A narrow stream bisecting the shallow valley below and the rugged mountain side rising to an imposing peak on the far end. The sun hits my back—surprisingly warm this early—as I lower myself on the rocky outcropping and dangle my legs off the ledge.

I'll allow myself just a few minutes to finish my breakfast and appreciate the beauty surrounding me, before I figure out what my next move is.

My gut says my sister was here, but where is she now? I haven't really looked around the site, it got dark too fast last night, but I know I'll need more than a firepit to convince law enforcement to take me seriously. Especially with her motorhome nowhere in sight. Still, something tells me she camped right here.

I wish she was sitting beside me, nudging my shoulder and trying to get me to crack a smile. Goading me to loosen up a little. She always tells me I'm too serious for my own good.

Someone had to be. I was twenty-five when Mom and Dad died, recently graduated, and landed the job I still hold eighteen years later as a research librarian at the College of the Rockies in Cranbrook. Pippa had just turned twenty-two and took our parents death hard.

Already a bit of a wild child, she seemed to become even more of an unguided missile after. I was the only stability she had in her life and felt I couldn't afford to let down my guard, even for a minute. At least that's what I told myself all these years.

If I'm honest, I'd have to admit it was probably easier to use Pippa as an excuse for my predictable and limiting lifestyle, when in reality it was my fear of living. Maybe I was too scared to put myself out there. Too afraid to take any risks.

Wow.

Who would've thought sitting on a rock in the wilderness by your lonesome could give you a clearer perspective?

I take a sip of my coffee and silently promise myself that if—no, *when*—I find Pippa, I'll let her drag me on one of her adventures. I always thought I had all the answers, but I'm starting to wonder if perhaps my sister did.

The hair on the back of my neck suddenly stands up when I hear the snap of a branch in the trees behind me. I scramble to my feet, splash coffee over my hand, and drop my half-eaten sandwich in the process.

Swinging around, I watch in horror as a large bear breaks through the underbrush and lumbers onto the rock. Then he stops, rises on his hind legs, and snorts as he sticks his snout in the air.

Panicked, I wrack my brain to remember the rules I read up on for an encounter with a bear.

Don't run: That one's easy, I have nowhere to go.

Don't go up a tree: Even if I had a hope of accomplishing that, bears are supposed to be better climbers anyway.

Make yourself as big and noisy as possible: Now that I can do. Although I'm not sure how much my five foot four is going to impress him, even with my arms waving wildly over my head.

"Shoo! Go away! Go home!"

The bear seems more puzzled than anything else and drops down on all fours.

Please go away. Please, please, please turn around and go away.

Its massive head starts bobbing from side to side and somehow, I instinctively know that can't be good.

Bear spray!

I totally forgot about the can on my belt and scramble to get it free, only to have it slip from my coffee drenched hand. My heart sinks in my chest when I hear the distinct clang of the can hitting rock and rolling off the edge.

The noise seems to jar the big animal and suddenly he starts heading this way, picking up speed.

"Stop! Go away!" I scream at the top of my lungs when I take an inadvertent step back and feel the ground disappear from underneath my feet.

Next thing I know I'm going down, my hands fruitlessly trying to find purchase on the rock wall.

Five

FLETCH

"Shoo!"

Shoo?

I hear but can't see her. Taking a step to the edge of the cliff, where I spotted the discarded travel mug, I peer down. There she is, sitting on a narrow ledge about twenty feet down, her surprised face tilted up and those hazel eyes staring right back at me.

"You?"

"What the hell are you doing down there?"

Her lips instantly disappear into a pissed-off line.

"Contemplating the meaning of life," she snaps back before clarifying. "I didn't get down here voluntarily; I slipped."

I curse under my breath. I swear the woman is a walking disaster.

"Stay put," I bark at her before retracing my steps to the truck.

I grab the rappelling pack I keep stored in the cargo box in the truck bed and return to the ledge. It takes me five minutes to find a sturdy tree and loop my tied runner around it and double strand my rope through the anchor. Then I fasten the harness and clip the loops of rope to the carabiner attached.

If the tree and the rope can hold me, they'll be able to hold her as I hoist her up.

"Coming down," I yell before planting my feet on the edge and lean my body back, testing the anchor.

Easing one loop of the rope, I slowly lower myself, walking my feet down the face of the rock until I reach the ledge.

"How did you know I was here?"

I notice her face is pale and drawn, and there are tear tracks down her cheeks. Suddenly I feel a hint of remorse for barking at her again. I don't know why this woman annoys me so much.

"I'm a tracker. It's what I do." I unclip the harness and step out of it. "Good thing too since you seem to have gotten yourself in a bit of a pickle."

"The bear got me into this pickle," she returns defensively.

"Bear? Is that what you were shooing at?" I snort. "Shouldn't have been out here in the first place without some kind of protection."

"I had bear spray but..." She hesitates and points to the valley below. "I'm afraid it's down there somewhere. It slipped from my fingers."

I step in front of her and she presses her back even farther into the rock face.

"Need to get you into this harness and then I'm gonna

haul you up. When you get to the top, unclip it and send it back down."

She shakes her head and I mistake it for fear.

"Nothing's going to happen to you. The rope was sturdy enough to hold me, it'll be fine for you. I'll do all the work; all you have to do is hang there."

"I can't."

I pinch my eyes closed and blow out an exasperated breath.

"Why the hell not?"

"Because I think my sister is down there somewhere."

She points at a boulder sticking out from the ledge. I take a step in that direction and immediately spot the blood. More than a drop but less than a puddle. Enough to indicate some damage.

"That blood could've been from anything. Maybe an eagle used that boulder as a perch to eat his prey. Why would you think that's your sister's?"

"Because I found this down here too."

She holds up a satellite phone, its screen smashed to smithereens. Then she flips it around revealing the sticker of a red maple leaf on the protective case.

"I recognize it. It's hers," she says before I can even question it.

Fuck.

"Okay. I believe you, but if she is down there somewhere, where the hell is her motorhome? Don't you think it's more likely she made her way up somehow and took off? Maybe you're right, and the blood is hers. Could be she's confused, which is why she hasn't shown up or called."

It seems like a reasonable scenario to me, but it's obvious she's not buying it as she shakes her head.

"She's here..."

To my alarm I see her eyes well up. *Jesus*. I'm not equipped for this.

"First, let's get off this ledge," I quickly suggest. "Then we'll have a look around the campsite. See if we can find something helpful."

I watch as she swallows hard and nods in agreement. Relieved to see she has a grip on her emotions, I quickly help her into the harness.

My arms and shoulders are sore by the time I pull myself safely to the top of the cliff. She has her arms wrapped around herself and is darting glances into the trees.

"He's long gone," I reassure her.

"I think he was after my PB&J sandwich," she mumbles.

"Probably." I roll up my ropes and stuff them into the backpack. "Wanna tell me what you were doing out here?"

"Looking for my sister." I can almost hear the mental eye-roll in her tone.

"I get that," I tell her impatiently. "But any reason why up here specifically?"

"I spoke to a woman at the last campground my sister stayed at. Pippa had mentioned wanting to boondock for a few nights and this was one of the places the woman suggested to her. I could tell she'd at least been here. The firepit was used and she left a stack of wood," she insists. "The phone confirms it."

I could point out the firewood may well have been someone else—other campers, or even hunters—but she's right; the phone confirms her sister at least had been here at some point. But the blood was concerning.

Concerning enough, I know I can't turn my back again.

There goes my bighorn tag.

I toss my pack over my shoulder and start walking toward the vehicles, but I don't hear her follow. When I stop and turn around, she's standing in the same spot with her arms crossed over her chest and a stubborn expression on her face.

At least she's wearing something a little more appropriate today. Jeans, a long-sleeved T-shirt, and a pair of hiking boots that look like they're brand new. Her shoulder-length hair is up in a messy bun and she looks a little more approachable.

Except perhaps for that scowl on her face.

"Let's go."

She shakes her head. "I'm not leaving until I find Pippa. With or without you."

I squeeze the bridge of my nose trying to stave off the beginnings of a headache.

"We can have a look around *after* I put my gear away. I also wouldn't mind a coffee."

Maybe that'll give her something to do while I check out the site for tracks.

"Fine," she grumbles, bending down to pick up her travel mug before following me to the vehicles.

Nella

While I wait for water to boil, I watch as Fletch slowly walks the site, every so often crouching down to run his fingers over something on the ground. Each time he does, I want to ask if he's found something, but I hold back.

I can tell he's annoyed. Heck, irritated appears to be the predominant trait in his personality. Of course, in addition to foul-tempered, moody, rude, and all-around unpleasant. I spoon some ground coffee into the French press I picked up before I add boiling water. Best coffee ever. I'm going to use this thing at home from now on too.

About twenty feet from my van, I see him walk into the new growth and crouch down again. This time he appears to pick something up. Since the coffee has to sit for a few minutes anyway, I wander over to see what he found.

"Got something?"

He glances over his shoulder.

"Maybe. But don't jump to conclusions."

I gasp when I recognize the BC license plate he holds up.

"Lots of Canadians come through here every summer."

"That's Pippa's."

"We don't know that."

Fear morphs into anger. At him.

"Would you stop treating me like some idiot? I know my sister's license plate number by heart." I point a finger in his direction. "And that is it."

"*Fuck,*" I hear him mumble under his breath.

Then he walks to his truck, where he reaches in and pulls out a radio.

"Ama, come in..."

At first there's a lot of static and then I hear a woman respond.

"*Boone?*"

"Yup. No reception up here. Need you to contact Wayne Ewing, tell him to head up logging road 4426 and hang a left all the way up Scenery Mountain. He'll see a couple of vehicles; my truck is one of 'em. Tell him to bring forensics."

"*Sorry, what was that last thing? You're breaking up...*"

"Tell Ewing to bring forensics."

"*God, tell me you didn't find a body up there...*"

His eyes dart to me before he responds.

"No, but we found some signs that missing woman may have been up here."

"*We?*"

I watch as he rolls his eyes before darting a look my way.

"Nella Freling is with me."

One of my eyebrows pulls up when he calls me Nella. My sister calls me Nella, but no one else.

"*You finally got a hold of her. Glad to know you pulled your head outta your—*"

"Right," he quickly interrupts her but I'm already grinning.

I really like that woman.

"Also, see if Sully can bring the bird up here."

"*Will do. That it?*"

"For now. Boone out."

"*Over and out.*"

"For the record," I start when he tosses the radio back in the truck. "My name is Antonella."

"Too long to remember. Nella works. Do you remember if she had front and back plates on the motorhome?" he abruptly changes direction.

"She would've. I'm positive."

"Be willing to bet there's another plate around here somewhere." Then he reaches back in the truck and comes out with a travel mug. "Fuel first," he says, jutting it at me.

There is so much I would like to say, but I'm afraid he'll just turn around, get in his truck, and drive back down the mountain. If my sister is wandering out there somewhere, I'm going to need him.

Each armed with a mug, we head out in opposite directions. I mimic him, staying within ten feet of the edge of the site. I may not be a tracker but I can recognize a license plate.

"Why do you think there'll be another one?" I call out.

"Heard of a couple of RV thefts recently. Someone took your sister's motorhome; I can see them switching out the plates before taking it on the road." He points at a spot in the thin layer of dust on the rock shield. "Aside from your van's tracks, those of my truck, and what I figure are those from the motorhome, I found a fourth set."

I'm trying to imagine what might've happened and I don't like the scenarios playing out in my head. In all of them my sister faces off with the thieves and none of them turn out well for her. It only makes me more convinced she's out here somewhere.

The sheriff's cruiser arrives fifteen minutes later, a second unmarked SUV behind him.

"Fucking hell, Boone. Quit calling me up on these damn dirt roads. We don't have enough budget to replace any vehicles."

"Ewing, meet Antonella Freling."

Guess he can remember my name after all. I push irritation away and shake hands with the sheriff.

"You've got a sister missing from these parts," he acknowledges.

"Yes. I'm surprised you know. No one seems to take me very seriously."

"Oh, I heard. Sheriff's Office has been keeping an eye out. Truth is, this is a big county, ma'am. We've got lots of ground to cover. Can't send search parties out when we don't know where she went missing from."

"We do now," I tell him. "She went missing right here."

Fletch drops the license plate on the hood of his cruiser.

"Don't touch," he warns the sheriff when he reaches for it. "Right now it only has my prints and those of whoever took it off the motorhome."

"Maybe it fell off? Caught on a branch?"

God, what is in the water here? Are all these people so stubborn they can't see what's right in front of them?

I reach in my pocket and pull out Pippa's satellite phone and lay it beside the license plate on the hood.

"I found that on a ridge back there." I crook my thumb over my shoulder. "Twenty feet down a cliff on a ledge about three feet wide. Found blood there too."

"Well, shit," he mumbles before turning around to a guy waiting beside the second SUV. "Hey, Cohen! Bring your kit!"

Twenty minutes later I'm standing beside the sheriff on the edge of the cliff looking down. Fletch is on the ledge with Cohen, who is testing the blood.

I feel like I'm going to be sick, but I shove it down.

"Human!" Cohen calls up.

I'm not surprised but it's still a shock to have it confirmed.

"Son of a bitch," the sheriff mumbles before turning to me. "Pardon my French."

"Will you look for her now?"

"We'd need to get a search party together. Set up a command post. It's gonna take some time."

I could scream I'm so frustrated, instead I turn around and head for the van and my backpack and water bottle. I'm not going to waste another minute waiting, and I don't care what either of these guys have to say.

Six

FLETCH

"What've we got?" Sully asks the moment he gets out of the truck.

"Missing woman. Could be injured, we found blood on a ledge twenty feet below the cliff."

I follow him around the vehicle where he lowers the gate to get his crazy-expensive drone. The thing is outfitted with rotating cameras for a three-hundred-and-sixty-degree view and a night-vision setting. It's the newest tracking tool we have in our arsenal and has already proved its worth a few times over.

I called the boss right after Sheriff Ewing announced a search party, and Jonas suggested he and Bo load up the horses and head this way to help.

"This the sister of that woman you've been dodging?" He wants to know as we lift the drone from the truck.

Fucking Ama and her big mouth. Love the woman, but she's like the annoying little sister at times. Living in a cabin on the ranch comes with perks but the downside is zero privacy. Should've gotten a place somewhere else like Bo did. Of course then I wouldn't have the convenience of walking to work, having a large pot of coffee or an occasional meal waiting in the big house, or always having family close by.

"It is. Found her license plates."

The sheriff actually found the second one in the trees near the cliff earlier.

"No shit?" Sully says, looking up. "You think her vehicle's stolen?"

"Wouldn't be the first one. Ewing mentioned there were five more thefts in the county this past month."

"Any violence?" He wants to know.

I know where his mind is going. Mine went there too.

"Not according to the sheriff, but that doesn't mean it couldn't have escalated to that. Who knows? She may have caught them in the act," I suggest.

"Maybe, or she fell, hit her head and when these guys happened upon the abandoned motorhome they seized the opportunity," Sully shares an alternate take.

"Possible, but that would mean she's been somewhere at the bottom of the drop and I haven't seen a single vulture around. In fact..." I remember the incident this morning I was told about earlier. "Nella had an encounter with a bear this morning who was after her sandwich."

Bears are opportunistic eaters, especially in the late summer and fall when they start fattening up for the winter. If there was a dead body nearby, this bear wouldn't have wasted his time on a piece of bread.

"Is she okay?"

"Yeah, she's fine."

He looks around. "Where is she?"

I follow his gaze. No sign of her by the van, where I

watched her stomp off to earlier, or anywhere else on the site.

"She must've gone down to the cliff with Ewing."

Even as I'm suggesting it, I realize the sheriff is sitting behind the wheel of his cruiser making phone calls. The forensics tech is taking pictures of some tire tracks not far from where I found the first license plate. There is no sign of Nella.

"Fuck."

"What?" Sully wants to know as I rush to my truck to grab my pack and rifle.

"Damn woman took off," I grumble. I hoist my pack on my back, clip my water flask to my hip, and sling the rifle over my shoulder. "She's gonna get herself killed."

Good thing I'm always prepared. I could wait for the rest of the team, but they won't be able to get the big trailer up here so will be picking a staging area at a lower elevation and ride in. That could take a while and I hate to think the kind of trouble she could get herself into in the meantime.

"Here!" Sully calls out, tossing me a walkie-talkie as I walk to the sheriff's cruiser. "I'll get the bird up and see if I can spot her."

With only my cell phone, which is useless out here, and the radio in my truck, I'm grateful for his foresight to bring these. We use the IC-SAT 100 when we're out in the field. It runs over a global satellite network and has a long battery life, although I hope I won't need it.

She can't be that far ahead.

I knock on the driver's side window.

"The sister, where did she go?"

Ewing startles, looking around the site.

"I thought she was with Cohen." He sticks his head out of the window. "Hey! Cohen! Where'd the woman go?"

The tech waves his hand toward the cliff and I start walking in that direction.

"How long?" I call out to him.

"Fifteen. Maybe twenty?" he yells back.

Good, it won't take me long to catch up.

The cliff is facing west, sloping up to the north, and down on the south side. She's heading down, trying to get to the valley below so I head south.

It isn't hard to follow her tracks, but the course she set is pretty steep and it looks like she slid in a few places. She's taken the most direct way to the valley below instead of the safest, and my annoyance with her grows. The woman is likely to get hurt at this rate and then I'm gonna have to haul her back up.

I try to listen for sounds of movement but I can't hear any. The trees get denser the farther down I go and I find myself holding onto the occasional tree trunk to stay on my feet.

"Pippa!"

I zoom in on the yell, which comes from below and to my right. Sounds like she managed to build up a lot more distance than I expected.

Following the direction of her voice, I make my way down the slope. Above me I can hear the high-pitched buzz of Sully's drone, but I'm not sure how much he'll be able to make out. The trees are dense and the canopy is pretty thick. Unless my team finds another way down, the horses will never be able to get down here.

Even if her sister is still miraculously alive somewhere, she's been exposed to the elements for over a week and won't be in good physical shape. We may have a hell of a time getting her out of here. Unless there's a break in the trees somewhere a helicopter could drop a basket, we'll likely have to carry her. The last thing we need is someone else hurt or incapacitated.

"Nella!" I holler. "Stay put, I'm coming to you."

I don't get a response at first and am about to yell again when I hear her call out, "Okay."

She's sitting on a rock at the bottom of the cliff, looking up through the trees. Her shoulders are slumped and her face pale.

"Are you trying to get killed?" I snap.

Then she turns her head to face me, and I catch the look of utter devastation in her eyes.

"She's not here."

My anger dissipates instantly, replaced by a wave of empathy for her. If the scenario played out as we suspect it may have, chances are slim her sister survived and I think Nella knows it. She's determined to find her sister, dead or alive.

"Let me have a look," I say, suddenly eager to give her even a small thread of hope.

Nella

After he radios someone to tell them he found me, he walks along the bottom of the cliff, alternately looking at the ground and up at the tree canopy.

I'm not sure what he's hoping to find, but then again, neither was I when I went blundering down the mountainside. It's only when I reached the bottom and couldn't see any sign of Pippa that it occurs to me, I was half expecting to find her body.

Assuming she went missing not long after her final phone call to me, she'll have been gone for two weeks tomorrow. Even if she simply wandered off, I highly doubt she'd have been able to survive two weeks out here on her own. Besides, she would've found a way to contact me.

Guilt overwhelms me. When she didn't show up on Monday, I should've left for Montana right away instead of waiting a couple of days to report her missing, and another few before deciding to look for her myself. I should've gotten in my van right away and come looking.

"Don't."

I look up to find Fletch standing in front of me, a stern look on his face.

"I know what you're thinking and it won't do you, or her, any good to let guilt paralyze you."

"How would you know?" I snap, irritated he seems to read me so easily.

He shrugs but his eyes get this faraway quality, like he's here but his mind is focused on something only he can see.

"You'll just have to trust I do."

Yeah, I have a sneaky suspicion maybe Fletcher Boone carries some guilt of his own. He surprises me when he holds out his hand.

"Come on. I have something to show you."

Reluctantly I allow him to pull me to my feet. He immediately releases me, and I follow him to the base of a large *Pinus albicaulis*, also called white bark or creeping pine. These pines don't tend to get nearly as tall as the fir or spruce since they're more frequently found at higher elevations, but this is a decent size.

The only reason I know a little about this is because one of the environmental science students at my college was doing a paper for her ecology course on the endangered tree and asked for help with research.

"What am I looking at?" I ask him.

He points up. "See those three branches?"

"I can see they're snapped," I comment.

"Yes. All on the side of the rock wall, and one below the other."

Then he points at some scrapes on the bark on the trunk of the tree right below the lowest branch.

"See these marks? I think those branches may have broken someone's fall, and they were able to climb down."

"Couldn't that have just been an animal? How would you know it's a person?"

Despite my hope sparking, I'm purposely being cautious. Hope can be painful.

"Because of these."

Now he crouches down and points at something on the ground. I'm not sure what he's looking at so I lower myself beside him. When he traces it with his finger, I can see the outline of a footprint.

"It's a hiking boot. My guess size seven men's, or a women's eight and a half."

That spark turns into a flame.

"Pippa is an eight and a half." If those are my sister's footprints, it means she was alive and walking. "Are there others?"

I immediately start looking around to see if I can find more of them. Fletch points out a partial one a few feet away. Then a third set of footprints, made by the same boots. It looks like they head farther into the valley.

"Where are you going?" he asks me when I start walking in that direction.

"Looking."

"Look, I know it looks like it might be her but we still can't be sure. Can you give me a second to at least report what we found?"

But I don't stop. Shaking my earlier doubts off, I feel resolve return.

I can hear him curse under his breath behind me before he calls someone named Sully on the walkie-talkie. His voice is clipped as he relays information, but I'm not really listening. My eyes are focused ahead.

I scan the ground in front of my feet for prints and the trees for any signs of disturbance. Broken branches, snapped twigs, a lock of hair, something—anything—to indicate my sister was here. I hear the crunch of boots behind me, telling me Fletch is catching up.

But by the time I feel a heavy hand fall on my shoulder, I have the proof in front of me.

"Hold up," he says. "Let me do my job. You could be heading in a totally wrong direction."

"I don't think so," I comment.

Then I turn around and point out the white piece of linen tied to a low pine branch.

"What's this?"

"Handkerchief."

"Didn't realize people still carried those," he observes.

I fish in my jeans pocket, pull an identical one out, and show him.

"I bet you you'll find the initials CMS embroidered."

I can see he's not yet a believer but he will be. He takes a closer look at the handkerchief before eying me suspiciously. I hold up my own so he can see the matching letters.

"What does it stand for?"

"My mom. Every Christmas my dad ordered a bunch of handkerchiefs for her. She always had a clean one on hand.

When she died she had close to fifty. My sister and I split them and now carry one of them every day." I look at him and see that his lukewarm interest in my sister's case has heated up a little. "Mom's name was Carmella Maria Scavo."

He drops his head, grabbing the back of his neck with his hand.

"Okay," he starts. "Here's the deal. I'll look for your sister if you head back up. It can be dangerous out here, there's no way to know what we're going to run into, and frankly, you don't know what the hell you're doing. You'll just be another liability."

Don't ask me how, but I get the sense his grumpy attitude is a front. He's hiding concern. Still, communication is clearly not part of his skill set. Not that any of it matters, because there's no way I'm turning back now.

"My sister needs me," I state firmly.

Then I turn on my heel and resume my search, hearing him mumble behind me. I only catch the last few words.

"*...giant pain in my ass.*"

Seven

FLETCH

The monogram isn't the only thing that stands out on the piece of linen. A bloody smear is visible on the knot used to tie it to the branch.

Why is it there in the first place?

People leave markers either so someone else can track them, or so they can retrace their own steps. The woman has been missing for almost two weeks. The last time someone spoke to her or saw her was on August twenty-sixth, thirteen days ago. However, it looks like she may have spent at least one night at the campsite.

Two weeks, that's a long time to be out here. She may be an experienced camper in her motorhome, but it's a different ballgame when it's just you and the elements. I have a feeling if we find her, it won't be alive.

Glancing up, I just catch a glimpse of Nella before she disappears from sight. The woman has more guts than sense.

"Sully."

The radio crackles to life.

"I'm here."

"Tell Sheriff Ewing we've found the missing woman's hanky. Tied to a pine branch about thirty feet from the base of the cliff. He'll want to send his forensics guy down here. I'm going after Nella."

"Will do. Also, I just flew the drone over the creek. Didn't see anything but she may have gone for water. It's not that far from where you are, about three-quarters of a mile northeast."

That's the general direction Nella took off in, so I quickly sign off and go after her.

She's not hard to find, I can easily hear her blundering through the underbrush ahead of me. Unfortunately, she's heading in the opposite direction of where Sully indicated the creek to be.

She doesn't even hear me when I catch up to her and startles when I put a hand on her shoulder.

"Hold up."

"I told you, I'm not waiting for a search party," she snaps.

The temptation is strong to react to her sharp tone but I force myself to take a calming breath. *I swear,* this woman pushes every button.

"There's a creek that way." I point behind me. "She'd have needed water to survive."

I can tell Nella is processing my words, her eyes drifting over my shoulder.

"A creek?"

"Yup."

I turn and start moving in the direction Sully indicated, hearing Nella fall into step behind me. My eyes are peeled for signs of anyone coming through here recently. Any tracks; broken branches, trampled underbrush, anything that might look out of place, but nothing stands out.

I wish James were here with his sharp eye and keen nose. He's the team's proverbial bloodhound, but I'm afraid we'd have trouble getting the horses through this dense forest. They would have to come in along the creek to be able to access this valley.

Nella seems to keep up, but by the time the trees start thinning out as we get closer to the creek, her breathing sounds labored.

"You okay?" I ask her over my shoulder.

"Fine," she pants, clearly struggling.

"We're getting close," I attempt to encourage her.

Unfortunately, the sun is already lower in the sky and pretty soon dusk will be setting in. We're going to have to decide soon whether to camp out here or head back to the vehicles. I'm a little concerned the trek back will be too much for her. It's one thing walking a couple of miles on level ground, but another altogether on this terrain. We'll also need some sustenance at some point and other than a few carefully wrapped protein bars in my pack I'm not carrying any food, and I doubt she is.

The creek is surprisingly swollen, it must've rained up here recently. That's the thing about living in the mountains, you can have fair weather in the valley and rain or snow up here, or vice versa. I know we haven't had much more than an occasional shower at the ranch these past few weeks, it's been more like an extended summer. Up here you can already feel a distinct chill in the air.

If there was any bank on the other side of the creek before, it's gone now. The mountain peak rises straight up from the water. Unless Nella's sister is a mountain goat, I seriously doubt she would've made her way up there. The more likely scenario—provided she's still alive—is that she headed downstream along the creek. It's what I would've done.

Any moderately experienced hiker knows that water follows the most direct route down the mountain.

From the corner of my eye, I notice Nella take a seat on a boulder and bend forward. I walk over and pull my flask of water from my pack.

"Have a drink," I instruct her, handing over the bottle.

Her eyes catch mine for a second before she puts the water to her mouth and takes a swig. I try not to look at her lush lips wrapping around the top of the bottle, but it's no use. When she's pissed her lips form a tight prissy line, but her mouth is a thing of beauty when relaxed. Every naughty librarian fantasy I've ever dreamed up comes flooding back.

"What do you do for a living?" I blurt out against better judgment.

I should leave well enough alone, but I remember her mentioning a book club and am suddenly hoping she's a dental hygienist or something equally unsexy.

She looks at me a little confused.

"I work at The College of the Rockies in Cranbrook. I'm a research librarian."

Of course she fucking is.

Giving myself a mental kick in the ass, I take the bottle she holds out to me and take a deep drink, only to remember her lips were just there.

In an effort to get my mind back on track, I start walking away from her toward the water, my eyes on the ground. The creek bank is mostly stone. It'll be tough getting any tracks, but if she came this way, she may have left something else behind.

Overhead I hear the high whine of Sully's drone passing just moments before the radio crackles.

"Heads up; you've got bad weather incoming. Heavy downpour on the other side of the peak."

My eyes dart up and I can just see the ridge of a dark, heavy cloud cover slide over the ridge.

Damn.

~

Nella

My clothes are plastered to my body by the time we reach the overhang Fletch pointed out. He barely got the warning out when the sky suddenly turned dark and rain started pouring.

I'm not usually afraid of a little rain, but this is ridiculous. It's like someone emptied a bathtub on us and it's still going.

"Stay here," Fletch orders me before ducking out in the downpour again.

The overhang offers some protection thanks to the large boulder blocking one side of it, preventing the rain from coming in. It's suddenly so dark, I have trouble seeing any farther than a few feet in front of me. All I see is water, either coming down or rushing by.

Fletch had guided me over a few large rocks to get across the creek to shelter. If he hadn't grabbed hold of me I'd have ended up in the drink, not that it would've made much of a difference since I'm soaked anyway.

As I try to catch a glimpse of Fletch, who disappeared into the darkness, a bolt of lightning suddenly brightens the sky and the landscape around me. It's followed closely by a heavy rumble I can feel in my bones, and I duck a little deeper under the overhang, pressing my back to the rock wall.

I hate thunderstorms. Have since a lightning strike hit our family home, causing the fire that killed my parents. Where before I thought storms were cozy, nowadays I get nervous and restless. This one is a doozy.

Squinting, I try and catch sight of Fletch, who is out there somewhere, every time the sky lights up. It's impossible to hear anything over the deep booms of thunder and relentless pounding of the rain. Is it my imagination or is the creek water flowing faster? It's definitely higher; reaching farther up the slab of rock I'm standing on.

What is probably just minutes feels like a really long time and panic is starting to set in. How much higher will it get? And where is Fletch?

Cold is starting to seep into my bones and I shove my hands in my pockets, encountering the familiar shape of my phone. I pull it out, worried it may have gotten soaked. Not that it would make much difference, I haven't been able to get a signal up on the ridge, I'm pretty sure I won't get one here. It's still alive, but sure enough, I have no bars. But what I do have is the built-in flashlight. I turn it on and aim my phone at the now raging water washing up on the ledge and getting closer to my feet.

Shit.

Already backed up to the rock wall, I inch my way closer to the boulder, wedging myself in the corner.

"Fletch!" I yell, panicked, as I use my phone to light up the other side of the creek.

Where the hell did he go?

A blinding flash is followed by a loud crack sounding

way too close for comfort. To my horror I watch as a large pine on the other side of the water starts falling in my direction, and I'm literally stuck between a rock and a hard place. I have nowhere to go.

Squeezing my eyes closed, I turn and press my face against the cold rock. The impact of the tree shakes the ground beneath my feet and when I peek over my shoulder, I'm confronted with a tangle of branches just inches from my face.

I'm trapped.

That water is going to come higher and I won't be able to get away.

My chest feels tight and my heart is racing. Each breath is more labored as I have trouble pulling in enough air. Little dots of light swim in front of my eyes and blood roars in my ears.

"Nella!"

The sound of my name is little more than a whisper and I'm afraid I've imagined it. Relief should flood me, but instead panic grabs a firmer hold. My knees buckle underneath me and my back slides down the rock until my ass hits the ground.

I'm so stupid, I should've listened. There's no one else to blame, I'm going to die here and there will be no one left to look for my sister.

Pippa.

The pain in my chest is overwhelming and I welcome the darkness pulling me in.

"...breathe with me. You're okay. In and out. Come on, Nella."

Cold, wet hands lift my face and I blink a few times. Fletch's dark brown eyes are just inches away, scrutinizing me with concern. Water is dripping down the salt-and-pepper lock of hair plastered to his forehead.

"Talk to me."

"I'm okay," I rasp.

"Good," Fletch says, grabbing my hands.

Then he gets to his feet, pulling me up with him. Over his shoulder, I catch sight of the tree which appears to have quite a few branches missing.

"How did you—"

"My KA-BAR knife. Always have it on me." He turns and pulls me to the gap he's created.

"Wait, what are you doing?"

I dig my heels in. The storm is still raging and as much as the close confines under this overhang scare me, going out in that weather terrifies me even more.

"I went out to find us a better shelter. The weather doesn't look like it'll let up any time soon. We need to get out of here."

"What do you mean we need to get out of here? Where are we gonna go?"

"Higher ground. There are crevices and caves all over the mountain. One that looks large enough just above us."

How on earth does he propose we get up there? Even if it wasn't storming outside, trying to get up that nearly sheer wall of rock would be madness.

"I can't."

I shake my head and pull my hand from his.

"We have no choice. At this rate we'll be knee-deep in water soon. Logs and debris are starting to come down in the creek and you could get knocked down and washed away."

Well, I definitely don't want to get swept off by the water, but I'm also not so sure if I'm ready to put my life in

Fletch's hands. He's not waiting for an answer though, and takes my hand again to pull me to his front.

"Up you go," he announces before grabbing me around the waist and lifting me up.

The last person to pick me up was my father when I was around twelve, which is why I'm so shocked, I can't get out a single word of protest. I'm a solid one seventy-five and this man lifts me right off my feet like it's nothing.

"Grab onto that fat branch above you," he instructs me.

I look up, blinking against the sheet of rain, and notice the branch he's talking about resting on the overhang above us.

"I'm right behind you," he says when I hesitate. "You pull up and I'll give you a shove. Grab it as high as you can and swing a leg over."

I almost laugh out loud at his suggestion.

"It won't hold."

"Yes, it will. Trust me."

"You can't seriously think I can climb up there."

I try to look behind me but only see part of the top of his head.

"Now, you're fucking giving up? Give me a break. You're the single-most stubborn woman I've ever met. Didn't take you for a quitter."

His tone is derisive and it burns because he's right. I'm not a quitter, at least not when it comes to my sister. Apparently, I lack the same drive when my own ass is on the line.

Motivated by embarrassment, I reach high and grab hold of the thick branch. Then, painfully aware of my less-than-athletic abilities, I attempt to swing a leg over the branch. Fletch's hands spread wide under my ass, shoving me higher. After a bit of a struggle, I manage to get upright, straddling the thick limb.

"Atta girl," he mumbles below me. The compliment wraps around me like a warm cloak. "Now shimmy up to the ledge. I'm right here."

I glance down at his upturned face, his dark eyes calm and reassuring. Oddly enough, I trust him. He won't let me fall. Then I look up to find the next hold for my hands and ungracefully make my way up the branch. By the time I reach the ledge, determination has taken the place of the sheer panic I felt earlier.

When I turn and look down, Fletch is already halfway up the branch, making it look shamefully easy.

Eight

Fletch

My plan had been to grab whatever dry wood I could find so we could get a fire going. It gets cold at night up here, especially when you're soaking wet. Unfortunately, that wood has probably washed down the creek by now.

I'd just been making my way across when I heard the crack and barely managed to jump out of the way when this damn tree came down. For a few minutes there my heart stopped until I was able to reach Nella. I was worried I'd find her crushed underneath.

Couldn't have handled another death on my conscience.

Another loud rumble of thunder outside has the woman across from me scuttle farther away from the opening. It's quite the storm and, so far, doesn't show signs of letting up. The crevice we've found shelter in isn't that big —probably not even enough room for me to stretch out in —but at least it's dry.

"Not a fan of thunderstorms?"

I barely see the shine of her eyes as she turns them to me.

"No," she confirms in a shaky voice.

"We're safe here," I assure her. "We just need to wait it out."

Which reminds me, I'd better let Sully know where we are.

"Sully, you there?"

"*...Affirma...*"

The weather is messing with the radio signal.

"We found shelter, west side of the creek. Do you have an update on the weather? Over."

"*Repeat.*"

I do as he asks, hoping enough of my message gets through.

"*...storms coming...north. Sh...early morning.*"

Fuck. Sounds like we'll be stuck here until daylight.

"Roger. Out."

I slip the radio back on my belt and unclip my backpack, pulling it in front of me. I want to take stock of our supplies, I'm sure the night will be a long one. First thing I grab is my flashlight, which I turn on before putting it down. Then, one by one, I empty the rest of my pack on the ground in front of me.

Water flask, three protein bars, a length of rope, my multi-purpose tool, first aid kit, a small mirror, matches and a flint, spare ammo, water purification tablets, fishing line and a hook, and at the bottom of the pack I find the solar blanket. I also have a compass on my watch and of course the radio. We're not doing too bad.

The sound of rustling has me look over at Nella, who is following my lead and is emptying out her smaller pack. It's basic, but not bad. She has some food and a water bottle as well, which along with mine, should be enough to sustain us through the night.

"Apple?"

I notice her hand holding up the fruit is still shaking but the panic has gone from her eyes. When I found her earlier, she was out of it—looked like she was having a panic attack—but all it took was a bit of coaxing for her to snap out of it. Not sure what triggered it in the first place, but it's clear she's not a fan of thunderstorms, and she did narrowly escape an unfortunate encounter with a tree. She may be shaking but she's tougher than I would've given her credit for.

"We can split," I suggest, using my blade to slice it in half before handing her portion back to her.

We eat the apple in silence, each lost to our own thoughts until Nella speaks up.

"I hope Pippa has shelter."

"She's been out here a while so I'm sure she has," I offer.

That is, if she's still alive, but I keep that to myself. Even if she is, our chances of tracking her down have been greatly reduced by this storm. Any traces will have been washed away by the time this is done.

A reasonably healthy person can survive without food for several weeks, but not without water. My gut tells me if Nella's sister is still alive, she won't have ventured too far from the creek. And if she's smart, she would've headed downstream.

Cedar Creek runs into the Kootenay River, just a few miles north of Libby. I'm guessing the distance from here to the river, which runs parallel to the US-2, is about four-and-a-half miles as the crow flies. Healthy, she should've been able to make that in a day, even in this terrain. But I've seen the blood, she may well be injured and hunkered down.

Or, she's dead.

A light clicking noise has me looking over at Nella. She has her knees pulled up to her chest and her arms wrapped tightly around them. The clicking is from her teeth chattering. She's freezing.

I grab the Mylar blanket and crawl over to her. When I touch the back of her hand it's like an ice cube. I'd intended to wrap her in the blanket, but feeling how cold she is I think better of it.

"Scoot forward a bit."

As soon as she moves, I slide behind her, my back against the rock wall as I pull her between my legs, covering us both with the blanket. She doesn't protest and seems to press herself into the heat still radiating from me.

"Tell me about your sister. What's she like?"

My real interest is in Nella herself, but I figure I could probably find out more about her this way than to ask her directly. Somewhere between our first face-to-face meeting and now, this woman has stirred my curiosity. I know she's tenacious, I know she has balls, and I know she's protective enough to step well out of her comfort zone to find her sister. I've also been able to deduce from remarks she made that they have no direct family left, that Pippa is the adventurous one of the two, and that Nella prefers the safety of a boring life.

Or so it appears.

"She's a mechanic," Nella surprises me by sharing. "She always marched to her own drum, sometimes to the despair of our parents. When I chose piano lessons, Pippa opted for the electrical guitar. She wanted to play soccer instead of the dance classes I was enrolled in." She chuckles softly, her back against my chest gently shaking. "She was determined to be unpredictable, but by the time she announced she wanted to fix cars for a living, not even my parents were surprised."

She's suddenly quiet and I immediately miss the soothing sound of her voice.

"You lost your parents," I prompt, interpreting her abrupt silence as grief.

I feel her nod.

"They've been gone for a long time," she confirms.

"You must've been young."

"I suppose. Although I'd graduated university and was already working at the time. My sister was still in college though. It was tough on her."

It doesn't take much imagination to deduce Nella took over the parental role, putting aside her own grief to help her sister through hers.

"She can't be that much younger than you are," I point out.

"Three years." Then she shifts slightly and twists her neck so she can look at me. "Is that your way of finding out how old I am without asking my age?"

My grin is involuntary at the unexpected tease.

"I'm forty-seven if that makes it easier," I confess and grin wider when her mouth falls open.

"Forty-seven? That is entirely unfair." She's clearly annoyed. "Why is it that men generally age better than women? It's like nature is determined to announce our gender has an expiration date when guys get unlimited shelf life. Gray hair enhances a man's looks, but we're supposed to dye it to hide the evidence. It's just wrong."

Amused, I pick up a strand of her hair. It's almost dry and shows the occasional silver strand.

"You don't dye yours," I point out. "I like it like this. It's real."

She huffs but doesn't say anything.

"Forty-eight?" I taunt her, knowing full well she can't be much over forty. Not with that flawless skin and those plump lips.

"I am not," she huffs, jerking away from my chest. "Forty-three, if you must know."

Chuckling softly, I ease her rigid spine back against me. She's long stopped shivering and seems to have forgotten about the continuing thunder outside.

Then I lean forward and put my lips by her ear.

"For your information, I wouldn't have given you a day over forty."

~

Nella

I startle awake and it takes me a moment to remember where I am.

The first thing I notice is the absolute silence. No wind, no rain, and no thunderstorm. Light is coming in from outside and I try to push myself up when my hand encounters firm muscle.

"Morning..."

Fletch's gruff voice sounds even raspier than normal, and far too close to be decent.

I catapult myself to the opposite side. When I look back at him, he's wearing a sardonic smile on his far-too handsome face. He's still sitting with his back against the rock, his hair standing on end—probably run through with his hand a few times—but it does little to dull the overall appeal.

I'm trying to come to terms with the fact I slept cuddled

up to this man, when my bladder suddenly announces itself. Urgently. I'm stuck in a hole in the rock the size of a generous closet...with Fletch, and I desperately need to pee.

Fletch gets to his feet and makes his way over to the opening, bracing himself with a hand as he sticks his head outside.

"Weather's cleared. We should be able to get out of here," he announces, turning back inside to grab his pack. "I'm just going to find us a safe way down. Won't be long, so do what you need to do."

Then he disappears outside.

He must've noticed me squirming. Normally I'd be mortified but the urge to relieve myself is too big. I retreat as far from the opening as I can get and struggle to get my jeans down. My clothes have dried on my body overnight and my hair is probably a bird's nest. I feel grimy but there's not much I can do about that so I quickly squat, holding onto the wall to keep my balance.

When I step out—feeling much better—the bright sun is almost blinding. Blinking a few times, I peek over the ledge to see the tree I clambered up last night and the creek below, still churning with debris. I'm not exactly looking forward to taking the same route down we came up. I look around me for other options. The ledge I'm standing on ends abruptly on one side but looks to extend for about twenty feet on the other, before it disappears where the rock face curves back.

That's where a few moments later Fletch steps into view.

"Ready?" he asks when he reaches me.

"Yes."

"Follow me and stick close to the wall."

I see why when we round the corner. The ledge narrows

to maybe half a foot and I hesitate, the drop is much farther here than where we were.

"Are you sure about this?"

"Yes," he says as he pulls the rope from his pack and ties one end around my waist. The other side he wraps around himself. "It's only a few feet before we get to the trees."

I glance around him to find the few feet he's talking about are at least twenty. That's a long way to be hanging over what has to be a thirty-or-forty-foot drop.

"Nella," he says firmly, and I pull my gaze from the drop to focus on his face. "I'm not gonna let anything happen to you. This is the safer option; you'll have to trust me on that."

The kicker is, I do—I have no reason not to—and I really don't want to go back down that tree. I give him a curt nod.

"Good. Like this," he says, spreading his arms and hugging the rock face. "Put your weight on the balls of your feet and keep your body close to the wall." He takes a few steps until the rope connecting us is almost taut. "You can do it. Keep your eyes on me."

I'm afraid to blink and lose my connection with his calm eyes as I inch my feet along the ledge. My face is pressed so hard into the wall, I'm sure I'll have scratches to show for it.

I'm a few steps from the other side where Fletch is waiting, when sudden loud static startles me and my front foot slips off the ledge. My fingertips claw into the unforgiving rock, desperately trying to find a hold, as I feel myself tip toward the drop.

"*Fuck,*" I hear Fletch curse as gravity pulls my body away from the mountain.

Time slows to a crawl as my arms windmill in an attempt to regain my balance and my other foot slides off

84

the edge. For a brief moment, my body is airborne before I'm jerked to a halt by the rope around my waist. I don't have time to brace when I slam hard into the rock face, letting out a painful yelp.

"Goddammit, Nella, you hang on," Fletch grunts above me. "Not on my fucking watch."

I glance up and watch him strain against my weight. He has one arm around the trunk of a tree, holding on for dear life, as he tries to pull me up with the other.

"Don't move," he barks when I try to grab on to a jutting piece of rock.

Inch by inch, he drags me higher until I'm eye level with his boots. Then in one heave he pulls me up and sandwiches my body between his and the trunk of the tree before my feet even touch the ground. His breath is labored against my ear and I feel his heart racing against my back.

"Jesus, woman. You're gonna be the death of me," he pants.

I close my eyes and welcome the rough bark pressing into my cheek and Fletch's safe weight behind me as I try to catch my own breath.

"Are you hurt?"

"I'm okay," I manage.

It's a lie—just breathing hurts—but my legs feel surprisingly steady.

"Good. Let's get away from the edge."

I feel the loss of his body the moment he moves away but he grabs a firm hold of my hand, pulling me farther into the trees.

The slope is steep as he leads me away from the edge toward a boulder where he forces me to sit. Then he takes out his radio and turns his back. I'm silently grateful for the reprieve, my jaw is clenched in pain.

"Sully, come in."

"...Talk to me."

"We're on the north side of the creek, heading downstream toward the highway. The water is still too dangerous to cross. Over."

"Figured as much. Ewing is getting a search party ready for this side of the creek, and I'm heading down the mountain to meet up with the team."

Fletch turns around and looks at me.

"I'm gonna need you to come toward us. Not sure if Nella can make it out. She's hurt."

I open my mouth to protest but he sharply shakes his head. I have no idea how he could possibly know.

"Hurt?"

"I suspect ribs. We'll keep moving the best we can. Over."

"Ten-four. We'll meet you up there."

He tucks away the radio, his eyes never leaving mine. Eventually, I start to squirm under his silent scrutiny.

"My legs are fine. I can walk," I tell him defensively.

"From here on in you tell me when you're hurting. Is that understood? Your heroics are dangerous out here."

I don't particularly care for his bossy tone, but in the past twenty-four hours this man has saved my bacon several times. I'm becoming well aware without him I'd be lost in more ways than one, so I nod my understanding.

When he holds out his hand, I don't hesitate to take it.

"We'll go slow and take regular breaks."

True to his word, he stops ten minutes later when I was about to call uncle. He has me sit on a fallen log and hands me a protein bar.

"Give me your water bottle, I'll refill them from the creek."

I watch as he makes his way down a steep incline toward the water before taking stock of my surroundings.

It looks like we've come down quite a bit, the ground appears a bit more level here. Behind me I notice a tall rock formation, partially covered by moss. In front of it is a large boulder and something about it catches my eye.

I tentatively get to my feet and walk over. The closer I get, the faster my heart starts beating. I could swear I smell the remnants of a fire. The markings I spotted on the rock look more like writing but it's not until I'm standing right in front of it, I recognize what it says.

HELP

"Fletch!"

Nine

My heart almost stops when I hear my name screamed.

She's not where I left her but is standing thirty feet away in front of a large boulder.

"She was here," she says in a wobbly voice when I reach her.

I catch sight of the message she's staring at.

"Anyone could've written that," I point out, but I don't really believe that myself.

I doubt many people would find their way out here and unless they were lost or missing, they wouldn't need to scribble 'help' on a rock unless they were lost. As far as I know, no one else is currently missing in these mountains.

My eyes immediately start scanning the surrounding area for any other signs and catch on a narrow crack in the rocks beyond.

"Wait here," I order Nella, but I'm not surprised when I hear her footsteps following me.

Fishing out my flashlight, I shine it into the crevice and my breath hitches when the light reflects off what I'm pretty sure is an emergency blanket. I clamp the flashlight in my teeth, shrug out of my backpack, and drop it to the ground as I try to wedge sideways into the tight opening.

"What did you find?" I hear Nella behind me, but I'm focused on the slight bump underneath the Mylar.

Once inside, the space opens up into a sizable cavern. Long dark hair peeks out from under the blanket, the strands draped over a hiking pack used as a pillow. My hand goes to the edge of the blanket but stops midair.

I'm not sure I'm ready for what I'll find underneath. I know for a fact Nella won't be.

"Fletch?"

I hear the rustle of her jacket as she squeezes through the opening.

Shit.

"Do me a favor, Babe. Stay where you are."

When I turn my head around, I see her nod, her face drawn and her mouth tight, but her eyes are fixed on the body on the ground. She's bracing.

Conjuring up every ounce of courage, I whip back the blanket.

Her back is toward me and her face is covered by hair. A dark, sticky patch the size of a pancake clumping the strands above her right ear. Her clothes are filthy and what is left of her body looks almost emaciated. She's short, like her sister.

I put a careful hand on her upper arm in order to roll her over. I expect her to be cold to the touch, but to my surprise she's almost hot. Then I notice a slight movement of her chest.

"Nella, I need my pack!"

"Is she alive?"

"My pack," I repeat sharply.

This woman may not be dead yet, but she's damn close.

I feel for a pulse which is a bit fast and thready. Shrugging out of my flannel shirt, I carefully wipe the hair back from her face. Her eyes are closed and her lips look chapped.

"Oh my God, Pippa..."

I grab my pack as Nella sags down to her knees beside me.

"She needs water. Little bits at a time."

As I suspected, her sister jumps into action right away when I give her a task. While I grab my own bottle and pour it over my shirt before covering her with it, Nella bends over her sister tilting her own, newly filled bottle, letting only a few drops at a time fall on Pippa's dry lips.

Aside from the fever ravaging her body, I'm sure she's dehydrated and her blood sugar levels are low, so I take one of the energy gel pouches from my first aid kit and hand it to Nella.

"See if you can give her a little of this. I need to get on the radio."

My primary concern has shifted from getting Nella looked at to keeping Pippa alive. It ramps up the urgency.

I won't be able to get a signal in here so I slip outside to radio my team.

"Are you on your way?" I ask when Sully answers my call.

Just riding out now.

"Did you bring King?"

Sure did.

I figured he would bring my horse, but wanted to make sure. Our horses are sturdy and are able to handle the weight of an extra rider. Which comes in handy when we have to transport someone out. Nella can ride with me, but someone else will have to take Pippa.

"Good. We found the sister, but barely alive. Unconscious, fever, dehydration. You'll need to hustle and get Ama on this frequency so she can have an ambulance waiting when we come out."

"Ten-four. I'll let Ewing know as well."

I forgot all about the sheriff and his search party. His resources are probably better spent elsewhere, like finding the woman's motorhome.

Ducking back inside the cave, I find Nella hunched over Pippa, examining a laceration on her scalp. It looks horrible; swollen, discolored, and oozing pus. It's clearly infected.

"There's disinfectant and antibiotic cream in my first aid kit, but it looks like the infection may have gone deeper than the surface."

"Are they coming?" she asks as she pulls supplies from my pack.

She sounds cool and collected, her hands surprisingly steady as she tends to her sister. Antonella Freling is made of stern stuff.

"On their way. I'm hoping they'll get here within the hour."

I crouch down beside Nella and sneak a peek at her face. It's drawn, her lips pressed tightly together showing stress, but her eyes are dry. I'm sure finding her sister wasn't quite the relief she'd hoped it would be. The woman is seriously ill, and I'm concerned she may not make it out of here.

"Maybe we should get her outside?" Nella suggests.

Not a bad idea. We could get her closer to the creek, we need water to cool her down. My only concern is the water may be too cold, which would only cause her internal thermostat to kick into higher gear. That is, if I can even carry her out of here.

"We'll have to do it together. The entrance is too narrow for me to carry her alone. You'll have to grab her feet. Once we're outside I can carry her by myself."

We switch positions. She takes hold of Pippa's ankles while I slip my hands under her arms. Nella slips out easily, but it's a bit of a struggle for me to get through. Outside I lift the unconscious woman in my arms, she barely weighs anything.

"Grab our backpacks," I instruct Nella as I start moving toward the bank of the creek.

There I lay her down, lifting my shirt from her chest and dunking it in the fast-moving water. By the time I have her covered again, Nella has joined me. She winces when she sinks to her knees by her sister's side, reminding me she's hurt herself.

"How are you feeling?"

"I'm fine."

She tucks a hank of hair hanging in her face behind her ear and turns those hazel eyes on me. They're dark with pain, telling me the real story. Stubborn woman even denies her own discomfort.

"You know you'll be no good to her if you don't look after yourself."

For a moment it looks like she's going to give me a piece of her mind but opts to silently dismiss me instead.

❧

Nella

. . .

It was on my lips to tell him to 'fuck off' but that would've required energy I have precious little of.

Energy I should devote to Pippa. Once we get her out of here and to proper medical care, I'll worry about me.

While Fletch resoaks his shirt occasionally to get her temperature down, I pour some more water in her mouth and try to get her to swallow some of that gel he gave me. Most of it drips from between her lips and I'm not sure how effective any of it is—I doubt much of it is going down—but at least I'm doing something.

Every so often I feel for her pulse, reassured when I can still find it. I can't lose her too, what would I have left to live for? I'm not sure I could survive. Each time my eyes start burning with tears I fight them back; they won't do anyone any good.

"Your sister is as resilient as you are," Fletch comments out of the blue, catching me completely off guard. "The fact she was able to keep herself alive for two weeks out here is impressive."

"My sister can do anything she puts her mind to."

It's true. Pippa is very capable, adapts quickly to new situations, and is absolutely fearless. I blame her in part for the premature gray in my hair, but I also envy her. Which is why I'm a little confused why Fletch would compare her to me. There is no comparison.

I'm about to tell him that when a large animal charges out of the underbrush and I launch myself backward, landing awkwardly on my side. I yelp in pain just as Fletch calls out.

"Max! Easy, buddy."

The animal turns out to be a large hairy dog, currently slobbering all over my face. Fletch pulls him off me and leans close.

"Did he hurt you?"

I shake my head; I don't think I'm hurt any more than I was before. Grabbing Fletch's hand, I let him pull me up, just as a group of riders appear out of the trees. The first one off his horse is a large man with tattoos peeking out of the pushed-up cuffs of his shirt. He doesn't even acknowledge me as his eyes lock in on my sister's prone body.

"Sully," Fletch identifies him.

Behind him I make out the bulky black cowboy I met at the ranch a few days ago. I think his name is Bo. He was smiling a lot then, but looks dead serious as he rushes to Pippa's side, dropping a large medical kit on the ground next to her.

Then I see the man pull an IV bag from the kit.

"Whoa." I surge toward him, trying to intervene, but Fletch grabs my arm and pulls me back.

"Bo has field training. He's a medic, let him do his job."

I'm half aware of a few other guys standing around but keep my eyes on what Bo is doing to my sister.

"Hard to find a vein," he comments, turning her arm.

He finally seems to settle on the inside of her upper arm and slides a large-looking needle under her skin. Pippa doesn't even flinch, but I do. I'm not a fan of needles in general. Bo quickly attaches the bag to the IV line and elevates it.

"I'll take her," Sully announces, bending down to lift my sister effortlessly off the ground.

She looks so small cradled in those bulging arms and a strained sound escapes me. I can feel Fletch close in behind me as she is carried to one of the large horses, and he puts a warm hand on my shoulder. The last of my energy drains and I find myself leaning back and letting Fletch take some of my weight. Then I watch Sully hand Pippa off to another man, get in the saddle, and reach for her again. He settles her sideways in front of him and takes the IV bag, holding it elevated.

"Come on, Babe, you're riding with me," Fletch mumbles in my ear.

I allow him to guide me to a horse. A very tall, very black, and very intimidating horse.

"Nella, meet King. He looks fierce, but he's a pussycat. I'll introduce you to the other guys once we get underway."

Yes. We need to get Pippa to the hospital. It's the only reason I don't balk when Fletch gives me a boost into the saddle. I cling to the horn like my life depends on it. Maybe it does. I've never been on a horse before.

Then Fletch swings on, sitting just behind the saddle, his arm firmly hooked around my waist.

I already feel safer and as he clicks his tongue, encouraging his horse to move, I allow myself to lean against his sturdy chest and let my head loll back to his shoulder. A few strands of my hair get caught where his bearded chin is pressed against my ear, but I'm suddenly too exhausted to care.

"The guy up ahead with the tan hat is Jonas Harvey. My boss," Fletch explains softly, pointing out the man leading the convoy. "You know Sully and Bo, and closing out the team behind us is James Watike. You met his wife, Ama, back at the ranch."

I'm comfortable where I am and don't want to turn around. I'll be polite later. Instead I tilt my head back slightly so I can look up. I catch Fletcher stealing a glance at me before focusing ahead.

"Didn't you have a hat?" I ask, noticing his mussed salt-and-pepper hair.

"Lost it in the creek when that tree came down. It's probably floating down the Kootenay River by now."

"I'll buy you a new one. It's the least I can do. Thank you."

He may have been grumpy and unpleasant at first, but despite that he's shown care and concern for me, and has been gentle with my sister.

"No need. I have another at home."

I nod my understanding, but the first chance I get I'm going to get him a new one anyway. It's the right thing to do to thank him for saving Pippa.

My eyes lock on Sully's broad back, the closest I can get to my sister.

"How does he steer?" I want to know when I notice the reins of his horse hang slack.

My voice sounds slurred with fatigue, and Fletch's arm around my middle tightens.

"His knees or his heels, but Cisko—that's his horse—can find his own way. All of our horses are calm, well-trained, and able to make their way back to the ranch on their own if need be. If anything were to happen, all you need to do is hold on."

My fingers instinctively tighten on the saddle horn. Fletch must've noticed because I hear his soft chuckle.

"You can relax, nothing's going to happen. I've got you."

Yes, he does. For someone who's used to relying on herself and doesn't trust easily, it's surprising how fast I've come to trust Fletch.

It's been an intense couple of days.

Ten

From the way her head gently rolls back and forth against my shoulder with King's easy gait, I can tell she's dozed off.

Not a surprise. Hell, I'm exhausted myself after the events of the past twenty-four hours. I could use a nap, if for anything, to get some perspective. The feel of Nella's soft hair brushing my beard is messing with my head.

I care about my brothers—my family at High Meadow —and of course Ama, but it's been many years since I've allowed myself to care about anyone else. There was a reason I hid out in the mountains around Fernie, British Columbia; I didn't *want* to care. Ultimately, I wasn't able to say no to Jonas when he found me, but even here in Montana, I mostly keep to myself. Purely out of self-preservation.

But in the past few days, this woman has broken through. Maybe I was an ass to her at first because I already felt that pull she seems to have on me. Not that she's actively tried to get in my good graces—hell no, quite the opposite—but somehow she made me care.

She's not what might be considered a knockout—she covers herself with this prim and proper shield—but her true beauty comes through in the strength of character she has shown. Nella is a total surprise. It may have been easy to dismiss her before, but I'm pretty sure ignoring her is no longer an option. Not when the feel of her warm body and faint scent of her shampoo is stirring my blood.

"She okay?"

James rides up alongside me, darting a glance at Nella.

"Exhausted."

"I bet," he acknowledges. "Ama called for an ambulance, but maybe we should've called for two. May not be a bad idea to get her checked out as well."

"I don't need an ambulance." Nella lifts her head from my shoulder and throws James a look. "I'm not leaving my sister."

"Fair enough," he says with a grin to her and a wink for me, before he lets his horse fall back in line again.

True enough, the ambulance is waiting right beside the ranch's horse trailer when we clear the woods. By the time I help Nella off King, EMTs have already strapped her sister to a stretcher and are rolling her to the rig. Nella rushes after them. Before I have a chance to follow her, she's already climbing in the back of the ambulance with Pippa.

Fuck. I don't have wheels.

"So I'm guessing you're staying?"

In the end it had been Sully who drove me to the hospital. I should probably have gotten a ride to pick up my truck on Scenery Mountain and gone back to the ranch, but I wanted to make sure Nella got herself checked out. My gut told me she'd likely ignore her own injuries and had no one to look after her.

Sully witnessed a heated exchange in the ER waiting room when we caught up with Nella. I won the argument and just watched her leave through the doors with the nurse I called over. She's pissed with me but that's nothing new, I realize. I seem to have that effect on her. She probably expects me to leave and maybe that's part of why I settle back in the uncomfortable chair, crossing my arms over my chest.

"Good guess," I answer Sully, who is leaning against the doorway.

"Figured as much," he mumbles, grinning when I glare at him.

"What do you suggest I do?" I snap defensively. "She doesn't know anyone here; she has no mode of transportation—her van is still up on the mountain—and we don't even know if the sister is gonna make it through."

Sully raises his hands in defense.

"You'll get no argument from me. I'm gonna swing by the ranch and grab a couple of the hands to help me fetch your truck and her vehicle. We can drop them off here."

I toss him my keys and inform him, "She probably has her keys on her."

"I'll see if I can grab them from her."

He's about to leave the room when I call after him.

"Just drop off my truck here. You can take her van to the ranch."

Not sure what the hell I'm thinking, but I don't like the idea of Nella getting another wild hair and taking off to sleep in that damn van somewhere. This way at least I have some control; the woman clearly needs a keeper.

"Want me to lie to her?" he asks, earning himself another glare.

"You don't have to fucking lie, just tell her you're getting her van and nothing else."

I know he's yanking my chain when the corner of his mouth starts twitching as he mock-salutes me before disappearing down the hall.

There are only a few other people in the waiting room but rather than awkwardly glance at each other every few minutes, I lean my head back against the wall and close my eyes. May as well catch a few z's while I can.

I wake up when someone nudges my knee. Sully is back, shoving a paper bag and a travel mug at me.

"Here, Sleeping Beauty. Lunch." He drops a bag on the floor by my feet. "And some clean clothes for you and your friend, all courtesy of Ama. She says she'll check in this afternoon. Van is parked outside your cabin, but we had to hotwire it. They wouldn't let me go back to see Nella. Where is she anyway?" He looks around the room.

"No fucking clue. How long were you gone?"

"An hour."

I get up and set the coffee and whatever Ama packed for lunch on my chair. Then I pull my change of clothes from the plastic bag, set those down too, and take the rest over to the nurses' station.

"Excuse me. I'm here with Antonella Freling and her sister, Pippa. Any news on either of them?"

The nurse looks at me over the rim of her glasses.

"Are you family?"

"Yes. I have some clean clothes for Antonella."

I don't elaborate on the lie, I just set the bag on the desk and stare right back at the woman.

"Let me have a look," she finally concedes, grabbing the clothes off her desk and disappearing through the door behind her.

A few minutes later she comes back.

"Ms. Freling should be done shortly and a doctor will be out to discuss her sister in a bit."

Not much information, but at least it sounds like Nella will be walking out of here.

I mumble my thanks and return to my seat.

"She should be out soon," I volunteer before digging into the paper bag.

"One of those is for Nella," he tells me when I pull one of the two huge, tightly-wrapped burritos from the bag.

Ama fills those suckers with everything but the kitchen sink, and I can't stop the groan when I sink my teeth into what tastes like pulled pork, roasted vegetables, and refried beans. I didn't realize how hungry I was until now.

Sully silently sits beside me while I devour my lunch. I have to resist starting on Nella's and instead grab my clean clothes.

"If she comes out, tell her I'll be right back."

I'm starting to smell myself, which is never a good thing, and quickly find a restroom, locking the door behind me. There's only so much you can do with antibacterial soap in a dispenser and a small sink, but I do my best. I use about half the supply of paper towels to dry off before getting dressed and instantly feel a ton better.

Stealing the liner from the garbage can, I dump my clothes in the bag and return to the waiting room. Nella is sitting beside Sully. She's wearing the clean clothes but looks surprised when she sees me.

"You came back."

"I never left," I correct her before dumping my soiled clothes on Sully's lap with a dirty look. "I just washed up a bit, which this asshole was supposed to tell you."

"Sorry, must've slipped my mind," the asshole in question says with a grin on his face.

Ignoring him, I sit down on Nella's other side.

"So what's the verdict on you?"

"A few cracked ribs. Nothing serious," she brushes me off.

That may well be, but I know from experience it hurts like a sonofabitch.

"Did they give you pain meds?"

"A prescription." She waves a piece of paper. "I don't think I need them, though."

Like hell.

I snatch the script from her hand and shove it at Sully.

"Sully will get it filled at the pharmacy in the main lobby. Won't you, Sully?"

"Sure thing."

He takes the paper and disappears down the hall.

Nella

"That was rude."

I turn to Fletch with a glare.

I'm half pissed at him, half pissed at myself for feeling abandoned just moments ago when I thought he'd left.

"Trust me, it's better to stay on top of the pain," he explains before pointing to the paper bag his friend set on the floor. "Ama packed lunch. You should eat something, keep your strength up."

He annoys me with his bossiness and I'm tempted to refuse, but the truth is I know I should eat. Waiting for the doctor to tell me what is happening with my sister has my stomach in knots though, and I only manage a few bites. When Fletch offers me his cup, I gratefully take a sip.

Warm coffee. I almost hum with the instant jolt of caffeine. Now that I could drink a vat of.

But the moment I hear my name called by an older doctor walking into the waiting room, my stomach instantly revolts. His face is so serious, I'm afraid of what he might have to say.

I'm not ready.

"Ms. Freling?" he repeats when Fletch waves him over.

I shoot to my feet, blindly feeling for something to hold on to when I encounter Fletch's hand and grab on for dear life.

"Yes?"

My voice is as wobbly as my knees.

"If you would follow me?"

Oh fuck. Oh no, that can't be good.

Fletch gives my fingers a squeeze, and I hold on tight as I force my feet to follow the doctor. I don't think I can do this alone.

We're led into a small office where the doctor invites us to take a seat. When we each sit down, I instantly miss the warmth of Fletch's strong hand gripping mine.

"As you know, your sister was brought in unconscious, severely undernourished, dehydrated, and with a head injury which had become infected. Do you know what happened?"

"We think she may have hit her head on a rock, but that would've been about two weeks ago," I fill him in.

Surely if Pippa hadn't survived he would've just told us so.

"That makes more sense. The wound looked like it hadn't just happened. We did a scan and discovered a very recent skull fracture that would likely have occurred at the same time." He sits down at the desk and flips through a file folder. "The EMTs noted she'd been missing for the same length of time?"

I gave the female EMT some background information while in the back of the ambulance.

"Yes."

"Hmm. I don't see how she could've survived all this time without water at the very least."

"We found her a couple of miles from where we think she hit her head," Fletch volunteers. "On the other side of a creek. She'd found shelter in a cave and left a few clues along the way, so she must've still been able to find her way there. Able to sustain herself."

The doctor nods. "That's the more likely scenario, and in a progressively weakened state her body wouldn't have been able to fight off the infection."

"Is she going to be all right?" I risk asking.

He sends me a sympathetic smile. "We're doing every-thing in our power. IV antibiotics and fluids, we're debriding the wound to remove all the dead and infected skin. We're also waiting for some more tests to come back. Once we have those, she'll be moved to the ICU and even though she hasn't woken up yet, we'll likely be keeping her in an induced coma."

"A coma?"

Fletch must've heard the fear in my voice because he

scoots his chair closer and puts his warm, calloused hand reassuringly on my clenched ones.

"Not unusual in a case like this, it gives her body a chance to heal before we take her upstairs. We'll be monitoring her closely in the ICU."

"Can I see her?"

"Once she's settled in, I'll make sure to tell one of the nurses to come and get you. It likely won't be for a while though, so if you wanted to step out, make sure you leave a number with the nurse at the ER desk so you can be reached."

With that he gets up and we automatically do the same, following him out of the room. By the doors to the ER waiting room, he stops and turns to me.

"I should get back, but I promise we'll take good care of her."

"Thank you, Doctor…"

He smiles. "Sorry, it's Osborne."

"Thank you, Dr. Osborne."

He nods at Fletch and then he walks down the hall and through a second pair of doors.

That's where she is. Pippa.

I'm not sure how he knows but before my knees have a chance to give out, Fletch already has me firmly in his arms.

Then the dam breaks.

Eleven

Damn, the woman can cry.

My shirt is still damp from the first bout when she turns and does another face plant in my chest.

"Maybe I shouldn't have come," Ama mutters uneasily over Nella's sobs.

Nella finally broke down after we left the doctor's office. I'd been waiting for it. The woman is so buttoned up, those emotions she'd been keeping a tight hold on had to burst free at some point. I led her to a quiet corner in the waiting room and let her cry it out. I'm sure fear, stress, and fatigue had her resistance understandably low. Since I was the only one there, it stands to reason she'd turn to me.

She'd been embarrassed when Sheriff Ewing walked in to get our story and avoided looking at me long after he left.

This time it was Ama who triggered this outburst. Unwittingly, she simply came to offer support, but I guess it's not something Nella is used to.

What shocks me is that instead of crying in Ama's arms, she picks mine again.

"You're fine," I tell Ama. "It's not you, it's just been a tough day."

"I can only imagine."

"I'm sorry," Nella sniffles in my shirt. "It's me; I'm a mess."

She lifts her head and makes a futile attempt to wipe at the wet spots on my shirt until I still her hands with my own.

"Leave it. It's fine."

She lifts her face and it strikes me she's no less pretty with a blotchy face and shiny eyes. For a moment, I let my gaze linger until Ama hands her a box of tissues she grabbed from a table.

"I want you to know I've made up the bed in one of our cottages. You can stay as long as you want. It comes fully equipped with your own bathroom and kitchen."

I close my eyes at Ama's words. I shouldn't be surprised she's making arrangements for Nella, Ama looks after everybody. What is a bit disconcerting is the fact my new neighbor will be a woman I'm already starting to find more difficult to resist.

"That's very kind but not necessary," she responds. "I can check with Martha Crandall at the Sandman to see if she has a vacancy."

"Nonsense," is Ama's predictable reaction. "Last thing you need is to worry about a motel room. Besides, you'd be hard-pressed to find any vacancies with the general hunting season opening up just days from now."

Shit. I'd almost forgotten about my bighorn tag. Only four days left on the bow hunt and I still have nothing to show for it.

"Surely there's something I could find closer to the hospital? Somewhere I could walk to? My van is still on the mountain."

Oh boy. Here it comes.

"Nope. Fletch already had the boys pick it up. It's parked at the ranch," Ama volunteers.

Nella flicks me a look. "You never mentioned that."

I shrug. "Didn't really have a chance."

Her eyes narrow. "Why park it at the ranch? Why not here at the hospital? That would make more sense."

I'm still trying to figure out how to respond to that—I don't really have a good answer—when she seems to come to a realization.

"Wait? How is that even possible? I have my keys in my..." She shoves a hand in the pair of yoga pants Ama leant her, coming up empty. "Shit. Where are my keys?"

I dig into my pocket and fish out the keyring I rescued when I stuffed her dirty clothes into the makeshift laundry bag Sully took with him.

"You left them in your jeans."

"Oh. But how am I going to get around?"

"Fletch will drive you," Ama offers, a sly smile on her face. I get the sense I'm about to get tossed under the bus. "His truck is parked right outside."

Nella's eyes dart from Ama to me, her eyebrows drawn close.

"You planned this?"

Before she can grill me for explanations, a nurse walks into the waiting room.

"Family for Fillippa Freling?"

Nella launches to her feet, my manipulations momentarily forgotten.

"I'm her sister."

"If you'd like you can see her now," the nurse tells her gently before taking note of Ama and me. "But I'm afraid only one person at a time and we have a fifteen-minute time limit."

Nella turns to me, her eyes unsure.

"Go ahead. I'll wait right here," I encourage her before giving her a little nudge in the small of her back.

When the nurse leads her through the double doors, I turn back to Ama.

"Stirring up trouble," I accuse her.

She doesn't seem fazed at all. Not much gets to Ama.

"Pffft. I'm helping, you just can't see it yet. You're the least communicative person I know—hell, you're worse than my James—but I'm telling you it'll trip you up eventually. You can ask my husband. Doesn't matter your incessant need to protect and control everyone and everything comes from a noble place, it wreaks havoc on relationships. Women don't like being managed."

Only one word sticks from what she just said.

"Then I have nothing to worry about, 'cause there is no relationship. Not sure where you got that idea."

She barks out a laugh. "Oh, I don't know. Maybe it's because instead of being out hunting that bighorn, you're here comforting a crying woman? Or the fact you had her curled up against you in the saddle like she belonged there? Do I need to go on?"

Fucking James. He's as much of a busybody as his wife.

"She's just a friend."

Ama snorts. "Newsflash: you don't have any friends other than the team, and no way in hell you'd give up a bighorn for them."

I sit down and fold my arms over my chest. There's no arguing with this woman so why waste energy trying.

"Fine. I'll leave you in peace, I've gotta get home, but I've got a big pot of stew back at the ranch. You both need to have a proper meal and some rest. You look like shit and she doesn't look much better."

Easier said than done. I doubt Nella will leave willingly but before I can tell Ama that she's already on her way out.

All I can do is wait for Nella and make the suggestion.

As a last resort, I can always pick her up and toss her over my shoulder.

Pretty sure that'll kill the rumors about any *relationship.*

Nella

She looks tiny.

Her face is almost as white as the sheets covering her, and the hand I'm holding in mine feels small and fragile.

Where is my strong, capable sister? The one who can take apart and rebuild any engine blindfolded, who could run like the wind, climb mountains, laugh without holding back, and who didn't take shit from anyone. A woman larger than life, despite her modest five foot four.

It kills me to see her like this.

The incessant beeping of the monitors she and some of her neighbors are hooked up to grate on my nerves and part of me wants to run out of this room, from the sound, from this woman I don't even recognize. But instead I sit here, holding onto her limp hand, praying silently for her eyes to open and her mouth to twitch into that lopsided smile of hers. I'd give anything to hear her customary, "Hey, Sis."

Maybe I should talk to her, but it feels awkward in this

otherwise empty cubicle. It's not like she can hear me, and besides, what do I say? I love you? She doesn't need me to tell her that, she already knows.

"I'm sorry..."

I startle in my seat when the same nurse from earlier sticks her head around the curtain.

"I gave you a few extra minutes but I'm afraid visiting time is over. You should probably get some rest. If you follow me to the nurses' station, I'll take down a number where you can be reached. If there is any change, I promise to call you right away."

It's hard to let go of Pippa's hand when I get to my feet, but I bend over her prone form and press a kiss to her forehead.

"Fight, Sissy. Fight like only you can," I whisper, before following the nurse from the room.

Fletch is right where I left him when I get back to the waiting room, but I don't see Ama. By the time I reach him, he's on his feet.

"She had to leave. They have a teenage daughter still at home."

It's a little unnerving Fletch apparently guesses where my mind wanders.

"Of course. It was nice of her to come," I mumble.

I feel bad. I never even thanked her in person.

"That's Ama for you. She mentioned saving us some dinner back at the ranch. Did you leave your number with the nurse?"

"I did, but I think I'll stay here. I don't want to keep you though. You should go."

"You can't even stand straight, you need rest," he grumbles.

I don't bother denying it, I can feel myself teetering on

my feet, my ribs hurt, and my eyes are gritty, but I can't bear to think of something happening to Pippa and me not being here.

"Look," he says in a softer tone as he puts a warm hand on my shoulder. "You did everything you could. Hell, you almost killed yourself trying to find your sister—but you did it. You found her. She's in good hands here. Best thing you can do right now is look after yourself. Make sure you're well-rested for when she wakes up. If anything happens, I can have you back here in minutes."

His dark brown eyes are almost mesmerizing and I find myself getting lost in their warmth and his deep, raspy voice.

"Please, Nella."

A warm meal, maybe a shower, and a bed sound so good right now.

"Okay," I finally agree after an internal battle between guilt and self-preservation.

"Good."

He grabs the bag of medication I've thus far ignored, and drapes an arm over my shoulder, steering me firmly toward the exit doors.

"Nella, we're here."

I blink my eyes at the sound of Fletch's voice. I must've dozed off.

We're parked in front of a cute little cabin. A small covered porch in front, and one window on either side of the front door. Someone left a light on inside.

"Where are we?" I ask, expecting the ranch.

"Your home for now," he says. "Don't think you're ready for the main house tonight. We'll worry about introductions tomorrow morning. Get yourself situated, grab a shower or whatever, and I'll go pick up dinner."

A few days ago, I thought this to be the most unpleasant

man I'd ever met, and although he's still mostly bossy and overbearing, he is also surprisingly insightful and considerate. Never mind ridiculously handsome, even with those circles under his eyes.

It's not exactly proper etiquette to eat and crash somewhere without at least introducing yourself to the owners, but I'm frankly too tired to concern myself with manners.

"That sounds good."

He looks almost startled by my compliance, but then quickly exits the truck and comes around to my side. I let him help me down and welcome his hand at my elbow as we walk up the flagstone path.

"Wait. Where is my van? I'll need some of my things," I point out when we step onto the small porch.

It's just wide enough for the two, side-by-side utilitarian chairs. A nice spot for morning coffee I guess. I'll have to check out the view in daylight. I can't see much tonight.

"Over there." Fletch points to the left of the cabin where I see the outline of a second cabin sheltered under a few tall trees. "It's parked on the other side. That's my place."

It's only about a hundred yards from this one. A little shiver of awareness pebbles my skin when I realize how close he'll be.

Fletch pushes the door open—I guess they don't keep it locked—and nudges me inside.

"Go have a shower. We've got good pressure out here and plenty of hot water. I'll go grab your bags and drop them just inside the door before I head over to the main house."

Before I have a chance to thank him, his long legs already have him halfway to his truck. I shut the door, turn around, and lean my back against it as I take in the space.

In the far-left corner of the open space is a small, L-shaped kitchen with a full-sized fridge and stove. An old square kitchen table with two chairs stands in the middle of the room, and to my immediate right is a sitting area with a love seat and an easy chair in front of a wood burning stove.

It's a bit more rustic but about the same size as my apartment, and surprisingly cozy.

My legs are heavy when I push away from the door. I'd love to sink down in that comfy couch but I'm afraid I won't be able to get up again if I do. Instead I push open the first door to my right and find the bedroom. Ama left a couple of towels folded at the foot of the bed and I grab those.

A light knock on the front door has me turn around as Fletch reaches in to drop my bag just inside the bedroom.

"Thank you," I call out.

He glances up and our eyes meet. For a second it looks like he's coming inside, but then he turns his head and grumbles, "Be back in ten," before he pulls the door shut.

I let out a deep breath and duck into the bathroom. I'm too tired to examine what just happened, but it feels like something did. Not that I'm all that experienced, but that glance he threw me sure looked smoldering.

True to his word, he's back by the time I come out of the bedroom, dressed in my own comfy lounge pants and slouchy T-shirt. I couldn't bring myself to put on proper clothes and these at least have me covered. I wouldn't want to give off the wrong signal and walk out in a nightie.

He's sitting at the table, two steaming bowls of something that smells delicious. A slight shiver tickles down my back as I take a seat across from him. The tension is thick. Trying to avoid his burning gaze, I tuck my damp hair behind my ear and sniff the fragrant stew.

"This looks so good," I comment, picking up the spoon he laid out.

"Ama's a great cook."

"Does she always cook for you?" I ask as I take my first bite.

I'm trying to make small talk but can barely keep from groaning when the taste hits my palate.

"For me? No. I mostly look after myself, but she does a lot of the cooking for the others. Among other things."

"You mean your team?"

"Among others. There's Jonas, Alex—that's his girl-friend—his father, Thomas, who all live at the ranch. Sully lives in the cabin closest to the big house and will eat at the big house most days as well. Dan, one of our ranch hands, and his mother, Gemma, have the cottage between this one and Sully's."

I can't imagine what that would be like, living alongside the people you work with. They must all get along really well. Funny, because Fletch strikes me as a loner, not that different from me.

Other than when I was growing up, and since then a short stint with my sister after our parents died, I've always lived alone and barely know my neighbors.

"Wow, I had no idea you all lived here."

"Not Bo, or Ama and James. They have their own places."

"You didn't want a place of your own?"

Fletch lowers his spoon and looks at me. The brief pause makes me uncomfortable and I wonder if I said something wrong.

"Don't need it," he finally responds. "I'm good where I am and everyone leaves me be."

Is that supposed to be some kind of warning? It's not

like I forced him to follow me on the mountain, or to stay with me at the hospital. That was his choice.

"Then I'll make sure not to disturb you," I tell him, a little prickly, before focusing on my stew.

"Look. I didn't—" He stops mid-sentence and grunts something unintelligible before bending down to his own dinner.

We quietly eat, the tension in the cabin suddenly of a different nature. Fletch is done first and immediately gets up.

"Get some rest," he says gruffly as he takes his bowl to the sink and quickly rinses it.

Even his back looks tense and I'm starting to feel bad for being snippy. I may have overreacted a tad but I'm about at the end of my rope.

He's already walking past me on his way to the door when I jump into action.

"Wait!"

His hand lets go of the knob and he turns around as I rush over.

"Thank you." I step up to him and awkwardly slip my arms around his waist. "I don't know what I would've done without you," I ramble in his shirt. "And I'm sorry if I was being nosy, and maybe bitchy—"

My weak apology is cut off when he lifts my face with a finger under my chin. His face is much closer than I expected and his eyes are dark with heat.

"Oh, fuck it," he mutters as his mouth closes over mine.

Twelve

I scowl at the empty spot where Nella's van was parked. She must've snuck off while I was in the shower, or I would've heard her leave.

Part of me expected something like this after I kissed her last night. Not sure what possessed me to do that.

At first, she responded like a dream, granting me access to her mouth as her hands grabbed onto my shirt at the small of my back. She pressed her body against me, and the last of my control went out the window. I had my tongue down her throat and my hand under her shirt covering one of her luscious tits, when I could feel her freeze up.

All she did was whisper a soft, "No," and I released her so fast she wavered on her feet. Then she mumbled an unnecessary apology and disappeared into the bedroom. My first instinct was to go after her but I could hardly barge into her bedroom, so I left without a word. It had been a long day, emotions were high, and I planned to have a chat with her this morning, but it looks like that's not going to happen.

I spent half the night rethinking that decision, and now it's not even seven o'clock and she's gone. I just don't know if she's gone for good.

Walking over to her cabin, I try the front door which is firmly locked. We don't normally lock doors here, but I guess Nella found the key by the side of the door. That would mean she intends to come back. I blow out a relieved puff of air before turning toward the main house. Better check in before I run after her. It'll give me a chance to cool down first.

Alex is standing by the stove in the large kitchen and Jonas and his dad are sharing a newspaper at the table. My stomach grumbles at the smell of frying bacon. No sign of any of the others yet.

"Morning."

Thomas is the first one to spot me.

"Morning," I echo as Alex turns around and throws me a smile.

"Scrambled okay for you?" she asks.

"Great. Thanks."

I take a seat beside Jonas, who eyes me conspicuously.

"Did you piss off our guest already?"

I wisely keep my mouth shut. The boss has an uncanny ability to see through any lie, and the truth is, I probably did piss her off last night when I groped her.

I guess he wasn't expecting a response because he continues, "Saw her sneak out of the cabin earlier and take off."

"Hospital would be my guess," I volunteer as Alex sets a mug of steaming coffee in front of me.

"And yet you're here, which makes me wonder."

"Leave him alone, Jonas," Alex admonishes him from the kitchen.

He mumbles something under his breath and dives back into his newspaper, but his father still has eyes on me.

"Pretty little thing, isn't she? I saw her from a distance. Too bad we haven't been introduced yet."

"The woman's had a tough two days," I snap. "She's walking around with broken ribs and her sister's in a coma. Cut her a break."

The old man seems to find my reaction amusing, and once again I feel his son's sharp eyes on me.

"Relax, my boy," Thomas says with a grin. "Not faulting her for anything. I just wondered why you'd been keeping her to yourself. And more importantly, why you let her go off on her own."

"That's quite enough out of you as well," Alex pipes up, sliding a plate in front of him.

"What did I do?" Thomas asks innocently, making Jonas chuckle.

To avoid any further discussion about Nella, I ask what's on the docket for today as Alex serves me a plate.

"We were supposed to move some of the foals to the south pasture," Jonas shares. "But I just got a call from the family of a missing hiker up on Mount Sterling and I'm waiting to hear back from the ranger station. Looks like we'll be heading out there so the foals will have to wait."

"I can take care of the foals," I volunteer, catching an odd look from him.

"I thought you were supposed to be off hunting bighorn," he points out.

It's the tenth of September today, four days left. I guess I could head out but, because of a pair of pretty hazel eyes and a lush mouth, I don't want to venture too far. I could pop into the hospital, make sure she's okay, and keep busy the rest of the day.

Before I can respond to Jonas, Ama bustles into the kitchen.

"Sorry I'm late. Una had a little episode this morning," she mutters as she pours herself a cup.

"Oh no. Is she all right?" Alex wants to know.

Ama flaps her hand. "She's fine, it's me who has the lasting effects."

Una is Ama and James's sixteen-year-old daughter, who has been acting out a bit lately and giving her parents a run for their money.

"Like I told you before, feel free to drop her off at the rescue any time. Lucy is good at cracking the whip," Alex offers before she announces to Jonas, "I should get going. I've got that blind appaloosa coming in this morning. Let me know if you go out on that search."

She's not kidding. Lucy is Alex's manager at Hart's Horse Rescue a few miles up the road. She's tiny—shorter than Nella—but is tougher than many a man I know. That woman can be intimidating.

"I'll walk you out."

Jonas gets up and follows Alex down the hall and I hear the front door close. I'm sure they'll be in a hefty lip-lock on the front porch. Those two seem to have trouble keeping their hands off each other. Even though they've been together for the past six months, this is the first time I envy their connection.

∼

I find Nella in the small ICU waiting room where the nurse directed me.

Apparently, visits on this floor are limited to fifteen minutes only a couple of times a day, and I'm guessing Nella already had her first visit in. She looks up and sees me.

I experience a rare pang of compassion at the forlorn look in her eyes and the remnants of my earlier anger at her for skipping out disappears.

"Hey."

"Hi," she answers in a soft voice.

"How's your sister?"

The waiting room is empty but I take the chair next to her.

She shrugs. "The same." Then she slumps back in her seat, her shoulder brushing mine. "She still has a fever so they were giving her another dose of something to try and bring it down."

She sounds dejected.

"Her body is weak yet, Nella. It makes sense she needs a little extra help and time to fight off the infection and the fever."

"I know."

She lists a little until she's leaning against me and my arm automatically rounds her, tucking her close. Her head rolls against my shoulder and I rest my chin against her hair.

We sit like that for a while in silence.

At some point she asks in a quiet voice, "Why did you come?"

I lift my head and look down at her, but she keeps her eyes fixed on the opposite wall.

"Checking in on you. You left before we had a chance to talk."

She tucks a hank of hair behind her ear. "I wanted to get here early."

It's not hard to hear the lie. I have a gut feeling she doesn't do it often so instead of calling her out on it, I let it go.

"Did you sleep at all?"

Now her head turns my way. "A little."

"We should talk...about last night." I feel her stiffen beside me but soldier on. "I probably shouldn't have kissed you."

~

Nella

I knew he would bring that up.

Last night was messed up. The kiss was definitely unexpected—handsome men don't go around kissing me with any regularity—and this one swept me right off my feet. For a moment he made me forget everything, I didn't even recognize myself. Then his hand was under my shirt and on my breast when I heard a horse neigh outside and reality suddenly hit me like a ton of bricks. I was at the ranch, losing myself to a tall, handsome cowboy while my sister was in a coma at the hospital.

The guilt had been so fast and thick, I could almost taste it. Still can.

I couldn't face him this morning. Couldn't imagine being introduced to the other people at the ranch, smiling and being polite, while I was feeling like the manure pile I'd spotted next to the barn when I was sitting on the porch watching the sun come up. So I bolted and came straight here.

But his words still sting. Reality must've hit him too, and he probably wants to make sure I don't have any expectations.

I don't know much about men. At least not men like Fletch. Maybe it was my lack of experience, or exhaustion, or the highly emotional events of the day that had me misinterpret the look I saw in his eyes as interest. Last night, I thought he'd instigated the kiss but this morning I realized I practically threw myself at him.

And yet, here I am again, snuggling into his side.

I probably shouldn't have kissed you.

With his words echoing in my mind, I abruptly stand up and move to a seat across from him, just to create a little distance. I'm like a moth to the flame when it comes to this man.

"I'm sorry." It feels like I'm always apologizing to him.

"What the hell are you talking about?" he snaps, his surly disposition back on display.

The man's moods are hard to keep track of. He makes me feel unbalanced.

"Last night. This morning. Everything."

His heavy eyebrows—barely visible under the brim of the hat he's wearing—draw together to form a stern line over his deep-set eyes.

"That's bullshit. In case you missed it, it was me kissing you last night." He flips off his hat with one hand before agitatedly running the other through his thick hair. "I took advantage of you. Fuck, I practically mauled you when you could barely stand on your own feet. That's not me."

I stare at him in disbelief. *Advantage of me?*

"I liked it," I blurt out, and I can't stop myself from adding, "a lot."

My confession is instantly followed by a flush of embarrassment as Fletch's eyebrows shoot up in surprise.

"You did."

It's more of a statement than a question, but I nod anyway.

"Well, I'll be damned," he mutters.

He leaves shortly after, citing some work he needs to do, but he first makes me promise to come back to the ranch after I see Pippa. He surprises me by dropping a kiss on the top of my head before he takes off.

This time when I sit down next to my sister's bed and the nurse closes the curtain to give us some privacy, I take her hand, lean close, and in a soft voice tell her all about this puzzling man I've met.

Two visits a day is all I get, so when the nurse alerts me my time is up, I kiss Pippa's forehead—the only place free from tubes and bandages—and promise her I'll be back tomorrow.

But when I walk out of the hospital a few minutes later, the rest of the afternoon and evening seem to stretch out in front of me. I'm not good at sitting around with nothing to do, but I've done plenty of it yesterday and today. All it does is make me focus on the negative. I need my hands to be busy.

Instead of turning the van left to go back to High Meadow, I turn right. My plan is to pick up some supplies for the cabin—other than coffee and creamer the fridge had been empty—and maybe bake a few pies as a thank you for letting me stay there. I'll also need some groceries so I can cook my own meals. I already owe these people so much; I don't want to infringe on their hospitality any further.

At Rosauers—the same grocery store I visited when I first got here—I fill my cart with enough food to last me the week. As an afterthought I pick up a few bottles of wine. Purely for medicinal purposes, in case I have trouble sleeping again. A glass of wine will knock me out, I'm a bit of a lightweight.

I can hardly believe it was only a week ago I arrived here. So much has happened, it feels like much longer.

As I pull out of the parking lot, I spot the sign for the Sandman Motel and remember the bench from my van which is still stored in Martha's garage. I might as well go pick it up, I think my boondocking days are over. Wouldn't be a bad idea to check for vacancies while I'm there.

I have no idea what is going to happen with Pippa or how long I'll be here, and I can't stay at the ranch forever. That reminds me, I should call work and let my boss know what's going on. Derek won't be happy to know I'll likely need longer than the two weeks he reluctantly granted me.

A pickup truck I recognize as Wyatt's, Martha's son, is parked in front of the garage when I pull up to the motel office. Maybe he has time to give me a hand. I get out, open the van's side door, and snag a bottle of wine from one of the grocery bags to give to Martha as a thank-you.

She's behind the counter when I walk in and her face lights up with a smile.

"The whole town's been abuzz about you finding your sister. How is she? What happened?"

Living in a small town myself, I'm not surprised the news has done the rounds. Even though I expected it, I still have to clear my throat at the mention of Pippa.

"She's in pretty rough shape. They're keeping her in a coma for now, so it's not clear what exactly happened yet."

Her smile is instantly replaced with a look of concern.

"Oh dear, I'm so sorry. I hope she pulls through."

I swallow hard before I respond.

"So do I." Then, eager to change the subject, I ask, "I notice the sign says no vacancies, when do you think you might have something available?"

"We're pretty booked up well into October, but let me have a look."

I mentally cross my fingers for something as she turns to her computer screen.

"For how long?" she wants to know.

"I'm really not sure. I hope once my sister improves, we'll have a clearer idea."

"I see. Well, the first available room I have is for October twelfth, and only for three nights before it's booked again." She glances at me with a sympathetic smile. "I told you, it's crazy here this time of year."

Rats. If we're still here in October, I might as well move because I'm pretty sure I won't have a job to return to.

"No worries," I tell her with a smile I have to plaster on. "If I leave you my number, could you let me know if there are any cancellations?"

"Of course."

She slides a notepad and pen across her desk and I quickly jot down the information.

"I appreciate it." Then I hand her the wine. "I appreciate everything you've done. I was also popping in to get my bench from your garage."

"That's mighty kind of you, but it was no trouble at all." She rolls back her chair. "Let me get Wyatt. He'll give you a hand with that."

I end up being sidelined when Wyatt insists he handle the bench by himself.

"You found her then?" he questions.

"We did."

"Was she lost or something?"

"Injured. She managed to keep herself alive though."

"Guess she's pretty lucky," he points out as he closes the van's back doors.

He's not wrong, I just hope her luck hasn't run out.

NELLA

"That's going to be a problem."

I keep a tight hold on my anger at Derek's sour tone.

Not a word of concern over Pippa's well-being. My boss is such an asshole.

"I'm sorry about that, but certainly you understand I can't leave my sister. I'll make sure to keep you informed," I tell him in a clipped tone.

I'm not one to take risks—which is probably why I've worked in the same place since getting my degree—but I've already proven I'll do anything for Pippa and I'm not about to stop now. If I lose my job, so be it. I have some money in savings and enough invested in mutual funds for my retirement. It wouldn't be too hard to access those—albeit at a loss—if I had to.

"Fall term just started so I'm afraid that won't be enough," Derek announces. "We're already stretched thin with you taking off last minute for two weeks. I'm going to have to insist you be back here Monday September nineteenth at eight in the morning on the dot, as previously agreed to, or don't bother coming back at all."

And there it is, I can't say part of me wasn't expecting it.

The law in British Columbia allows for an employer to fire me for no specified reason as long as they give sufficient notice or pay an adequate amount of severance, which depends on years of service. Of course if I don't show up, he could try and claim work abandonment, but either way, I'll be out of a job.

I'm waiting for the panic to hit, but to my surprise I feel oddly calm at the prospect. Somewhere in the past week, it would appear, my perspective on life has changed. Before, most of my identity had been connected to the work I did, but these past days have been an eye-opener. I'm discovering an entirely new person inside. One who doesn't need work to identify herself.

Pippa would be proud.

The realization has me respond with a new sense of freedom, "Do what you must."

I end the call just as the oven pings, alerting me the flapper pie is done. I opted for butter tarts and flapper pie for a Canadian touch. Both are pretty easy and they don't take too long to make. The butter tarts have been cooling while I browned the meringue on the custard-filled pie.

Five minutes later I'm on my way to the main house, a little self-conscious about just knocking on the door. The thing is, I can't, in good conscience, let another day go by without properly introducing myself. I just hope Ama is still there to break the ice.

An older gentleman opens the door, a smile deepening the prominent lines in his face.

"Finally," he exclaims. "Come in."

"Oh, I'm just dropping these off. Is Ama here?"

The man relieves me of the pie and with his free hand waves me in.

"She's in the kitchen."

He starts walking down the hallway to the rear of the house and I have no choice but to follow. The kitchen is massive compared to what I'm used to. It opens up to a dining room and what I assume to be a living room beyond. Large windows all along the back of the house provide gorgeous views of the landscape.

Somewhat intimidated, I throw Ama—who is standing by a massive island—a small smile.

"I'm sorry to barge in," I start. "I wanted to—"

"Your timing is perfect. Dinner is in twenty minutes," she interrupts before glancing at the flapper pie the older man slides on the counter in front of her. "What's this?"

"Flapper pie, it's a traditional Canadian pie. And these are butter tarts. As a thank-you for your hospitality." I set the plate of tarts on the island before turning to the man and holding out my hand. "I should introduce myself; I'm Antonella Freling, pleased to meet you."

"I know," he says with a sparkle in his eyes as he grabs my hand. "Thomas Harvey, and I assure you the pleasure is all mine."

"That's Jonas's father. Never mind him," Ama says, bumping Thomas with her hip. "He doesn't get out much."

The old man grins in response, not appearing at all offended by her words. Ama turns back to the vegetables she was slicing.

"Well, I'll get out of your hair."

I take a step toward the door when Ama announces,

"Nonsense. You'll stay for dinner. We'll have your baking for dessert."

Before I have a chance to turn around, the front door flies open and the large dog I met up on the mountain comes charging toward me. Someone yells, "Max!" but it's too late. He jumps up and knocks me right on my ass.

"Get off, you big galoot," a deep voice sounds above me as a large, wet tongue laps at my face.

The next moment he's gone, pulled back by Fletch's boss, Jonas.

"Looks like he's taken a shine to you," he comments as he holds out his hand for me to grab on to.

With no apparent effort at all, he pulls me to my feet.

"You all right?"

A little embarrassed, I wipe the seat of my pants. "I'm fine, thank you."

Other than humiliated.

I'm not used to dogs—never had a pet in my life—and to be honest, the large animal scares me a little, but he does seem friendly enough.

"Let me get you a drink. What would you like?" Jonas offers.

"I should prob—" I start declining when Thomas pipes up.

"Come sit by me," he says, patting the stool beside his. "I want to know how your sister is doing."

Five minutes later, I'm sitting at the kitchen island, a large glass of white wine in front of me, listening to Jonas recount how the team found a missing hiker this afternoon, when the front door opens and Sully walks in. Bo and James are right behind him, but I'm fixed on Fletch who's the last one through the door. His face shows no reaction to my being here as he comes straight for me, and I'm starting to wonder if I overstepped in some way.

"She's staying for dinner," Thomas shares as Fletch stops in front of me.

"Actually I was just dropping off some pie and tarts. I didn't mean to—"

"Pie?"

I turn my head to catch Bo trying to grab one of my butter tarts, but Ama is faster, snatching the plate out of his reach.

"Hands off. That's for dessert," she admonishes.

"You baked?"

Fletch's voice is low but I have no trouble hearing it over the lively discussion that ensues in the kitchen. When I turn back to him his eyes are warm, little crinkles fanning out from their corners.

"Just as a thank-you for letting me stay here," I clarify.

His lips stretch in a slow smile which—if possible—makes him even more devastatingly handsome.

Oh, dear...I'm in trouble.

"You bake," he echoes, except this time it's not so much a question as it is a statement.

"I know he doesn't look the part, but Fletch has a serious sweet tooth," Ama volunteers, grinning at me as her husband tucks her under his arm.

She's right; I wouldn't have associated a penchant for sweets with the generally broody man. But when he smiles like this? A warm sensation spreads through my body and I find myself smiling back.

"I do."

I'm not sure if it's the glass of wine she nursed all through dinner, the fact her sister is looked after, or both, but I'm liking this more relaxed Nella.

Everyone hung around for dinner—even James and Ama stayed, something they rarely do—and for once I wasn't in a hurry to get back to my place. So it's already pretty dark out by the time I walk Nella back to her cabin.

She's still beaming with the compliments she received on the dessert she provided.

"Gotta say, you sure know your way around the oven," I comment, eager to keep that smile on her face a little longer. "I can cook, but never mastered baking. Probably a good thing, or I'd have a gut by now."

Sure enough, her smile brightens and the color on her cheeks deepens at the compliment. Not sure how I initially missed how pretty she is.

"It's relaxing," she shares. "More of a hobby, but I give most of it away, or I'd be the one with the gut. Lord knows I don't need the extra padding, there's enough of it already."

And as far as I can see, every ounce of it perfectly distributed. It's what makes her a pleasure to hold, soft and warm, molding easily to the rougher angles of my body. But I don't tell her that. Not yet.

What I do say is, "Ever thought of making it a business?"

I can tell from the pause before she responds, it's at least crossed her mind before.

"I've fantasized, but it's hardly practical. I don't have any formal training though, and bakeries are a dime a dozen."

We've arrived at her door when I ease her around to face me.

"Not in Libby. At least not with desserts like yours."

I'm not sure where my head is at when I blurt that out and neither does she, judging by the look of confusion on her face.

"But I don't even live here."

I shrug. "So move."

Before my mouth runs away with me even further, I find a better use for it. I slide a hand along the side of her face and into her hair, tilting her chin up with the light press of my thumb. Then I take those amazing lips of hers and slip my tongue between, finding hers ready to tangle.

Her hands come up to my chest, my heart beating against her palm as I wrap my free arm around her waist, tugging her closer. She tastes like that butter tart she had for dessert, her flavor sweet and rich. I can't get enough of her and find myself sliding down a path I never intended to go down.

"Get a room!"

I tear my lips from hers and look up, seeing a grinning Sully slip into his place.

"I should—"

I cut her off with another kiss, while I reach for her doorknob. I thank my lucky stars when I find the door unlocked this time, and ease her backward into the cabin.

She doesn't even seem to notice as I press her up against the wall and lash her tongue with mine in an effort to still this burning hunger I have for more. More of this...of her. Of those little sounds she makes as her fingers curl in my shirt.

Fuck, this woman is messing with my head. She's already hard to resist when she's being straitlaced and stuffy, but downright impossible to steer clear of when she's relaxed and burning hot like this. I can't wait to get her out of these buttoned-up clothes.

I tug at her shirt, trying to free it from the waistband of her pants so I can slide my hand over her silky soft skin. I'd love to drive her wild with my hands and mouth, see that pretty flush build and watch her come apart under my touch.

Her shirttail finally freed, I yank her shirt up and plump her breast in my palm. Breaking our kiss I bend down and close my lips over the pert nipple poking through her dainty lace bra.

"Fletch..."

"Fuck, you taste good, Babe," I mumble against her skin before sinking to my knees.

I fully intend to get her out of those pants and sample more of her when she suddenly digs the fingers of one hand in my hair and pulls my head back.

"Fletch, I have to take this."

In her other hand she has her ringing cell phone.

Jesus. I hadn't even noticed.

Here I am on my fucking knees with a dick so hard it hurts, while she pulls her shirt down, walks into the kitchen area, and answers her phone.

"Hello?" She turns and I notice the fear on her face, just as I get to my feet. "This is she. Is my sister all right?"

Damn, it's the hospital. No wonder she looks terrified.

I ignore my dick and join her in the kitchen, putting a supporting arm around her shoulders.

"Okay. I'll be there. Thanks for calling."

Then she ends the call, dumps her phone on the counter, and turns her body into mine. I'm surprised to see a smile when she lifts her face.

"What happened?"

"She's doing better. The doctor apparently just came by to check on her and wants to start trying to wake her up first thing tomorrow morning. That was her nurse, Tracy. She wanted to make sure I knew so I could be there early."

This time I'm guessing the tears pooling in her eyes are happy ones.

"That's great news, Nella."

She nods. "I know. I'm trying hard not to get too excited. Tracy warned me not to expect too much, there's a possibility she may not wake up. Even if she does, she could have sustained damage that wasn't noticeable before."

I tuck her head under my chin and mumble, "I think you should let yourself be excited. Every step forward is a bonus, right?"

"Yeah."

My body stirs when she snuggles closer, but my head realizes it's probably just comfort she's looking for.

"What time did you plan on going?"

She tilts her head back to look up at me.

"To the hospital? I want to be there by seven. Why?"

"Because I'm coming."

"Weren't you going hunting tomorrow?"

The guys had given me a hard time over dinner about wasting my tag, and when Nella heard she insisted I should go while I can. I eventually conceded since things seemed pretty stable with her sister, but I hadn't planned on going far.

"I was, but I can go later. Or the day after tomorrow."

The truth is I don't want her to be alone if it turns out her sister has some kind of permanent damage, if she even opens her eyes.

"I appreciate it, but you really don't have to hold my hand."

The way she looks up at me with those pretty eyes sparkling and that mouth spread in a smile, has me turn into someone I don't even fucking recognize.

"What if I want to?"

Fourteen

Nella

"Who are you?"

I never expected that to be the first thing out of my sister's mouth, or the blank expression on her face when she turned her eyes on me.

"Sure you're okay?" Fletch asks for the umpteenth time since leaving the hospital.

"I'm fine," I snap irritably.

Except, I'm not. Not by a long shot.

It had been closing in on noon when Pippa finally started showing signs of stirring and by the time she answered a few basic questions by the doctor coherently, my heart was soaring and my eyes leaking. But then she turned her head and looked at me without the slightest hint of recognition. She also had no clue where she was, what happened to her, or what she was doing in Montana. She recognized she was in a hospital, knew her name, her date of birth, and that she was Canadian, and that was it. She couldn't even recall the calendar year.

I could see the panic in her eyes as she tried to remember and it killed me. I couldn't help myself and filled in the gaps for her, which only got her more agitated. Dr. Osborne kindly but firmly led me from the room and into his office, where he sat me down and suggested perhaps it was better to give Pippa some time to get her bearings. He assured me she was doing well physically, that memory loss is not unusual and often resolves itself with time, but that stress could hamper that recovery.

Then he sent me home.

Fletch jumped up when I walked into the waiting room and although I'm grateful for his concern, I almost wished he hadn't come. It wasn't easy to tell him Pippa has no idea who I am, and when he tried to wrap me in his arms, I quickly turned for the exit.

If I give in to any show of kindness now, I will crumble. The one person I have left in this entire big world—who loves me as I am and always has my back—doesn't know I exist. I'm terrified. What if she never remembers?

The deep ache in my chest makes it difficult to breathe. I need to get back to the cabin, grab my van, and find something to keep me busy before I have a full-fledged panic attack.

Fletch pulls his truck up in front of my cabin and before the wheels have stopped rolling, I already have the door open.

"At least fucking wait until I stop," he grumbles, jerking the vehicle in park as he throws a glare my way.

"Sorry, I've gotta go," I mutter, as I get out of the cab.

"What's the hurry?"

"I thought I'd do some shopping," I lie, but add as an

afterthought. "I appreciate you coming with me to the hospital. Maybe there's still time for you to go hunting?"

When he doesn't respond, I toss him a forced smile and rush to the front door, throwing a final look right before I'm about to go inside. He's standing in front of his truck, glaring at me. Oddly enough I'd rather have this grumpy version of him than the warm-eyed, caring one I've seen glimpses of. It's so tempting to let myself lean on him, but I can't. In the end I'll just have myself to depend on anyway.

Tearing my eyes from his strong, handsome face, I head inside and shut the door behind me, leaning my back against it. It takes me another few minutes after I hear his truck drive away to get my breathing under control. Then I grab my computer bag, snag my car keys, and head straight back out the door.

Bean There is a small coffee shop I spotted on the main drag in Libby. The sign outside boasted Wi-Fi so I pulled into the parking lot.

I found a quiet table in the far corner, away from foot traffic walking up to the counter. I sip the latte the young barista made me as I look around. It's a cute place, trendy, and looks to be popular judging by the steady flow of people walking in. Mostly for takeout, though, only a few tables are occupied.

No one appears to be paying me much attention as I pull out my laptop and turn it on, logging into the network listed on a blackboard over the counter.

I'd formulated a plan on my drive into town; to find my sister's motorhome. It's been her home for a while and all she owns in this world is in that rig. I'm hoping if I can locate it, there'll be something among her possessions that might trigger her memory. It's farfetched, I know, but it's not like I have anything better to do.

Trying to put myself in the shoes of the thieves, I imagine they'd want to sell her motorhome quickly. Online seems to be the most logical place for that so I'm checking any 'For Sale' listings for a 2018 Jayco Redhawk as I jot down information I find on a notepad.

I'm so focused I don't notice the barista walking over to my table.

"Can I get you a refill?"

I startle and look up at her before she redirects my attention to my empty coffee cup.

"That would be lovely, thank you." I'll probably be awake most of the night, but right now I don't care.

"Anything to eat? We have muffins, a few Danish, or a sandwich. I make a pretty good chicken salad sandwich, if I say so myself."

She smiles hopefully and I don't have the heart to say no. I should probably eat something anyway; it looks like I missed lunch completely. The earlier rush of customers seems to have slowed down.

"Chicken salad sounds delicious."

"Coming right up."

As she returns to the counter, I look over my notes. So far, I've found three Jayco Redhawks for sale in and around Libby, but only one listed as a 2018 model. The pictures with that last listing didn't look like my sister's though, but from what I've noticed these ads often use generic images. It could still be hers.

Hundreds more of them show up for sale, but not necessarily locally. I realize just because it was stolen here doesn't mean they'll try to sell it around here as well. In fact, now that I think about it, that might actually make more sense. It's only a few hours' drive to Canada or into Idaho.

Geeze, I may have bit off a little more than I can chew.

I remember the sheriff mentioning some other stolen RVs. Maybe I should go have a talk with him, see if he'll tell me if they have any leads, although I doubt he'd be willing to share. I'm equally sure he won't be happy if I'm sticking my nose into his investigation, but I figure I can pose as an interested buyer. No one would have reason to question me and I might get more answers than when a sheriff's deputy or police officer showed up. Besides, the sheriff doesn't need to know what I'm doing in my spare time.

It would help to know the model names for any of the other stolen RVs. Maybe I can track down my sister's if I manage to find one of the others.

"Here you go."

I shove my laptop aside to make room for my lunch. It looks amazing and I tell her so.

"Thank you," she says, clearly pleased.

I glance at the name tag on her shirt before responding.

"Well, Kaylie, if it tastes anywhere near as good as it looks, I should be thanking you."

She glances at the screen of my open laptop and her eyes light up.

"Are you looking for an RV? You should go see my uncle. He has an RV place right up the road. Sells new and used ones," she offers.

That would almost be too easy, but it wouldn't hurt to check.

"Really? I'd love to go have a look."

"It's called Rick's RVs—that's my uncle's name—he does repairs and stuff too."

I jot the name down on my notepad. Perhaps I'll drop in there after I stop by the sheriff's office.

~

Fletch

The big ram lifts his head and appears to be looking right at me.

I bypassed a few smaller ones in the valley below. They would've been easy pickings but there would've been no sport in that. No, I was determined to hold out for a more mature ram. One a bit more experienced detecting a threat and would require some skill to take down.

I'd just made my way on top of the ridge when I noticed him standing apart from a small herd of about ten or eleven bighorn. Most of them are bedded down, but the big ram is still up and clearly alert.

Bighorn sheep have keen eyesight, so I stay as still as I can. He's a few hundred yards from where I'm crouched down, so I wouldn't have a shot at him at this distance anyway. The sheep are predictable though. Creatures of habit who will follow the same migratory path and use the same bedding spots to rest for generations. Meaning even if I can't bag that ram today, I'll likely find this herd right back here tomorrow when they go down for an afternoon nap.

I'll wait them out and try to get a little closer when I have a chance. By the time they go look for food at dusk again, I'll be in a better position to take a shot at the big guy.

This is a good distraction and I needed it, because that thing with Nella earlier was fucked up.

I went with her to offer support should she need it, but

then when she did, she practically ignored me. Granted, having her sister wake up and not recognize her must've been a shock and I get she needs some time to process, but she could've just said that instead of pretending all is fine when obviously it's not.

Pissed me right off, her handing me that fake little polite smile as she lied to my face. *I'm fine*, my ass. It's killing her, and the kicker is, it's killing me to know that and not be able to do anything about it.

Hunting seemed like a good idea, given there are just three more days left on my tag. I just wish I could stop thinking about what she might be up to, and enjoy what I'm doing.

The big ram finally settles in with the herd and I start inching my way closer, while making sure to be quiet and stay out of sight.

It's not an easy route; I have to slide down a cliff, try not to knock loose any rocks, and traverse a few protruding boulders on my way to the bottom. There I manage to stay under the cover of the sparse trees, crawling low to the ground when I move from one to the next, and every so often I peek out at the herd to see if they noticed me.

So far so good, but in order to get a decent shot off I have to be within twenty-five or so yards and their bedding area is at least forty yards from the last tree I'm sitting under. Still, dusk is setting in and I'll miss my shot if I don't try to get closer.

Going down on my stomach, I belly-crawl another ten or so yards before peeking over the brush again. I find the large ram with his head up, staring right back at me and I freeze.

Fuck.

A magnificent animal, his nostrils flare as he tests the air for scent and I notice his ears scanning for sound. Staying absolutely still is something that comes as second nature to me, but after a while even my muscles start cramping. So when he finally turns his head in another direction and gets to his feet, I let out a breath of relief.

Following the large ram's lead, the rest of the herd stands up and I use the distraction to line up my bow, keeping an eye on my target. I would've liked to have been another five to ten feet closer, but beggars can't be choosers and I figure this may be the best shot I'll get.

I wait until the ram makes a hard right turn and starts moving straight west from my position. I have a good view of his left shoulder and flank.

Then I take in a breath, hold it, and release my arrow.

It's almost ten when I finally pull up to my cabin and notice Nella's van is parked outside hers, but all the lights are off.

I did the best I could out in the field by the waning light. Normally I might've called in some help to carry the entire ram out, but it was already getting late and I decided to take only what I would use. It took me a couple of trips to carry out just the meat and the head. I left the rest of the carcass where he fell for the predators to take care of. It'll be gone in no time. I have no interest in trophies and only carried out the head because I need to present it at the game warden's office. I did take some pictures before I started field dressing, in case the warden has questions. The meat I stored in the two large coolers I have under the tarp in the back of my truck.

Luckily with the sun down the temperature dropped significantly as well, but I'd still like to get the coolers into the spare bedroom where I can run the window AC to make sure it stays under thirty-seven degrees. It's not an ideal situation, but it'll do until I can hang the meat to age in the breeding barn in the morning. We have a cold room to store the sperm we collect that sometimes doubles as a meat locker, but the place is locked tight for the night. Believe it or not, horse sperm is valuable and there is a thriving black market for the stuff.

I'm not the only one who brings home game from time to time and Jonas doesn't mind us using the breeding barn to hang the meat. Proper aging makes all the difference in taste, and I plan to leave it hanging for about ten days before I process and pack it for the freezer.

"I see you got one?"

I look up to see Sully approach as I pull the first cooler from the back of the truck.

"Yeah. I'm guessing somewhere between two seventy-five and three hundred," I inform him.

"Nice." He grabs one side of the cooler and helps me carry it inside. "I was wondering where you'd gone when I saw her after dinner," he nudges toward Nella's cabin. "I figured you'd be together."

"No."

I can feel his eyes on me but I'm not about to elaborate.

"How's the sister?" he changes the subject.

We set the cooler down under the window unit and I turn it on high. Then we head out for the second one.

"Awake, but she seems to have trouble remembering anything."

"Nothing?"

"Her name and birthday but that's about it. She didn't even recognize Nella."

"Damn, that must've been tough on her."

I ignore the pang of guilt as we haul the second cooler down.

"Yeah. She needed some time to process."

"And you went hunting?'

I can clearly hear the disbelief and accusation in Sully's voice and my defenses go up instantly. I lower my side of the cooler on the porch before turning on him.

"Not that it's any of your fucking business but she asked me to. She didn't want me around so I went."

The asshole raises an eyebrow, shakes his head, and easily lifts the entire cooler by himself, brushing past me as he walks inside.

My temper flaring, I want to plant my fist in his face, but I opt for the doorpost instead. It turns out to be a lot less forgiving.

"Fuck!"

Nella

"How are you feeling?"

Pippa turns her eyes on me and I brace for the blank look in them, but instead I see curiosity.

I called the hospital a few times yesterday to check in on her. The nurses were friendly, letting me know she had eaten, had been out of bed to use the bathroom with help, and did a lot of sleeping. Then at just after six this morning, Tracy—the nurse from earlier on the weekend—called me to let me know Pippa asked to see me. For a moment, hope flared perhaps some memory had come back but I quickly nipped that in the bud. If my sister had remembered me, she would've called herself.

"I'm all right, I guess."

I take a seat beside her bed and resist taking her hand in mine. Something that under normal circumstances would come naturally, but might be perceived as invasive now.

Instead I fold my hands in my lap and wait her out. After all, she's the one who invited me here.

"Tracy mentioned you're the one who found me?"

"Fletch and I did," I correct her, not wanting to take all the credit. "Fletcher Boone; I got his name from a friend back in Cranbrook. He's a professional tracker."

"You hired a tracker to find me?" There's a hint of disbelief in her voice.

"Of course, you're my—" I snap my mouth shut, remembering her reaction to me yesterday.

"Sister," she finishes for me. "I'm sorry I don't recognize you. It wasn't until I found you'd been looking for me for a while I realized this has to be difficult for you too."

I swallow hard, making a mental note to thank Tracy.

"I'm just grateful you're recovering, awake, and talking," I reassure her, earning a faint smile.

"Too bad I don't remember much."

This time I don't resist the urge to grab her hand.

"It'll come. Don't force it," I echo Dr. Osborne's words to me yesterday as I give her hand a squeeze before releasing it.

"Okay, but will you tell me a little bit?"

The vulnerability in her voice tears at my insides, but my voice is steady when I answer, "Of course."

I feel a ton lighter when I walk out of the hospital half an hour later.

Pippa had tired quickly. I'd tried not to overwhelm her by cramming our entire history down her throat, but it still proved to be a lot to take in. So when I saw her eyes get heavy; I told her to get some rest and promised I'd be back later this afternoon to see how she's doing.

There'd been a change of shift while I was with my sister and Tracy had already left for home. I found out at the nurses' station Pippa would likely be moved to a regular room after morning rounds, and the nurse I spoke to promised to give me a call with her new room number.

I briefly consider going back to the cabin to catch another hour or so of sleep, but I have too much energy buzzing through my body. After what was a very tough day yesterday—and three-quarters of a bottle of wine to help me sleep—this morning definitely lifted my spirits, despite the mild hangover headache lingering.

Instead I pull my notebook from my computer bag the moment I get behind the wheel of my van. I'll just pick up where I'd left off last night.

Sheriff Ewing surprised me by inviting me right into his office when I'd stopped by yesterday afternoon. He seemed genuinely pleased at the news Pippa was awake, but his mood sobered when I informed him she was suffering memory loss. Apparently, Ewing had hoped her statement might offer them some fresh leads on their investigation into the RV thefts.

I made a few general inquiries about the case he willingly responded to, but when my questions became more detailed—makes and years of any other stolen trailers and motorhomes—and he clued in I was making notes, he clammed up.

"I hope you're not getting any ideas about playing amateur sleuth, Ms. Freling," he'd cautioned me. *"I understand your persistence in finding your sister, but I'd appreciate it if you left the investigating to professionals."*

He cut our chat short pretty quickly after that, but I

wasn't too discouraged. I still had Rick's RVs to visit and whatever information I didn't get from the sheriff, Kaylie's uncle was able to fill in. Apparently, law enforcement had already been by there for a chat. I walked away with a list of model names and years.

Last night I was able to link my laptop to my phone's data network and through simple Google searches was able to find mention of five of the stolen RVs, including my sister's, on the Lincoln County Sheriff's Office blotter. That gave me dates and locations of those thefts and with that I was able to pull up some newspaper articles, which provided me with a few more details on some of the incidents.

There had been a story on Pippa as well, but by then I was too emotional and halfway drunk on the wine I'd consumed, so I saved that for another day. I fell asleep, exhausted the moment my head hit the pillow, but when I woke up at four with a lightweight's hangover and the headache that went with it, I hadn't been able to get back to sleep. Against better judgment I read the story in bed.

The focus had been Pippa's dramatic rescue and it was clear the writer of the story had done his job because not only was HMT—High Mountain Trackers—mentioned, but Fletch was named specifically. Of course that got me thinking about him, something I'd tried to avoid doing the night before, and the guilt set in. If not for him, I don't think Pippa would be alive. He had saved my bacon more than once, I'd been an active participant in the heated kisses we've shared, and then I'd brushed him off. It's not fair to keep avoiding him.

But first I want to make a few stops in town.

~

My mood hasn't improved much when I walk into the barn after lunch.

I was pissed to see Nella's van missing again this morning when I stepped outside. At the main house I asked Thomas if he'd seen her leave but he hadn't. I'm annoyed I have no idea where she was yesterday or where she could've gone off to before seven in the morning. If I hadn't seen her van parked right outside the cabin last night when I got back, I'd have thought she'd packed up without a word.

Instead of waiting around for breakfast, I'd gone home and cooked some myself. Then I'd loaded the meat into the bed of my truck and went to hang it in the breeding barn. Trying to stay busy, I cleaned out the coolers when I got back at the cabin, left them upside down on my porch to dry, and headed into town to drop off the head with the game warden.

I just got back, hoping Nella might have returned but her van is still missing.

"Get into it with someone?"

Jonas points at my hand, which looks pretty beaten up. Guess the doorpost won.

"Banged it," I tell him by way of explanation.

Not sure he's buying. I figure Sully probably blabbed already; things tend to get around quickly.

"Looks sore."

"It's fine." I flex a few times to prove it. "Ama mentioned you were looking for me?"

"Yeah. Have you talked to Nella?"

I don't like the stern look on his face.

"Not since yesterday. Why?"

"Got a call from Wayne Ewing earlier. He's a little concerned. She stopped by his office yesterday afternoon, asking about the investigation and apparently was taking notes."

Fuck. What do you want to bet she's decided to do a little investigating of her own? I swear, I've never met a more headstrong woman in my life.

Frustrated, I whip my hat off and slap it against my thigh. I'm going to have to have a word with her. Jonas's next words bring that home in a big way.

"A hiker found two bodies about fifty yards from a dispersed camping site on Forest Road 176, just north of Troy, early this morning. They'd been there for a while, predators got at them."

"Jesus."

I know what that looks like and it's not pretty. What I don't know is what this has to do with Nella, but before I can ask, Jonas volunteers the answer.

"Yeah. Ewing was calling from the scene and says a pair of fairly new camp chairs and an ax were left around a firepit at the nearby camp site. He thinks this may be connected to the RV thefts."

And it looks like Nella is poking around that investigation. I'm gonna have to shut that down.

"I'll talk to her."

"That'd be good, but are you sure she'll listen to you?" He looks at me with an eyebrow raised.

"I'll make her," I growl.

Fucking Sully.

"Been trying to call you for the past hour."

She almost jumps and drops her bag on the floor at her feet.

"You scared me!"

I get up from the kitchen table where I've been waiting since I let myself in. She'd locked the door but that hadn't been too much of a deterrent. I wasn't going to sit on the porch in full view of the entire ranch or tongues would never stop wagging. Then I stalk toward her.

"How did you get in here anyway?"

"What've you been up to, Nella?"

"I asked you first," she says, sticking her chin out when I stop inches away from her.

"Lock's a piece of shit. Where have you been?" I push.

"Out."

"Nella..."

She tilts her head defiantly and I suddenly feel the need to kiss her. So I do.

Her lips open in shock when I wrap an arm around her waist and I grab the opportunity. The moment my tongue touches hers, her hands curl around my neck and she pulls me closer.

And just like that, prim and proper Nella is on fire.

"Easy," I mumble into her mouth, but more to myself than to her. I'm about two seconds from losing my last thread of control.

I came here to have a serious talk with her and instead her hand is slipping into the waistband of my pants. I've reached my breaking point when she digs her fingers into my ass cheek. Groaning, I lift my head and look down into her flushed face.

"Only one way this can end with your hand on my ass, Babe," I growl in warning.

Something flares in her eyes and I close mine as she pulls her hand from my pants.

Shit. I'm going to need an ice bath to freeze my junk, or I won't be able to walk with this raging hard-on in my jeans.

But then I feel her hand take mine and my eyes snap open as she starts moving us toward the bedroom. The moment we cross the threshold, she lets go and moves to the side of the bed, turning around to face me.

"I didn't mean to come off as ungrateful yesterday," she says, even as she lifts her hands to her top button closed tightly at the base of her slim neck. "I was overwhelmed and needed..."

I barely register the rest of her words as she methodically unbuttons the rest of her shirt and shrugs out of it. Then she folds it neatly and places it on the nightstand. I completely miss what she says next when she reaches behind her to unclip her bra, letting it slide down her arms before placing it neatly on top of her shirt. Her creamy skin looks as soft as I remember it being, and all I can think of is tasting every last inch of her.

"Fletch? Are you listening?" she asks sharply.

My gaze meets her accusing one. *Damn*, even that angry scowl is sexy. At odds with her prudish appearance, she seems completely unbothered by her nudity as she plants a fist in her side. The woman is a walking contradiction and I'm discovering I like it.

A whole fucking lot.

"Seriously? Babe, the moment you started taking your clothes off my ears stopped working."

She rolls her eyes before repeating, "I said I was sorry for never properly thanking you for all you've done."

Her words act like a cold shower.

That's what this is? Gratitude?

Suddenly I'm pissed.

"So this is your idea of thanking me?" I wave my hand in front of me. "You're gonna fuck me out of gratitude?"

Her mouth falls open and her eyes bulge. My crass words shocked her. *Good*.

I turn on my heel and am about to walk out of here. As much as she turns me on, I have a little pride left and I'm not about to become someone's equivalent to a mercy fuck.

"No!" Her voice stops me in my tracks. "I mean yes, I'm grateful, but that's not why—"

Before she can say another word, I bridge the few steps between us as I rip my shirt over my head and toss it on the floor. I reach for her and the next moment my mouth is on hers, her fingers are clawing on my back, and all of that glorious, silky skin is pressed against my chest.

"Bed," I mumble when I come up for air.

Her pretty eyes are dark and shiny with heat as she nods before climbing onto the mattress. Her scorching gaze never leaves me as I toe off my boots, shuck my jeans and boxers, and peel off my socks before putting a knee in the bed. Her hands are fumbling with her zipper and I brush them aside, making quick work of her pants, yanking them and her panties down in one move.

Fuck me. She looks like a wet dream; sturdy thighs, rounds hips, the soft swell of a belly, and the pink blush slowly covering her upper chest and face as I drink her in.

I reach for my jeans only to realize I'm no longer the guy who walks around prepared for any opportunity with a condom in his wallet. Haven't been that guy in years.

"What's wrong?"

I look at her, mentally cursing myself as I formulate an apology but all I can manage is, "Condom."

The color on her cheeks deepens. "My computer bag,"

she says, her eyes drifting over my shoulder. "I picked up a box this morning."

I'm instantly hit with an image of Nella, all buttoned up, walking up to the counter at the drugstore in town carrying a box of condoms. It puts a smile on my face as I bend down to kiss her stomach before darting out of the room to grab her bag. I'm back in a flash with the box.

"You bought a bulk pack," I point out, ripping it open and pulling a strip free. I toss the box on the nightstand and slide in bed beside her, propping my head on my hand as I look down on her.

"I grabbed the first thing I saw," she admits with a smirk on her lips as she glances down my body. "Be grateful they're not extra-small."

"Oh, I'm not complaining," I assure her, running my palm over her skin from her neck to the patch of hair between her legs.

I love the way she sinks her teeth into that plump bottom lip and moans softly as I dip between her thighs and play with her. Liquid heat coats my fingers.

"Look at you...all pretty and flushed. Your body is ready, but are you?"

By way of an answer, she reaches out and wraps a firm hand around my shaft.

Oh, fuck yeah, she's ready.

It takes less than two seconds to roll on a condom and kneel between her legs. I use my hands and mouth to show her how much I love her body as I slowly stretch out on top of her. Shifting her legs she makes room for me, but then throws me a curveball when she plants a foot in the mattress, flipping me on my back.

As she climbs on top of me, she has her bottom lip between her teeth again but she avoids looking at me.

"Do you mind? I've always wanted—"

"Whatever you want, Nella," I tell her, my voice strangled as I keep myself from taking charge.

Then I get her eyes, hot and intense, as she carefully guides me inside her. I grind my teeth when she sinks down on me and suddenly freezes.

"You feel incredible," I mumble digging my fingers in her hips. "But you're gonna kill me if you don't move."

I groan when she finally does. Tentatively at first, but once she finds her rhythm, she seems to shed every inhibition and rides me wild. I've never seen a woman smile when she comes, but Nella is smiling as she cries out her release.

Fucking magnificent.

Sixteen

I'm not going to lie and say I'm not concerned.

Learning over an early dinner we slapped together last night—after a mind-blowing afternoon in my bed—two people may have lost their lives at the hands of the same thieves who stole my sister's motorhome, sent shivers down my spine. And not the good kind.

The problem is, I'm not ready to give up my search yet. Not after talking to the nice couple whose thirty-eight-foot Class-A was stolen from—according to Lorna and Jim Carmichael—the loveliest spot along the Kootenay River, just a few miles north of the Libby Dam, where Lake Koocanusa flows back into the Kootenay River on the US side of the border.

I got the names from the editor at the Libby Press, who had written the few short pieces I found on the thefts. In one of the articles she'd described the Carmichaels as a retired couple from Spruce Grove, Alberta—a small town just west of Edmonton—so they weren't too hard to find.

Jim and his wife were quite willing to talk to me, especially after I mentioned what happened to my sister. They shared they'd stayed a few nights at Timberlane, the same campground I discovered Pippa stayed at, except the Carmichaels were there back in early July.

Still, it was a bit of a coincidence and I'd intended to see if I could connect with one of the other victims yesterday afternoon but got a little distracted.

I can't stop the smile pulling at the corners of my mouth as I look at Fletch's back standing at my stove, cooking us breakfast. He was already cooking when I walked out of the bedroom five minutes ago.

He'd stayed the night.

Other than that one time in college when my then boyfriend and I had fallen asleep after a night of too much drinking, I've never had a man sleep over. My choice, I never wanted the commitments that would inevitably follow. My life was balanced and predictable, which is the way I preferred it.

I never met a man I was willing to rock the boat for. Until now, I guess. In part because of Fletch, but perhaps a little more so because I'm starting to like who I am without the boundaries I set myself years ago. I certainly let go yesterday.

"What's the smile for?"

He's looking at me over his shoulder.

"Nothing in particular."

He grunts, but despite the scowl on his face, I notice his eyes are dancing.

"That smells good. I'm getting hungry."

My attempt to redirect the conversation proves successful when he turns back to the stove.

"It's about done."

Two minutes later he slides breakfast in front of me: a fluffy cheese, mushroom, and bacon omelet topped with thinly sliced tomatoes. I take my first bite as he returns with the coffeepot and tops me up before he sits down across from me at the tiny kitchen table.

"Tastes even better."

He looks up and one corner of his mouth tilts up. "Good." Then he digs into his own.

We eat in companionable silence until I catch the time on the stove clock. It's already after eight.

"You don't have to work?"

"Not until Thursday, unless something comes up. Why?"

I put down my fork and lean my elbows on the table.

"I want to visit Pippa this morning, but I was wondering if you'd want to go on a drive in the country with me after?"

He'd been very adamant last night, after telling me about the sheriff's caution, I leave the investigating to the experts, but I'd really like to explore if this connection to Timberlane may prove to be a lead. I'll happily hand it over to the authorities if I can tie a third stolen vehicle to the campground. Only two could just be coincidence, but three makes a pattern.

Fletch narrows his eyes at me.

"Where are you suggesting we go?"

Lying has never been my strong suit, and clearly the whole 'drive in the country' ploy didn't fly, so I opt for the truth instead. I mentioned my visit to the newspaper and the phone call with the Carmichaels to him last night.

"I'd like to stop by Timberlane Campground. I'm hoping the manager remembers if Janice Laszlo was ever there."

That was the second name the editor at the paper had passed on to me. The only problem is no one answered the contact number she gave me when I tried calling yesterday and I wasn't able to leave a message because the mailbox was full. Janice's twenty-eight-foot travel trailer was actually stolen from a site not far from where the dead couple was found.

"Nella..." he growls.

"Well, what do you expect me to do; twiddle my thumbs? I have to do something, Fletcher. I want to help Pippa get her memory back. All her belongings are in that motorhome, maybe something will trigger her recollection. That's not going to be a priority for the sheriff, especially now he has two bodies to worry about."

He blows out a breath through pursed lips.

"Dammit, Nella."

"Does that mean you have plans already?" I ask innocently, to which he scowls even harder.

"It means I should've known you wouldn't give up."

"I'm persistent."

"You mean stubborn," he grumbles.

Thirty minutes later I get into Fletch's truck, grinning.

Fletch

I don't like the guy.

Chuck Yates is a sleazeball.

I don't trust the middle-aged, pot-bellied campground manager with the greasy ponytail on sight. For one thing, I don't like the way he looks at Nella, but what really sticks in my craw is how he pushes her for information on her sister. His interest is as fake as a three-dollar bill. Luckily Nella isn't buying it either.

"Feel free to write her a note and I'll be happy to deliver it to her."

"I'd like to send her flowers," he responds, trying to sway her with a saccharine smile.

"That's very kind of you, but I assure you, not necessary." Her smile is tight and is gone in a flash. "But that's not the reason I'm here. Does the name Janice Laszlo ring a bell?"

"I don't believe it does." He darts a look my way and then shakes his head as if he's contemplating the question. "No, it's not familiar."

"She would've stayed here probably late June?" Nella pushes.

He shakes his head again. "I've got so many people staying here over the summer, it's impossible to remember names."

I've had enough of whatever fucking game the guy is playing and speak up for the first time.

"You don't keep a registry? I thought that was mandatory?" I pull out my phone. "Never mind. I'm sure my buddy, Wayne Ewing, can answer that question."

Everybody in Lincoln County knows that name. Wayne was just reelected last year for his third term in the Sheriff's Office. Obviously, Chuck does as well.

"No, no, you don't have to do that." He holds out a hand to stop me. "I'll have a quick look."

He ducks inside the tiny office as Nella sidles up to me.

"Did you just threaten him?" she whispers, her eyes sparkling.

"Technically, no. And only someone with something to hide would take it as one."

It doesn't take long for Chuck to reappear, waving a piece of paper.

"June twenty-second through twenty-ninth," he announces, handing me the note.

It lists the name, the make of Janice Laszlo's trailer, the license plate number, and a phone number. I show the latter to Nella. "Same number you've been trying?"

"Yes."

"I remember her now," Chuck volunteers. "Pretty girl."

"That all you remember?"

My tone is purposely sarcastic, but the idiot doesn't even seem to clue in.

"She had a dog. One of those little ones. Bit of a yapper if I recall correctly. Oh, and I remember she had some problems with her fridge. She came by to pick up bags of ice and I gave her a few names of reputable places that might be able to help her with that."

I put question marks by the label of reputable from Chuck's mouth, but he does open up another possibility to pursue. Nella comes to the same conclusion and beats me to it.

"Which places would that be?"

"A buddy of mine owns an RV dealership in town. Rick's RVs? He does repairs too. Advanced Truck and RV services just south of town would've been another one. And Mobilife in Happys Inn."

I watch Nella pull out her phone and make a note of those names. Not that I'll let her do anything other than pass those names on to Ewing. I intend to hold her to her promise.

"Did my sister ever mention needing repairs?"

Chuck seems to think a moment before shaking his head.

"Not to me." Then a lewd smile forms on his face. "If she had I would definitely have remembered."

I can almost feel Nella bristle beside me, but neither of us have a chance to react when an older lady walks up.

"Back already, Betsy?" the manager greets her.

"Too many idiot yahoos at Kootenai River."

"Hunting season, Bets. Could'a told you that."

The woman grumbles something and darts a glance at me before focusing on Nella.

"You're the one from last week. Looking for your sister?"

"That was me. Hi, Betsy, how have you been?" Nella replies politely.

"Weather's gettin' colder so the arthritis gets worse. Old age sucks and don't let anyone tell you otherwise. So, your sister was found? A miracle, that is. Not many who could survive bein' out there as long as she had. How is she?"

"Well, she was in rough shape and it was touch and go for a while, but it looks like she'll pull through."

"Lucky girl, walking away unscathed."

"Not quite," Nella volunteers. "Unfortunately, she's suffering from some kind of amnesia. We hope it'll just be temporary though."

I keep a close eye on Chuck during the exchange, and I'm not a fan of how closely he's listening in.

"We should go," I announce, putting a hand on Nella's elbow.

"It was nice seeing you again." She holds out her hand to Betsy.

"You too. I reckon you'll be taking your sister home soon?"

The old woman's question startles me, although I guess it would make sense. I hadn't really thought about it much, but enough to know I don't like that idea at all. I focus all my attention on Nella, eagerly waiting for her response.

"She's still in the hospital so it depends on when she'll be released." She darts a quick glance my way. "And what she wants to do."

It's on my lips to ask Nella what *she* wants. But it's way too fucking early to be talking about shit like that, even after spending the night with my nose buried in her hair with the claw marks of her unexpected passion still marking my back. Not something I want to discuss in front of these two either. So I swallow it down.

"Motel must be getting expensive," Chuck observes. "If you need a cheaper place to stay, I have a rental trailer on site 114, full services, I can give you for a steal. It's the least I can do."

"Like hell—" I start but Nella grabs my arm, digging her fingers in deep.

"I appreciate the offer," she interrupts. "But there's no need. I've been offered temporary lodging at High Meadow Ranch. Everyone's been very kind."

Chuck's eyes shoot an indecipherable look my way before turning back to Nella.

"Offer stands if you need it."

"Thank you." Then she slips her entire arm through mine. "We'd really best get going. Appreciate your help." She gives Betsy a little wave with her free hand. "See you, Betsy. Thanks again."

"Sheriff's Office?" I prompt her when we get in my truck.

"Hospital first," she returns.

The neurologist had been in with Pippa when we got there this morning. He wanted to have a few tests done so we weren't able to visit with her and were asked to come back later.

"Sooner the sheriff has the information the faster he can do something with it."

For a moment it looks like she'll protest but instead she lets out a deep sigh.

"Fine. Sheriff first. I don't trust Yates," she adds. I can't say I disagree. "It's a bit of a coincidence, isn't it? That they all stayed at Timberlane?"

"Three of them," I correct her.

I'm not sure how many of these thefts are connected but she's right; three makes it worth looking into.

We just catch Ewing coming out of his office. He starts waving us off the moment he sees us.

"I'm sorry, folks. Don't have time right now."

"Five minutes, Wayne, then we'll be out of your hair. It may be worth your while."

He looks at me, before eyeing Nella with narrowed eyes.

"Been sleuthing again, Ms. Freling?"

Nella wisely keeps her mouth shut.

"Fine," he continues. "Five minutes. Not a second more."

Then he turns on his heel and leads us into his office.

"Pippa, the Carmichaels, and Janice Laszlo all stayed at Timberlane Campground in the days before their vehicles were stolen," Nella lays out.

"What in the fresh hell? Where did you get those names?" Ewing barks at her.

She doesn't seem too impressed and shrugs her shoulders.

"Research. It's what I'm good at," she says dryly.

"Your sister is in the hospital and I just had to notify a family over the phone their loved ones won't be coming home because they're on a cold slab in the morgue," he snaps at her and my hackles go up.

"Hey," I intervene. "Easy does it, Ewing."

That gets his attention.

"Easy? These guys went from theft, to attempted murder, to murder, Boone. We have our hands full already, last thing we need is a civilian poking around stirring up more trouble."

Then he turns back to Nella and wags his finger in her face.

"You're playing a high stakes game, Ms. Freling."

NELLA

I'm still walking funny when I enter Pippa's room.

Fletch kept me busy yesterday. I think he was making sure I had no time to go against the sheriff's clear instruction, which basically was to butt out of his investigation.

He'd left me at my door the night before with a peck on the lips and a warning to get a good night's sleep in because he'd have a surprise for me in the morning. I'll admit, I was a bit disappointed but it did give me a chance to boot up my laptop and check out online ads for older model Jayco Redhawks. Sheriff Ewing said not to butt into the investigation, but he can hardly stop me from checking out previously owned motorhomes. I found a few promising listings; one in Eureka, and the other one near Sturgeon in neighboring Idaho and I planned to call yesterday morning, but I never got the chance.

It was barely eight in the morning when Fletch knocked on my door yesterday. My insides did a little squeeze at the sight of him leaning against my doorpost. The black Stetson he's been wearing since he lost his old one in the creek, a white Henley under a loose plaid shirt, but the showstopper had to be the chaps encasing the legs of his threadbare jeans. It wasn't so much what they covered, but rather how they framed what was left uncovered that got my full attention.

That was, until I heard snorting and looked beyond him to find two horses tied to the railing of my porch.

"No."

"You can't visit Montana and not go riding."

He's trying to sway me with that rare grin he flashes, but I'm not falling for it.

"Sure I can," I fire back. "People fall off horses and break things. I've seen enough of Libby's hospital, thank you very much."

"Says the woman who took off into the wilderness by herself, faced off with a bear, spent the night in a cave, and dangled off the side of a mountain. Heck, you climbed on King with me, don't tell me old Buttercup here scares you. She rides like a comfy chair."

He points at the—admittedly—docile-looking chestnut standing next to his horse. She looks friendly enough but she's almost as tall as King, and the thought of getting on the powerful animal by myself is a bit daunting.

"Fine," I snap, unable to resist the challenge in his words. It should probably bother me he seems to know me well enough to recognize I wouldn't be able to.

He'd been right, riding Buttercup was surprisingly comfortable. I had no trouble keeping up with him as he showed me the beauty of Montana from a new vantage point. He'd even packed sandwiches and water, which we had sitting on the edge of a cliff overlooking Fisher River below.

It wasn't until we got back to the barn—and I was starting to feel the effects of being in the saddle for an extended period—I realized Fletch had been quiet, even for him. I'd done most of the talking and he'd been listening but hadn't really said much. There hadn't been much touching either.

He came with me to the hospital for a visit, suggested a local bar and grill not far from the hospital for an elk burger and a piece of huckleberry pie after, and by the time we got back to the ranch it was dark outside. He dropped me at my door with a brush of his lips and announced he'd be back to work in the morning. That was it.

I'm far from an expert on relationships, but something told me whatever happened between us was a little more temporary than I had thought. I'm not going to lie, it hurt, but somewhere halfway through the restless night I decided I was too practical to let a handful of kisses and one mind-blowing sexual experience throw me off.

After all, I'm the one who bought the condoms and it was me getting naked, practically throwing myself at him. Hell, I didn't even take the time to explore—all I remember was the sparse hair on his chest and the feel of his muscles under my hands—and went straight for the goods. Sure, he seemed a willing participant, but my guess is most guys would be under those circumstances. Maybe I'd read too much into the fact he stayed the night and cooked me breakfast. Maybe that's just something he does because he's a good guy.

A really good guy.

Or maybe he's just not that into me.

I plaster a smile on my face for Pippa's sake.

"What happened to you?" she asks, noting my somewhat awkward gait. "Fun night?"

The comment is a small glimpse of the Pippa I used to know. She would regularly encourage me to let loose and have some fun. Often accused me of being a stick-in-the-mud. There is only a shadow of the familiar disarming grin on the face of the woman sitting at the small table by the window, but I'll take it.

"No such luck," I tell her, as I join her and take a tentative seat. "Went horseback riding yesterday. Woke up bowlegged this morning," I explain.

"Still, sounds like fun. It's been a while since—" She abruptly stops and turns to me, wide-eyed. "I've been horseback riding?"

"Every chance you got," I clear up, trying not to burst out crying at the small glimpse of memory returning. "You actually joined a cattle drive in Wyoming earlier this summer."

I watch her closely to see how she reacts to my prompt. She'd been so excited when she called me after that adventure. Told me she was seriously considering changing her career from mechanic to cowboy. Or cowperson, whatever the appropriate term is these days.

"Bitterroot Ranch," she mumbles, her gaze drifting past me. "Winston..." Her eyes come back to me. "The horse they assigned me to. I remember now. It made me think of—"

"Winston Churchill," I finish for her, my voice cracking. "My cat."

I'd been fifteen when I came home with the scrawny little kitten I'd found rummaging around the dumpster at the fast-food restaurant where I worked a few shifts after school. My parents had been less than enthused but I'd promised to pay for its care myself and they were finally swayed. Pippa had been over the moon.

"Black with four white socks," she whispers and all I can do is nod. "He would always sleep in your laundry hamper."

"Unless you lured him into your room with Mom's tuna salad," I remind her, my voice thick with emotion.

I've never seen my sister more beautiful than in this moment, her face lighting up with a smile as each memory seems to trigger another.

"Winston was the only one who liked it anyway," she recalls.

She's right, Mom's tuna salad was even worse than her chicken salad, and that was bad enough.

"Mom was always a far better baker than she was a cook," I reminisce.

I definitely inherited my love for baking from her, but I'd like to think I get my cooking skills from my father, who took care of a lot of the meals in our house. Probably self-preservation.

"I would do anything for a slice of her pecan pie," Pippa sighs.

"I'll make you a whole one. I still use her recipe."

She turns to me, trying to smile through the tears coursing down her face.

"I'd like that."

"I'll do it tonight," I promise, myself a sobbing mess by now.

"They're gone, aren't they?"

"Eighteen years."

She nods. "I remember."

It's heartbreaking to see the pain of their loss play out on Pippa's face as if she only just received the news. The next moment I'm on my knees beside her chair—ignoring my muscles' loud protest—and wrap my arms around her.

That's how Dr. Osborne finds us when he walks in moments later.

∼

Fletch

"What the fuck is wrong with you?"

Bo, who hardly ever gets bent out of shape, is pissed. At me, to be clear. I'm a few inches taller and no slouch, but when I try to brush past him, he easily blocks me with his solid mass.

"Move," I bark, but he's not budging.

"Not until you talk."

That's the last thing I want to do. I've had an internal argument running for the past two days, with my head and my heart on opposing sides. It's fucking exhausting.

There's a reason I don't allow myself to get emotionally involved. It fucks with my head. My current situation is a case in point. I *knew* I should've kept my distance from Nella. Not sure why I didn't, but those damn words from the sheriff's mouth were quick to remind me.

"You're playing a high stakes game."

Ewing directed them at Nella but I heard them loud and clear. It was like a bucket of ice water.

I was told the same thing once and didn't listen, with detrimental results. I'm not about to make the same mistake again.

"What's going on?" Jonas pokes his head in the tack room. It only takes him a second to read the situation. "Someone better fucking tell me."

"Bo won't fucking get out of my way," I spit out like

some five-year-old on a temper tantrum, but I can't seem to help myself.

"You've been a dick all damn day," Bo fires back. "Off in your head somewhere, not paying attention. Losing it on Dan in the breeding barn for no good reason."

"He dropped the goddamn sleeve!"

I get up in Bo's face but he doesn't back down.

"Only because you didn't have control of Blitz. Your head was too far up your own ass!"

"Fuck off!"

I plant both my hands on his chest and shove, but Bo is like a fucking tree trunk, he doesn't even waver.

"Told ya, not until you talk."

"This about the woman?" Jonas asks, stepping up beside Bo.

Great, now I have both of them fucking blocking my way out.

I turn my back, my hands in fists by my side as I try to resist the urge to use them.

"Sully, get the bourbon from my office, will ya? And grab James and join us in here," Jonas calls out.

"Sure, let's make this a goddamn party," I mutter.

"Not a party, a *team*. Or have you forgotten? We're only as strong as our weakest link, and right now that's you. Now take a damn seat and start talking."

Five minutes later, there's barely enough room to breathe in the tack room. I'm sitting on an inverted feed bucket, taking a deep tug from the tumbler someone shoved in my hand.

"Brother, not for anything, but Ama has a massive tray of enchiladas waiting inside and I'm getting hangry," James announces. "So I'm gonna make this easy for ya. Nella is not Sandy."

My eyes snap up to him but I don't trust myself to say anything. It still unnerves me how easily these men can see through my shields.

I only had about six months left in Afghanistan when I was reassigned to assist in the search and extraction of a Red Cross worker. She had gone missing from the Pul-e Khishti Bazaar, an open-air market in Kabul, in broad daylight. It took me five fucking days to track her down, but I found her.

She was kept in a cave in the mountains by a group of insurgents, whose ultimate goal turned out to be drawing as many US service personnel into their trap as possible. Sandy had been the bait. As the daughter of a US senator her disappearance drew a lot of attention, which is exactly what those assholes were after.

The rescue was a clusterfuck from beginning to end. The only reason she and I weren't blown to bits along with the rest of the extraction team and the Humvees was because Sandy tripped about thirty feet from our getaway vehicle and I was helping her up when the first RPG round hit.

"I don't need to tell you how high the stakes are, Fletcher."

I could still hear the senator's words as I managed to throw myself on top of her. I was able to shield her from the worst of it but I didn't get away scot-free.

After we were pulled from that ditch, I ended up at the Daoud Khan Military Hospital in Kabul while Sandy was whisked off on a military transport to meet up with her father, who was waiting Stateside.

Except, she never made it. The woman who only three months prior had agreed to marry me, killed herself in the small airplane washroom.

That fucks with a man's head.

I was still in the hospital in Kabul five days later when

James found me and told me she was gone. No one contacted me. Not even Senator Galvas—Sandy's father— had bothered to notify me.

"I fucking know that."

"Do you?" Jonas questions. "'Cause we all know what happened last time you cared for a woman. We saw the aftermath when we found you in that mountain shack in Canada living like fucking Grizzly Adams. Although 'living' may be an overstatement. You were more like an angry bear then too."

"Then I don't have to explain, do I?" I counter, pointing at James and Jonas. "This relationship bullshit may work for you two, but some of us are just too fucking messed up to try. She deserves better than damaged goods."

"Hey, speak for yourself," Sully pipes up. "I may be messed up but for the right woman I'd give it a shot."

Jonas tosses back his bourbon and gets to his feet.

"Sounds like you're making excuses. You can pretend all you want this is some noble attempt to protect Nella from your bad self, but this has got nothing to do with her and you know it."

"What the hell are you talking about?"

Agitated, I stand as well, feeling a little less vulnerable when I can look Jonas straight in the eye.

"It's fear, Fletch. The only one you're trying to protect is you."

Moments later I'm alone in the tack room with the bottle of bourbon they left behind.

NELLA

"That's amazing. I'm so happy for you."

Ama smiles big as she slides a glass of wine across the island.

I was so eager to tell someone the good news, I ended up knocking on Fletch's door but no one answered. So instead I turned to the main house where I found Ama alone in the kitchen.

I just filled her in on the latest news.

"Don't tell me you'll be hurrying back to Canada?"

I've considered it. It certainly seems like the most logical move, but Pippa will need continued care and rehab until she has full functionality back. She's experiencing problems with balance, concentration, coordination, and despite some of her memory coming back, there are still huge chunks missing. I hesitate to drag her back to Cranbrook and transfer her care there. It would mean more tests, more prying and prodding, and she's had enough of that over the past week or so.

But staying here means not only finding a place for us to stay, but giving the college my notice. I'll probably have to do that anyway, since Pippa will need my help wherever we end up.

"I honestly don't know what to do. Either way, I'm going to have to quit my job, but other than that I don't want to rush into any decision. If I could find a short-term rental in town that would be perfect."

"A rental? You can stay here as long as you want," she offers.

Very kind, but I'm sure Jonas would have something to say about that. Besides, the cabin is a little small for the two of us with only one bedroom. I also think it's better to create some distance from Fletch, it makes for a cleaner— maybe less painful—break.

"I really appreciate your hospitality but I think in addition to needing a little more space, I've probably overstayed my welcome already."

"What's going on?"

Thomas, Jonas's father walks in with Alex right on his heels.

"Nella's sister is being released tomorrow," Ama volunteers.

"That's great news!" Alex walks over and gives my shoulder a squeeze. "You must be so happy."

Her smile is contagious and I flash one back.

"I am. Her memory actually started coming back today. She knows who I am, she is starting to remember little things from our past."

"Couldn't be more pleased for you, girl," Jonas's father weighs in. "Is your sister a looker like you?"

"Christ, Thomas." Alex swats his shoulder. "Did you not hear your cardiologist just now? You need to slow your strut."

I sip my wine and listen with half an ear to the three of them exchange banter.

It'll be hard to leave here and not just because of Fletch. The only two actually related by blood are Jonas and his father, but everyone here is family and for a while I could imagine being part of it too.

So yes, I'm sad for losing that fantasy I allowed myself, but I have to focus on Pippa. I'm her family and she needs me.

"...can meet Lucy."

I only catch half of what Alex says to me. "Sorry?"

"Ama mentioned you need a place big enough for the two of you and I have a solution. You know I own the horse rescue on the way into Libby?"

I nod. "Hart's Horse Rescue. Yes, I've seen the sign in passing."

"My manager and good friend, Lucy, lives there alone since I moved out earlier this summer. It's a big rambling farmhouse with plenty of empty space. I was just saying you should come with me tomorrow morning and meet with Lucy. She's been talking about getting a roommate, and if the space suits you, it may be a great solution for everyone."

It takes me a moment to process what she's saying, but she's right; it would be perfect. We'd be closer to Libby, have lots of room to give each other space, we'd still be close to nature, which I know Pippa would like, plus...there are horses, which she loves.

So perfect in fact, it prompts me to ask, "How much?"

"You'll have to haggle with Lucy over money, that's her decision. How about I pick you up early; seven okay with you? I'll give Lucy a heads-up tonight and we can get all that sorted out over breakfast. Lucy's a great cook, but it wouldn't hurt to bring her a sample of your baking," Alex suggests with a wink.

I mentally take stock of the supplies I have left at the cabin just as the group of men floods into the kitchen. Everyone except Fletch, that is.

It takes me ten minutes to untangle myself politely and hustle out the door, but Sully catches me on the porch.

"Good to hear your sister's gonna be released."

"Yeah, it's great news."

"So what's the plan? You sticking around for a bit, or rushing off right away?"

There's an odd weight to his question, borderline accusatory. A deep groove between his heavy eyebrows shows his intensity and almost has me feeling guilty.

"We'll probably be around for a little while. Give Pippa a chance to get her feet back under her."

He seems almost relieved at my response.

"Good. Fletch is a good man. Salt of the earth. I don't like to see him hurt."

Hang on a second. What exactly is going on here?

"I don't like to see anyone hurt," I counter but I doubt if he hears me, he's already heading back inside.

Was he implying I did something to Fletch? That's laughable. I'm the *dumpee* here, if you want to put it that way. I'm not sure what he's been telling his buddies, but I aim to find out.

I'm hopeful when I see Fletch's truck still parked out front—at least he hasn't gone far—but when I try his door, there's still no answer. Looks like I won't get an answer tonight, but if the man wants to avoid me there's not much

I can do. Hopefully by the end of tomorrow I can start forgetting about him.

Although the thick lump in my throat tells me it might not be as easy as that.

~

Fletch

Jesus Christ.

I don't only feel like shit, I smell like it too.

When I crack an eye, the first thing I see is the bottom of an empty bottle.

Right. Guess I owe Jonas a bottle of good bourbon.

Beyond the bottle I see a familiar pair of horse hooves standing in straw. How the hell did I get in here?

"Still here?"

I roll on my back and end up staring at King's underside, which does nothing for my churning stomach. Struggling to sit up, I find Bo hanging over the stable door.

"What time is it?"

"It's almost nine. You're a fucking mess, brother."

He doesn't need to tell me that. I lean my head in my hand, encountering a clump of something in my hair. I need a fistful of Tylenol and a shower.

"Where is everyone?"

Bo's booming laugh reverberates in my skull as he walks away.

I understand why when I finally stumble out of the stable and everyone is standing around the corral watching Dan work with a young, feisty colt. Every eye turns my way.

Pretty tough walking with your head held high when it feels like your brains are leaking from your ears.

"You owe me a bottle," Jonas mumbles when I pass him.

"Yeah."

Ducking my head farther, I make my way to my cabin, hoping like hell Nella isn't witnessing my walk of shame from somewhere. I've pretty much decided I'll have to talk to her, but I'd prefer doing it without alcohol leeching from my pores and horseshit stuck to my hair.

Forty-fucking-seven years old. You'd think I'd be past drowning myself in a bottle.

My shower lasts close to half an hour, long enough to clear some of the cobwebs and scrub the stench of bourbon and manure from my skin. Clean, somewhat coherent with the aid of a strong cup of coffee, and with a vague idea of what I'm going to say, I knock on Nella's door.

"You missed her."

I turn to see Sully standing on his porch.

"Van's here," I return.

"She left with Alex hours ago."

"Where to?"

"They didn't say, I didn't ask." He starts to move inside but leans back at the last minute. "Oh, I almost forgot— Jonas is looking for you. He needs you in the breeding barn."

That's where I spend the next few hours, keeping my head down and human interactions to a minimum. When a report comes in late afternoon of a colt breaking through the fence around one of the rear pastures, I volunteer to go chase him down. King needs some exercise anyway and I feel like I have some penance to do, I've been an ass.

The fresh air does me good. I have the colt rounded up and back on the right side of the fence in no time, and manage to patch the hole in the setting sun. The lights of the ranch are already on, providing a beacon in the dusk, and I realize how much of a home this place has become.

A home that now includes Nella as well.

I leave King in his stall with a pile of fresh hay and head for the cabins, determined to straighten a few things out with her. It doesn't take a genius to figure out she's not home—her van isn't parked outside—but I knock on her door anyway. When there's no answer, I show myself in to confirm what part of me already suspects.

There is no sign of her. No shoes by the door, book on the coffee table, or sweater tossed over the back of a kitchen chair. The fridge is empty, as is the bathroom, and the bed is stripped bare.

Fuck.

She's gone.

NELLA

"I'm just going to grab a wheelchair."

The nurse darts out of the room while I read over the sheet of appointments she just handed me. Starting on Monday it looks like there'll be a lot of driving back and forth. Good thing I moved my stuff to Hart's Rescue this afternoon, which is closer to town.

I loved the rescue. The house is older and definitely smaller than the ranch, but that makes it more intimate. I instantly felt at home. Lucy had a lot to do with that too. She actually reminds me a little of Pippa, outspoken and unapologetic, although Lucy seems to have a little more of an edge. I could see the two of them getting along just fine.

That's why it wasn't hard to come to a decision when Lucy quoted a number for a weekly rent a lot more suitable to my budget than an extended stay at the motel would've been. I accepted on a handshake right away. Packing up my belongings didn't take much, just some groceries and my travel bag. I did end up stopping in town at a thrift store to pick up a few items for Pippa, but we're going to need to go into a larger town for a Walmart or something like that.

I knock on the door to the bathroom where Pippa disappeared with the thrift store clothes I picked up for her.

"Are you okay in there?"

"Yeah, I won't be long."

I thought it was a bit unusual for Pippa to be released this late in the day but we had to wait for the neurologist to look at the latest tests before signing off on her release. Besides, as Dr. Osborne told us, if at all possible they prefer to send people home before the weekend.

It's funny, Pippa never asked where we were staying. She seems to trust I have it covered, which is the way things used to be between us. Not in recent years, but back before she met, married, and ultimately scraped off the waste of space whose name shall not be mentioned. Those are years I wouldn't mind if she never remembered. I'm certainly not about to refresh her memory.

By the time the nurse comes back with the wheelchair, Pippa has surfaced from the bathroom. She's looking a little white around the gills. I'm guessing she didn't count on something simple, like getting dressed, taking so much out of her. She doesn't object to the wheelchair and allows the nurse to wheel her from the room. I follow behind with her meager belongings in a plastic bag.

Down the hall I see them slip into the waiting elevator when I hear behind me, "I was hoping to catch you."

I swing around to find Tracy, one of Pippa's nurses, walking toward me.

"Nella?"

I turn back to see my sister blocking the elevator doors.

"Go on. I'll grab the stairs." I wave them off.

"Sorry about that," Tracy says. "I just wanted to make sure your sister's boyfriend managed to get a hold of you?" My surprise must've been visible on my face because Tracy immediately follows it up with, "He wanted to know how she was doing and I told him I couldn't give out that information and suggested he get in touch with you. I'm guessing he didn't call you?"

This is weird. Surely if Pippa had someone important in her life she would've told me. Also, if she has a boyfriend, why the hell isn't he here?

"No. I wasn't even aware she had a boyfriend," I tell Tracy. "Did you give him my number?"

She shakes her head. "He said he had it."

Getting stranger by the minute and it's making me feel uneasy, I'd better catch up with Pippa.

"I appreciate the heads-up. I'm sure he'll get in touch at some point, but if he should call again, could you let me know?"

"Sure, I'll put a note up at the nurses' station."

"Thanks, Tracy."

I find the stairwell and hustle downstairs where they're waiting for me at the exit doors. It takes me two minutes to fetch the van.

It's not until I pull out of the parking lot Pippa speaks up.

"What did Tracy want back there?"

"Someone claiming to be your boyfriend apparently called."

I glance over at her to gauge her reaction. She looks confused.

"I don't..." She shakes her head. "At least I don't think... I have a boyfriend?"

"I don't know. You never mentioned a man to me and

I'd like to think you would have."

"Yeah, for sure," she mumbles, but she doesn't sound convinced.

"Look..." I reach over to give her knee a squeeze. "We're not going to worry about that now. I haven't told you where we're staying yet," I offer as a distraction.

"Where?"

"A horse rescue. It's run by two women. Alex, who lives with Jonas Harvey at High Meadow Ranch, and Lucy, who manages the place. She's the one who actually lives at the rescue in a gorgeous old farmhouse. You'll love it. The land is very pretty and the views are to die for. Oh, and they have two rescue dogs and a donkey as well."

I know I'm rambling but I can't seem to help myself. I'm suddenly wondering if I made the right choice and it feels important to have Pippa's approval.

"Horses? I love horses."

Thank God.

Her face lights up and the weight of responsibility seems to slide right off my shoulders. Looks like this will work out.

"That was amazing," Pippa gushes as she pushes her empty plate away.

"Compared to the bland hospital fare you've been eating these past weeks, I'm sure an old shoe sole would've been an improvement," Lucy points out, clearly uncomfortable with compliments.

"Actually, I've been eating pretty well, but I have to agree with my sister; that was delicious."

Lucy waves a hand to brush me off as she collects our plates and carries them to the sink.

When we drove up to the farmhouse, she'd been waiting on the porch, two dogs—Chief and Scout—sitting beside her. I'd been a little apprehensive when I'd realized we'd be living with dogs, but Pippa had no such reservations. She was always the one who connected easily with people and animals alike, and already had two new four-legged friends before we even breached the front door.

Lucy insisted on cooking us a light meal for which she'd already made preparations. The smoked salmon fettuccini Alfredo she put together was a thing of beauty.

"Just so you know, my talents in the kitchen are more geared toward baking than cooking," I admit. "But I get by and am happy to do my share."

"I can cook," Pippa offers before turning to me with a question on her face. "At least it feels like I can."

"You're a better cook than I am," I confirm with a smile.

"Don't get me wrong, I love putzing around the kitchen, feeding people," Lucy volunteers. "It beats cooking for one all the time, but I have to admit it would be nice not to have to worry about dinner every once in a while."

I get up to give her a hand washing the dishes, when the dogs suddenly rush to the front door and start barking. Lucy is already moving in that direction when there's a loud rap on the door.

From my vantage point I can't see who it is, but that mystery is quickly solved when I hear a familiar voice.

"I'm here for Nella."

~

Fletch

. . .

I was fully prepared to drive to Canada if Sully hadn't flagged me down.

He directed me to the rescue, where apparently Nella made arrangements to stay.

I'm relieved she didn't head back home. Maybe there's hope for me yet, although it's probably narcissistic to think the reason she's sticking close has anything to do with me. That doesn't stop me from heading directly to the rescue though.

Lucy shakes her head when I tell her I'm here looking for Nella.

"You guys are so fucking predictable," she mutters as she steps aside to let me in.

I have no idea what that means, but I'm pretty sure I don't want to poke the bear by asking.

I never realized how much the sisters look alike until my eye first catches Pippa, who is sitting at the table. It only takes a sardonic lift of her eyebrow to have my focus shift to her sister, who is standing by the sink. She looks equal parts confused, hurt, and angry. I own that.

I wish we weren't standing in the middle of Lucy's living room with an audience listening, but if this is where we need to clear the air, so be it. I owe her that much.

"I've been an ass."

Lucy snorts behind me.

"You have a dick, so of course you've been an ass. I think the two are genetically entwined."

Pippa snickers at the comment, but Nella's face is stoic. Except for her eyes, those show a storm of emotions.

"Can we talk?"

Nella's body gives a little jerk at my question. Then she appears to straighten her shoulders and jut out her chin.

"I'm not sure there's much to say."

More snickers from the peanut gallery and I'm starting to feel grossly outnumbered.

"Maybe not, but I have to try."

I hope like fuck she'll give me this shot. Not that I plan to leave without saying what I need to say anyway, but I'd rather she listen voluntarily.

She makes me wait a few uncomfortable moments before nodding.

"Fine. We can talk outside."

I watch her walk toward me, her back ramrod straight and her mouth tight. I let her pass before following her out onto the porch and pull the front door shut behind me. She stops and turns to face me, folding her arms over her chest. I'm far from an expert in body language, but her pose screams 'keep your distance.' I will...for now.

"Take a walk with me?"

Without giving her a chance to answer, I head down the steps, waiting to hear her footsteps coming down the stairs behind me. When she catches up with me, I turn right toward the barn.

"So talk."

Easier said than done, I'm not quite sure where to start.

"I have scars." I guess it's as good a place as any.

Not something I usually talk about, although some women have asked over the years. Nella never asked though, and I'd started to think maybe she'd missed them the one night I spent at her place. It had been dark; we'd been a little preoccupied. It's possible.

I glance over to find her looking at me with eyebrows raised.

"I had my hands on you, so yeah, I know you have scars." She says it matter-of-factly, like she's confirming I have dark hair.

"You never asked."

That seems to surprise her even more.

"I figured they were part of you and that if it was important for me to know how you got them, you would tell me."

That's a really fucking good answer.

"I got them trying to rescue my fiancée from her Afghani captors. My unit was decimated." Nella's hand shoots out, stopping me in my tracks, the question all over her face. "She survived, only to kill herself after."

I walk over to the fence where a small donkey looks to be dozing on his feet.

"Why?"

Her voice is soft as is the light touch on my back.

"That's the million-dollar question. Wish I knew, maybe then it wouldn't feel like I fucked up somehow."

I tell her about my stay at the hospital in Kabul, how I found out she was dead, and the lack of communication from her father, Senator Galvas.

"That's a horrible thing to have happen, I'm so sorry," Nella says. "And I appreciate you telling me, but I'm not entirely clear on how that relates to me, or makes you act like an ass."

She doesn't hold back, and I have to remind myself it's one of the things I like about her. She also makes a good point; I haven't exactly explained myself well. I'm not sure I know how.

"I'm not that clear myself," I confess, turning my head to find her hazel eyes fixed on me. "I guess in a nutshell; that experience fucked me up and I've tried to steer clear of people because of it. Don't like anyone getting too close."

"I see," she mumbles, nodding slightly like she's weighing my words before she adds sharply. "That explains your actions in the beginning, but I'm pretty sure that was you who cooked me breakfast after voluntarily spending the night in my bed, only to avoid me like the plague in the days following."

"Yup, that was me," I admit, feeling like the worst kind of scum when I see the hurt in her eyes.

She confirms how much with her next words.

"You know, you could've just told me you're not interested. Did you have to be an asshole about it?"

I lift my hands to her face and lower my head until our noses are just inches apart.

"Babe, you're so far off the mark it's not even funny. The truth is, I freaked out because I care about you."

"You have a unique way of showing that," she comments dryly, making me grin.

"I've been told my delivery needs some work. Question is, will you give me another chance?"

She grabs onto my wrists and pulls my hands away from her face before she turns her back on me. *Shit.* Too little too late, I guess.

"Another chance for what? Because I don't know if you've noticed, but I've got some stuff going on in my life—some major stuff—and I'm feeling vulnerable enough as it is." I try to reach for her but she takes a step back, shaking her head. "There's a reason I've avoided relationships like the plague. When there are no emotions, there are no expectations, and therefore no hurt or disappointment. I let go with you. Against my judgment I let you in and already you've been able to both hurt *and* disappoint me. With everything else going on, I don't know if I have the resilience to take that chance again."

Fuck, I really did a number on her. A nobler man would back off, but that's not me. Especially not after hearing her admit I got under her skin as much as she got under mine.

"We're not so different, you and I. But—as I've recently been made aware—those walls we have up for protection also limit us. I know how big the risk is I'm asking you to take because I'm taking one as well, but I, for one, no longer want fear to dictate my life."

I invade her space and kiss her forehead, before delivering my parting shot.

"You may wanna think on that."

I don't know if I said the right thing—if she heard me—but I'm hopeful when I hear her running footsteps catch up with me.

"Wait..."

I turn around just as she slides to a stop right in front of me, a little out of breath. Then she rises up on her tiptoes and brushes a kiss at the corner of my mouth.

"Give me some time."

Twenty

"I'm sorry you feel that way, Derek."

I grind my teeth and fix my eyes out the window where Lucy is introducing Pippa to one of the rescue horses. She spent a lot of yesterday napping, but this morning she announced she wanted to get some fresh air.

"Not as sorry as I am. Your lack of loyalty to the college after all these years is a disappointment."

That makes me laugh. Out loud.

"Lack of...loyalty? In my almost twenty years with the college I have missed a grand total of seven days. I have volunteered...no, you know what? I'm not even going to waste energy on this. This was a courtesy call, but you do what you need to do, Derek. I'll be in touch with Human Resources first thing tomorrow morning."

Then I hang up, grab my jacket from the coatrack, and head outside to talk to my sister.

"Did you know about Lucy's plans?" she asks when I join them.

"What plans?"

"She's training Hope here as a therapy horse."

Pippa is rubbing the animal's nose, clearly in her element.

I turn to Lucy. "Therapy horse?"

She shrugs. "It's a dream I don't know will ever come true—we'd need more than one trained horse for that—but we've gotta start somewhere. I thought eventually we could maybe offer a therapy program here for people with mental health problems or suffering from trauma. I already connected with a local psychotherapist who would be interested in developing a program. Equine therapy has shown to be effective for people with anxiety and depression, as well as for adults or kids on the autism spectrum."

"Wow. That's a lofty undertaking," I comment. "And using rescued horses is almost poetic. I love the idea."

"I want to help," Pippa announces with more excitement than I've seen from her in a while.

It's on my lips to remind her she's still recovering, but I swallow it down. My sister's not stupid and who knows, maybe it'll do her good.

"As soon as your doctor gives you the all-clear," Lucy says, earning a grateful smile from me.

"I'm already going stir-crazy," Pippa complains.

She never could sit still for long.

"We could hit up that Walmart in Ponderay," I suggest. "If you're sure you're up for it."

Half an hour later we're on our way.

I'm less concerned about the drive than Pippa's ability to roam the store for any length of time, but I assume they'll have a wheelchair I can push around. The reason I suggested the Idaho store over the one in Kalispell is that Ponderay is not far from where I found a motorhome similar to Pippa's for sale. We'll see how she does shopping first, but if she has enough left in the tank maybe we can go have a look.

"After we hit up Walmart, I want to make one more stop if you feel up to it."

"Sure. Where are we stopping?"

"I found a few ads for motorhomes similar to yours a couple of days ago. One of the addresses is half an hour south of Ponderay. I wouldn't mind checking it out."

She shifts in her seat to look at me.

"You think it's mine?"

Even though some of her memories have come back, most of those are from years ago. I'm the one who told her she owned a motorhome that was missing. I also told her under what circumstances we found her, hoping that might trigger something, but so far the past few years still seem to be a blur.

"I don't know. Like I said, this is only one ad I found, there's another one near Eureka I'd love to check out."

"Shouldn't the police be looking into that?"

"The sheriff's office, yes, but they have their hands full."

In addition, someone selling used—possibly stolen—RVs may not be so willing to help out law enforcement, but they might be a little more relaxed with a potential buyer. Who knows, I may be able to find some useful information I can pass on to the authorities. I'm sure Sheriff Ewing won't be too pleased, but I can't sit still.

Anything that provides a distraction from my churning thoughts. I've been going around in mental circles since Fletch's visit the other night. Some of what he said really resonated with me. His comment that he and I aren't that different struck me hard and gave me a better understanding of his motivations. He was protecting himself, which is something I recognize. I'm doing the same thing myself, which is why I've been hesitant to let him in again.

I'm not holding a grudge—he's already forgiven—but that doesn't mean I'm eager to put my heart on the line again. I wasn't lying when I told him with my entire life on shaky ground I didn't think I could risk incurring another blow. Hell, I don't even know where I'll be or what I'll be doing tomorrow. I need to get a bit of a foothold on what is left of my life first, and if he's as serious about me as he says he is, he'll wait.

I hope.

"I just realized, I don't have money," Pippa says when we finally pull into the Walmart parking lot.

"Don't worry about that. We can sort all that out this week. We should make a list of things to do anyway, and that includes calling your bank." I unclip my seat belt and open my door. "Hang tight, I'm just going to grab a wheelchair."

An elderly Walmart greeter points me in the right direction and a few minutes later I'm helping a grumbling Pippa in the seat.

Her mood is quickly lifted when I wheel her over to the clothing department. She always was more of a shopper than me. In no time she has clothes piled on her lap, both for herself and some she picked for me. We spend some time in the dressing room where she has me try things on I never would've chosen for myself. Yet somehow the clothes fit this new version of me.

I'm grateful for the space my van offers when I load our bags in the back. It didn't take long to make a dent in my budget, but I'm not going to worry about that now. Sorting out my finances is something I need to sit down for this coming week as well.

Pippa has her head leaned back against the seat, her eyes closed. Maybe this was too much, too soon for her.

"Ready to go home?"

"Didn't you have another stop?"

"That can wait."

It really can't. In fact, the motorhome may already be gone. Those chances go up the longer we wait, but I'm not about to put that kind of pressure on Pippa.

"We're out here anyway. Let's go have a look."

The address is a weird exit off the highway for an auto repair shop. The road starts off paved but when it leads into the woods it turns into packed dirt. I'm starting to wonder if this was a good idea.

I have half an eye open for a good place to turn around, when the trees thin out on the right side of the road, revealing what looks like a junkyard.

"Yikes. That doesn't look too promising," Pippa remarks.

It sure doesn't, but my fleeting hopes come back to life when I spot about half a dozen tent trailers and a couple of motorhomes parked outside a building. I focus on one that looks very much like the Jayco Redhawk my sister owned.

I pull the van up behind it when an older man walks out of the building, wiping his hands on a rag.

"Can I help you?"

The question is friendly enough, despite the squinted look he shoots our way when we get out of the vehicle.

"I called about the Jayco a few days ago? Is this it?"

"That's it. You're lucky it's still here. I've had a lot of interest. A couple of folks are coming to have a look tomorrow."

That could be true, although it's a common ploy to try and push a sale. Still, I'll try and use it to my advantage.

"Do you think we could have a look inside?"

He gestures to the camper. "Be my guest. Door is open."

I follow Pippa up the steps and into the motorhome. To my relief, the guy stays outside.

The interior looks fairly clean and smells like bleach. I've only been inside Pippa's place once, but I'm assuming they all look the same. Generic flooring, cabinetry, window coverings, I can't see anything personalized.

"Do you recognize anything?" I whisper at my sister.

"Not really."

She opens the small kitchen cabinets and peers inside. I start opening doors and drawers as well, but everything looks to have been cleaned out. I turn to the truck cab and check in the center console, cupholders, and behind the sun visors without any luck, when I notice something sticking out from under the floor mat on the driver's side.

"Everything all right in here?"

The man's voice startles me just as I close my fingers on the corner of a white piece of paper and pull.

"Yup," I chirp, a little too high-pitched. "Just checking the odometer."

It looks to be a receipt and I promptly shove it in my pocket before I back out of the cab.

The guy is standing in the door opening and is watching Pippa step into the small bathroom.

"What year is it again?"

He turns my way. "Just four years old. Well-maintained, as you can see. Only reason you'd be getting a deal on this beauty is because it's got close to forty thousand miles on the clock."

We both turn to Pippa, who is backing out of the bathroom. When she turns I notice her face is pale.

"Everything okay?"

Her eyes snap to me.

"Yeah. Fine."

I'm not buying it. She looks like she's seen a ghost, but I'm not going to push it. She's darting nervous glances at the man.

"Your price is as listed in the ad?" I ask, trying to divert his attention from Pippa.

"Firm. Like I said, it's a steal."

It's a steal all right. One of the reasons a red flag went up when I spotted this listing in the first place was the low price. The average asking price for this year and model is mid-to-high seventies.

"Do you provide financing?"

I already know the answer to that but I want to get out of here.

"Cash, money order, or bank check only," is his curt answer before he backs away from the door.

"Fair enough. Let me think on this."

Grabbing Pippa's hand I exit the motorhome, eager to get to my van.

"Better think fast. At this price it won't last."

"I understand. Appreciate your time."

It's not until we turn back onto the highway that I finally relax a little.

"What happened back there?" I ask Pippa who hasn't said a word yet. "You looked like you saw a ghost."

"Smell this," she says, sticking her hand under my nose.

The faintly familiar scent of hand lotion wafts up.

"That smells like that stuff you always used."

"Khiel's aloe and green tea hand cream," she confirms. "My favorite."

"Yeah, I remember."

I recall a disagreement she and I had once. She swore by

Khiel's, whereas I felt the thirty or forty dollars for a bit of hand lotion was outrageous when simple bag balm would do the trick.

"I found a tube in the medicine cabinet back there. I think..." She turns to look at me. "I think that may have been my rig."

～

Fletch

"Why the sudden interest in Esther Grimshaw's place?"

I guide King around a couple of trees before sidling up to James again.

We're out this morning to search for a couple of hunters who haven't been seen or heard from for four days. They were staying at a local motel and hadn't been back to their room either. Having hunters reported missing happens all the time, and is often simply a matter of poor communication. These guys are out in the mountains, cell reception is bad or nonexistent, and half the time they turn the sound off so they don't alert wildlife. In this case, however, the father of one of the guys had a massive stroke and is not expected to live. The family is desperately trying to get word to his son, hoping he'll have a chance to say his goodbyes, and hired us to find him.

I noticed the for sale sign when we drove by Esther's place this morning.

"Just curious, that's all. I thought it was sold already."

A neighbor as long as I've been here, Esther was getting up there in age and decided a couple of months ago to sell her property. I suspect it was getting to be a bit much for her to handle. The ten or so acres of land had been left to lie fallow since her husband passed away years ago, but even just the upkeep of the house and the yard would be a challenge for someone well into their seventies. Besides, she's a fair distance from town and emergency services if anything were to happen.

"I hear the deal fell through. For sale sign went back up last week."

"That's too bad."

"It sure is. She's supposed to close on a small single level a block from the hospital in three weeks. She's in a hurry to sell."

I grunt and process the information.

The property is halfway between High Meadow and the horse rescue. Great location, house is in decent condition, and I believe it has a good-sized barn as well.

Never really felt the urge to buy a place of my own—the cabin at the ranch worked just fine—but maybe it's time to consider a change. Hell, it's not like I can't afford it, all I do is sock away money. It wouldn't take much to free up the funds. It would also be conveniently close to the ranch. I bet I could find some trails back there and ride an ATV to work.

"Are you looking?" James prompts.

I shrug. I wasn't, or at least I didn't realize I was, but for some reason this feels like an opportunity I need to jump on for a multitude of reasons. Some of which I don't feel like examining too closely, not yet anyway.

"I'm interested," I admit a bit reluctantly.

"Anything in particular bring this on?"

I'm not about to discuss my motivations, but as it turns out, I don't need to when Bo decides to weigh in.

"He's got a woman now," he pipes up from behind us. "That is, if he ever gets his head dislodged from his ass."

"You can fuck right off, Rivera," I fire over my shoulder, which seems to amuse James.

"Hey, I'm just saying I get it," Bo persists. "A woman like that deserves more than a one-bedroom shack in the woods."

"A woman like what?" Sully asks, who took point when we set out but has let us catch up.

"Nella," Bo answers. "Fletch is thinking of buying the Grimshaw place for her."

"*Jesus Christ*, you guys are worse than a bunch of hens. I never said that."

"Maybe not, but we all recognize the first signs of domestication," James shares.

I'm about to deny when Jonas's booming, disembodied voice comes from somewhere to my left.

"If you ladies are done with your bickering, you may wanna have a look at this."

When we join him in the gully, he points out a strip of camouflage material tied to the branch of a young tree. Ten minutes later we find a second one. Close to two hours after that we find the slightly disoriented hunters near a small creek.

The two had been tracking a black bear and not only lost the bear, but their way back to the trail as well. Little did they know that the trail was a mere twenty feet from where they'd left their markers in the gully. They got wise after they found a source of water and stayed put, but they sure went into these mountains unprepared.

After a lecture from Jonas on proper gear and emergency equipment, we explained our reason for looking for them in the first place. The mood was quite subdued as we guided the men back to the trailhead where we'd found their truck.

Driving back home, we pass Hart's Horse Rescue. It's late afternoon and I can't help wonder what Nella is doing now. I'm tempted to grab my truck when we get to the ranch and drive back here to check on her, but she asked for time and it hasn't even been two days. Patience isn't my strong suit.

The realtor's sign is still on the front lawn when we pass the Grimshaw place.

Maybe I can swing by and check on Esther instead.

Twenty-One

Nella

"Ms. Freling...you are relentless."

The sheriff sounds exhausted.

"Determined," I counter.

"Reckless, you mean. What were you thinking? Never mind," he adds immediately. "I don't even want to know. Andrew's Auto Repair is not only outside of my county, it's in flipping Idaho."

"Does that mean you're doing nothing?"

I hear him sigh deeply.

"A tube of hand cream in a medicine cabinet is hardly a smoking gun, Ms. Freling. I can contact local law enforcement, ask them to go have a look at the vehicle, hope the VIN number is still legible but I can't make any promises as to when that will be. That'll be up to the locals."

I glance inside where Pippa is pulling our purchases out of the bags to show Lucy.

"My sister remembers it. The hand cream is hers, as is the motorhome, what more do you need?"

"With all due respect, your sister couldn't remember her own blood a few days ago. Her recollection seems at the very least unpredictable, if not outright unreliable. Look, I'm not saying I won't follow up, but my department is spread thin as it is. I have to prioritize."

I get it, I do, but that doesn't make me any less annoyed.

"What about—" I start asking when Ewing cuts me off.

"Ms. Freling, I'm sorry but I really have to go. I will be in touch but in the meantime, I'll ask you again; please don't interfere with the investigation."

I puff out a frustrated breath and lean back in the rocking chair, watching Hope chase Daisy the donkey away from the fresh pile of hay Lucy dumped in the paddock earlier.

Ewing may not want me involved, but if nothing is done, that motorhome will be gone and so will anything linking it to Andrew's Auto Repair. I'm so stupid, I could've taken some pictures. I'm contemplating making the two-hour drive back there, but the sun's already setting and I'm not comfortable sneaking onto private property in the dark.

"Are you coming in? Dinner's ready."

I twist my head to see Pippa standing in the open door.

"Be right there."

She disappears inside and I get to my feet, tucking my phone in my back pocket, but it seems to catch on something. I shove my hand down and retrieve the piece of paper I found stuck under the floor mat in the motorhome. Almost forgot about that.

It's a gas receipt for twenty-seven and a half gallons of unleaded and five gallons of propane. Cash payment. None of that would be particularly unusual, not with the gas station address listed as Chain Lakes Inn, Highway 2, Libby, Montana. I know it's south of here. Pippa may well have come through there.

Not on September sixth, though—the date on the receipt—because by then my sister had already been missing for at least a week.

I hesitate for a minute, wondering if I should risk bothering Sheriff Ewing but the likelihood is he'll just brush me off again. No, next time I contact him it'll be with something he can't ignore.

In the meantime, I'll drive out to the gas station tomorrow, ask around and see if anyone remembers seeing Pippa's rig.

"Those are the tiniest cinnamon buns I've ever seen." Pippa's critical eye scans the cooled display case with maybe half a dozen pastries. "Who does your baking?"

"We get them from Rosauers."

Pippa was craving something sweet so I thought stopping in at Bean There would be a good idea. We just spent over two hours at the bank to get her finances sorted, and I for one could use a large latte and a pastry.

"The grocery store? There's no designated bakery in town?"

My sister glances at me and waggles her eyebrows. More and more of the old Pippa comes to the surface. It's not new for her to try and coax me into doing something more interesting with my life. Something I can be passionate about like baking. My canned response used to be that research was my passion, but I don't think that was ever true. I enjoyed my job and was good at it, absolutely, but now that I'm without I'm not exactly heartbroken about it.

"Not really. The only place they actually bake fresh is at Rosauers," Kaylie volunteers.

"See?" Pippa smiles at me. "It's a sign."

Wishful thinking is Pippa's department; she's always been the dreamer, the eternal optimist. I'm supposed to be the logical, practical sister. However, as of this morning I'm also officially without employment, which is the only reason I'm allowing myself to even entertain my sister's suggestion.

"There are so many reasons why that would be impossible, Sissy. For one, I live in Cranbrook."

"So?" She shrugs. "Move. It's not like you have a job keeping you there. All you have to do is give your landlord notice."

"For another, I'm not a US citizen. I don't think I'd be able to set up shop here just like that."

"One mocha," Kaylie interrupts, sliding a takeout cup in front of my sister.

"Thank you," she says before turning back to me. "So find out what steps you'd need to take."

Yeah, I remember this Pippa. She's a bulldozer.

"I wouldn't know the first thing about running a bakery, Pippa."

"You're a baker?" Kaylie asks as she hands me my latte.

"No."

"*Yes*," Pippa says at the same time. "She's an amazing baker."

Ten minutes later I finally manage to herd my sister out of the coffee shop. She's already late for her first appointment at the rehabilitation clinic next to the hospital. The clinic offers a variety of therapies—physical, speech, occupational, cognitive—which will hopefully benefit her.

My plan is to drop her off and drive down to Happys Inn to check out that gas station. I have the receipt in my pocket and have tried to come up with a possible cover story but I'm not a very good liar. I'm probably better off sticking as close to the truth as I can.

I walk my sister into the clinic and leave my number with the front desk. I'm told Pippa should be done by four thirty, which gives me enough time to poke around.

The drive to Happys Inn is about forty minutes away. It's not really a town, more a concentration of population with a bar by the same name at its core, but is still technically part of Libby. There are several signs boasting cabin rentals and resorts on the handful of lakes south of the highway.

The gas station is actually just two pumps in front of the bar. Smart choice, judging by the busy parking lot. It's a mix of trucks, cars, recreational vehicles, and bikes. A lot of bikes. In addition to the bar, part of the front of the building looks to be a convenience store of sorts. A sign on the gas pumps indicates to prepay inside.

When I drive past the entrance, I spot a sign beside the door advertising live music. I've never heard of the band listed, but I guess they're popular enough to draw a respectable crowd on a regular Monday afternoon. A pickup truck is backing out in front of the convenience store and I slip the van in the vacated spot.

I get out of the van and immediately check the front of the building for security cameras. I spot two; one over the entrance and another one mounted on the post that holds the bar and roadhouse sign.

As soon as I enter the building, I'm glad I wore my hiking boots and the new clothes Pippa picked for me. I would've stood out like a sore thumb otherwise. Walking in, the entrance to the bar is straight ahead, a heavy drumbeat filtering through the doors. To my left is a single door into the convenience store.

A bell sounds when I push the door open and behind the counter a young kid—I'm guessing late teens or early twenties—looks up from the screen of his phone. No one else looks to be in the small store.

"Can I help you?"

"I hope so." I walk up to the counter and pull the picture of Pippa in front of her rig from my purse. "Do you by chance remember seeing this motorhome?" I slide the image across the counter at him. "It would've been almost two weeks ago. September six? Were you working then?"

On a shelving unit behind the counter, I notice a small screen showing the feed from the camera above the front door. Part of my van is visible, as is the bike I parked next to. As I look, a man walks into the frame from between the vehicles and takes the steps up to the entrance. My head automatically swivels around to see him walk in the lobby and head straight for the doors to the bar.

"What day was that?" he wants to know.

"It would've been a Tuesday."

"Yeah, I work Tuesdays. Can't remember seeing her though." He points at Pippa and then looks at me. "Are you sisters or something?"

"Yeah. She wouldn't have been here. Just the motorhome."

He gives me a long glance before he turns back to the image, picking it up for a closer look.

"Hard to tell. We get quite a few through here. Aside from walk-ins for the roadhouse, there's a repair place as well as a campground not too far from here, and we have the only pumps close by. We even put in the propane fueling station in the back. Lots of traffic through here.”

I fish the receipt from my pocket and show him.

“Does this ring a bell? They paid in cash and the time stamp is for eleven forty-five in the morning on the sixth.”

“It would’ve been me working at that time,” he confirms. “But cash payments aren’t that uncommon. Heck, the guys from Mobilife do it all the time.”

“Mobilife?”

“RV repair place just up past the church. Those guys are here all the time.”

Fletch

“Everything all right?”

I’m leading King out of the stable when Jonas intercepts me.

“Yeah, one of the hands checking the fence line at Spring Creek gully thought he spotted one of the mares limping. I’m just heading out there to have a look.”

“Good, but I meant with you. Ama said you had an appointment in town.”

I swear, as much as I keep to myself, there is no fucking privacy here at the ranch. Don’t get me wrong, the concern comes from a good place, but it gets annoying.

“Yup. Bank. Getting some stuff sorted.”

“Grimshaw place?”

Jesus. Up in my business.

“What of it?”

"Nothing." Jonas lifts a defensive hand. "But if you need anything to pull that together, come talk to me."

The unexpected offer instantly deflates my growing annoyance.

"Appreciate the offer, but I'm good. Needed to shift some things around is all."

The truth is, I could probably buy Esther's place outright, but I know dick-all about investments, which is why I wanted to talk to my financial guy first. With a plan in place, I stopped in at the realtor's office to put in an offer.

Esther let me look around the place last night when I dropped by. The house is in need of some repairs and I wouldn't mind doing a few upgrades, but the bones look solid. It's a pretty piece of land. The view from the highway doesn't do the property justice because you can't see that the house sits on a ridge overlooking a small valley behind it. I haven't seen it by daylight, but if the views are as good as I imagine, a large deck will be the first upgrade I'll invest in.

"A lot to consider," he observes.

"Already put the offer in, Jonas. Not dicking around."

He nods thoughtfully before narrowing his eyes on me.

"What if she wants to go back to Canada?"

He's not a fool. He knows if it wasn't for Nella showing up in my life, buying a house would probably not have been on my radar.

"Fuck, I don't even know if she wants me in her life at all, but I'm determined to make that choice easier for her."

Jonas grins and claps me on the shoulder.

"Never thought I'd see you fall. Bo, for sure, he works that charm hard. Heck, even Sully with his inflated sense of responsibility. But you? Never. Pleased as fuck for you though, brother."

At my age the pat on the shoulder shouldn't matter as

much as it does, but it lingers through the afternoon while I chase down the injured mare.

I finally locate her in the shadows of a copse of trees, segregated from the rest of the herd. I'm surprised to see it's Ginger, the alpha mare. She looks to have gotten tangled up with some predator, a mountain lion, judging by the wounds on her hind quarter.

Mountain lion attacks are pretty rare, but not unheard of. Horses have three possible predators out here; bear, wolves, and mountain lions. They don't make for an easy prey though, so for a big alpha mare like Ginger to be targeted means the lion was either young and stupid, or desperate. Maybe even injured itself. Whatever the case may be, they could pose a threat to the entire herd.

I radio in for backup. The best thing to do for now is to move the herd closer to the ranch before nightfall. The alternative is taking in just Ginger to get her looked after, but then we'd leave the rest of them vulnerable. Safer to bring them all in.

Mountain lions are territorial and can claim anywhere from fifty to a few hundred square miles. But I'd bet the one that got a chunk out of Ginger hasn't moved too far away from the food source, especially since we're heading toward the colder months.

"James and Bo are already heading your way. *Over.*"

"Can we get a trailer up here for the injured mare? Not sure how far she's gonna get under her own steam. Closest would be the forest road parallel to Fisher River. Radio me when you get close, I can get her there."

"Ten-four."

The mare is skittish and not keen on me getting too close, so it takes me a good half hour to get a halter on her. By that time Bo and James have arrived and they're already rounding up the herd when Sully lets me know he's getting close.

"Lucy called the ranch looking for you," Sully announces when I meet up with him.

"Lucy?" I repeat, instantly on alert. "Why?"

The only reason I can think of for her to call me is if something is up with Nella or her sister. Sully doesn't hesitate to confirm my suspicions.

"She called just before I rolled out. They're looking for Nella, can't get hold of her. She was supposed to pick up her sister at rehab at four thirty but she didn't show."

I quickly glance at my watch, it's almost six now.

Twenty-Two

Nella

Stupid, stupid, stupid.

I was so excited to have another lead to follow, I didn't stop to think it through.

I recognized the name immediately—it's one of the places Chuck Yates at Timberlane mentioned—but I may have made a big mistake coming here. *Big* mistake.

At least I had the foresight to do a drive-by first, but after that it was bad decision after bad decision.

The tarp alerted me; it was clearly covering a large Class A RV which was parked flush against the rear of the main building. If I hadn't been doing a drive-by, I would not have seen it and my mind immediately went to the latest theft. The one where the couple lost their lives. From what I understand they had a Class-A that was stolen.

What seems clear enough to me I'm pretty sure the sheriff will think is far-fetched. He'll want to see concrete evidence before he'll even consider looking into it, which is why I thought it was a good idea to take a few pictures.

I ended up turning onto a dirt road past Mobilife and followed it a few hundred feet before I found a place to park the van in the shadow of a large boulder. Then I started backtracking on foot.

The rear of the building was only about fifty or so feet from the tree line, but from that angle I couldn't see much of the RV. From the edge of the trees to the tarped vehicle, two tent trailers and a pop-up partially blocked my view. Looking from my vantage point, I was able to see along the side of the shop to part of the parking lot in front where I saw the same two parked vehicles as when I drove by. There was no movement at all and I wondered if the place was even open.

Keeping the closest tent trailer between me and the building, I left the cover of the trees. All I wanted was a few photos of anything recognizable on the motorhome. Anything to get Sheriff Ewing out here, although I suspect he'd have a thing or two to say to me first.

It's when I round the second trailer, I hear the sound of an engine and freeze. The only thing between me and the tarp is the small pop-up trailer, but that doesn't provide a lot of cover. I contemplate turning back when I hear the crunch of wheels on gravel coming around the side of the building.

I panic and try to duck between the trailers when I trip and take a nosedive, just as a pickup truck rounds the corner. My phone goes flying, the crack of the screen on the gravel sounds loud as a gunshot to me even as I land awkwardly on my hands. I have to bite my lip to keep from crying out as sharp stones dig into my palms and knees.

I startle at the sound of a door slamming followed by a

second one, and I drop my head to the ground. Fear has my heart beating out of my chest and breathing is difficult. I press my cheek into the dirt, facing away, and squeeze my eyes shut. Maybe if I can't see them, they won't be able to see me.

Two sets of footsteps crunch on the gravel surface before I hear the rustle of the tarp on the other side of the pop-up trailer. Muffled noises follow. It sounds like maybe they are inside the RV. I cautiously lift and turn my head.

I'm just a few feet from the small trailer, peeking underneath, and I can see my busted phone out in the open on the other side. Glancing beyond, I notice the tarp is partially pulled away from the motorhome, exposing the back half. The RV door is wide open and I hear the sounds of cabinet doors opening and closing.

Next thing I know something is tossed out the door. A pile of clothes, or maybe it's bedding. More follows, and it looks like they're cleaning out any personal belongings. I'd really like to get pictures of that, but I'm not sure my phone survived. Besides, I'd be an even bigger idiot than I already am if I exposed myself just to grab it, even if they appear to be distracted.

Instead, I push up on hands and knees, using the opportunity to back up toward the tent trailer behind me. I need to get away and try to find a phone so I can contact Sheriff Ewing before they completely strip the motorhome of anything recognizable. I've lost sight of the door, but I can still hear things being tossed on the growing pile. I hope it's enough to cover any noise I make. If I can make it back to my van, I can get to the roadhouse and alert the sheriff's office from there.

Once I reach the back of the trailer, I pull myself up to my feet and poke my head around the side to make sure whoever is in the RV is still out of sight. I wasn't able to see the pickup truck parked behind it before, but I see it now and it looks exactly like one I've seen before.

I just have trouble believing it.

Then movement catches my eye as a guy—I'm guessing late teens early twenties—comes down the steps of the RV, carrying what looks to be an air fryer or something in his arms to the back of the truck. I'm so relieved I don't recognize him; I close my eyes and drop my forehead against the trailer.

So I miss the second person stepping into view, but snap my head up when I recognize the voice.

"Hey, Willy! Grab the pliers from the center console, would ya? Can't get the damn glove compartment open."

Oh, my God.

I twist away from the edge and swing around, pressing my back against the camper as I try to suck in air. How is this even possible?

I freeze when I hear footsteps heading in this direction. Every hair on my body stands on end as I flatten myself against the metal, waiting to be discovered, but then they stop. I hear the soft scrape of flint hitting steel, before the scent of a freshly lit cigarette wafts my way.

"Yo! Willy! Did you lose your phone?"

My feet are moving before my brain has a chance to engage, and sheer panic has me bolting for the trees.

"Hey! What the hell?"

I've never been a particularly athletic person, but my legs are pumping like an Olympic sprinter as I tear into the woods like the devil is on my tail. Branches slap my face as I dart between the trees, but I'm afraid to slow down. This is like waking up in a nightmare, where people you thought you knew suddenly turn on you. Not even facing down the bear up on Scenery Mountain was I this terrified.

Up ahead I see the outline of the boulder behind which I parked the van.

Then the bark splinters on the tree trunk beside me only a fraction of a second before I hear the reverberation.

I'm being shot at.

The next moment I feel something hit the back of my leg, hard enough to take me down.

Fletch

I don't even fucking know where to start.

I ended up taking the truck and trailer with Ginger back to the ranch, and left King with Sully so he could help the others herd the horses to a pasture a little closer to home.

Jonas has already alerted Doc Evans by the time I get there. I give him a hand unloading Ginger and tell him about Lucy's phone call.

"What the fuck are you still doing here, then? Get going and let us know if you need help."

I jog to my truck and start the engine, but I'm not sure where I'm going. I dial Lucy.

"Fletch, I've been—"

"I know. I was out of range," I cut her off. "Talk to me."

"Nella dropped her sister off at the clinic for her one thirty appointment and was supposed to pick her up at four thirty, but never showed up. She's not answering her phone. I just got back to the rescue with Pippa, we drove around town a little, looking for her van. We'd hoped maybe she came home in the meantime, but no luck."

"Can I talk to Pippa?"

"Sure."

There's a light rustle of the phone exchanging hands and then Nella's sister comes on, sounding just like her.

"Fletch?"

"Right here. Listen, any idea where she may have gone? Anything you talked about before she dropped you off? Errands, groceries, anything like that?"

"Nothing like that, but I know she was frustrated with the sheriff. I thought maybe she came to see you."

"Why frustrated with the sheriff?" That's the part I'm most interested in now.

"Didn't sound like he took her seriously when she told him we found my rig."

They found her...what?

"You'd better start explaining. I'm heading your way."

By the time I pull into the rescue, I'm fuming. Not sure who I'm more pissed with, Nella, her sister, or fucking Wayne Ewing. Or maybe I'm pissed at myself for giving her space instead of planting my ass on her doorstep. I should've known she wouldn't stop pursuing her own investigation, but going across state lines and pulling her sister into it is taking things a little too far, even for Nella.

Scout and Chief—the rescue's dogs—come running up when I get out of the truck. I give them each a little attention before I turn to the porch, where Lucy and Pippa are already waiting for me.

"What do you remember?" I ask Pippa, not bothering with hellos. "You said the hand cream you found was a trigger."

"Uhh, I remembered my rig. It felt like mine, but I've

been trying to remember staying in it, or traveling in it, and I just get flashes. Like a slideshow of snapshots I can't really place in any kind of context."

"So nothing relating to the theft?"

I climb up the steps and lean against the pillar, and I'm struck once again by the similarities between Nella and her sister. Pippa is still way too skinny, but her face is no longer as gaunt and her hair has a healthy sheen. Right now worry lines make her look years older than she is.

"No."

"Okay, let's figure what we do know."

It's only been three hours since she was supposed to pick her sister up at the clinic and I doubt the sheriff would consider this a matter of concern but, like Pippa, I'm worried. Nella would never have left her sister waiting. Not voluntarily, anyway.

"Last night after she talked to the sheriff, she mentioned wanting to check out the gas station."

"Gas station?" I'm not sure what she's talking about.

"Yeah, she found a gas receipt in the front of the rig dated September sixth."

I can see how that would've sparked her interest; Nella was already here looking for her sister by then. Someone else must've driven the motorhome.

"Which gas station?"

"I'm not sure. She said it was south of here."

Closest gas stations I know are in and around Libby which is north. I can't think of many south of us unless you drive a ways.

"In Happys Inn," Lucy supplies. "The roadhouse has a few pumps outside."

That's right, they do. Bo dragged all of us out there last

year for some beers and live music. Good grub too, as I recall.

Nella would've had plenty of time to get from the clinic to the roadhouse and be back in time to pick up her sister. It's a possibility.

Heck, it's the only thing I have to go on.

"Where are you going?" Pippa wants to know when I turn and head down the steps.

"Gonna look for her," I throw over my shoulder without slowing my pace.

"I'm coming."

That stops me in my tracks and I swing around as she comes toward me.

"Like hell you are. You just got out of the hospital and look like a stiff wind could blow you over. Besides, someone has to stay here in case she shows up."

"Lucy will be here."

I recognize the stubborn tilt of her chin, I've seen it before on her sister, but there's no way in hell she's coming.

"No." I put a hand on her shoulder and drop my head down to eye level. "I need my full focus on finding Nella and you'd be a distraction."

Harsh, perhaps, but the truth. Who knows what I'll bump into, and the last thing I need is having to worry about Pippa.

I can see it costs her as she presses her lips together, but she nods her understanding.

"I'll stay in touch. Call me if you hear anything."

Another nod, and this time I release her to continue to my truck.

As I pull away from the rescue, I pull up Ewing's number. There may not be enough cause for him to take this seriously, but I want him to know I do.

"What do you want now, Boone?" I can hear sirens in the background. "I'm up to my last remaining hair follicles here. Don't need you adding to my fucking stress."

"Courtesy call only. I'm heading out to look for Nella, who's missing. She was supposed to pick up her sister at four thirty but never showed. I just wanted to give you a heads-up I'm driving down to Happys Inn to look for her."

"You have gotta be fuckin' kidding me!"

His outburst gives me an uneasy feeling.

"Not kidding, why?"

"Because that's where I'm heading. Got a disturbance call, possible shots fired."

My foot instantly presses the accelerator down to the floorboard.

Twenty-Three

FLETCH

It's not hard to find Ewing.

I can see his flashing lights from across the road when I pull up to the pumps. Doing a quick loop through the parking lot, I don't see the familiar van so I wait for a break in traffic to get across to the other side of the highway.

The sheriff's SUV is parked beside another cruiser behind the church—kitty-corner from the roadhouse—so I pull up right behind them.

"What's going on?"

Both Ewing and the deputy turn their heads in my direction.

"Waiting for Jethro. He's the church caretaker who called it in, but lives in a trailer on the back end of the property. He's heading this way on his ATV."

A few minutes later I can hear the higher whine of a small engine as a four-wheeler comes barreling out of the woods behind the church, driven by an older man wearing a do-rag wrapped around his head and an entire arsenal strapped to his chest and back.

"Jesus Christ, Jethro," Ewing grumbles.

I guess the sheriff knows who he's dealing with.

"Oh, keep yer shorts on, Sheriff," the old man shoots back. "I got a right to defend church property. Only got a warning shot off. *Sumbitch* shooter was gone by the time I got to where I thought it was comin' from. Sounded close to Clayton's place but that's supposed to be closed on Mondays, so I stopped in to check on it. Looks like someone may have been there. Not sure what he was shootin' at, where he went, or how he took off. Only thing I know is something went down behind the RV shop and there's an abandoned *vee-hickle* sittin' in the driveway next to my trailer. Made sure it wasn't goin' anywhere though."

He pulls a large hunting knife from his belt and flicks the sharp edge with a nail like some fucking geriatric Rambo.

"Where?" Ewing asks.

"Dirt road runs right along the north side of Clayton's property. I ain't never seen it before, no one I know would be found dead in one of them mommy missiles."

My feet are already carrying me to my truck.

"Hold your fucking horses, Boone," the sheriff yells behind me.

Like hell I'm gonna wait, not when I'd wager my left nut that *mommy missile* Jethro mentioned is Nella's fucking minivan.

I almost blast by it. She'd pulled off on the far side of a large boulder obscuring it from view in this direction.

Fuck. Nella's van.

Giving not even a single shit I'm blocking the dirt road for anyone else; I slam my truck in park right behind her vehicle which is listing oddly. Looks like Jethro did a number on her tires.

Instead of waiting for Ewing to catch up with me, I start heading through the woods toward the back of Mobilife RV Repairs, as the sign along the road indicated. It doesn't take an astrophysicist to figure out that was Nella's target.

Goddamn, woman. What have you gotten yourself into now?

I cup my hands around my mouth and bellow her name.

~

Nella

It's probably not even that cold but I'm shivering.

That may have something to do with the blood leaking from my leg.

I'm not a fan. Either of blood, or it leaking from holes in my body that don't belong. I was hit, I know that much.

The impact took me down to the ground as more shots rang out over my head. Staying as low as I could, I managed to crawl to a fallen tree and I was just able to wedge myself underneath. Good thing, because not too long later I started hearing rustling in the underbrush.

It became clear they were looking for me when after a while I could hear two voices come closer.

"Where the hell did she go?"

"Better find her. You know how Graham feels about leaving witnesses behind."

I remember taking in a breath and holding it as I was looking at a set of running shoes walking up and stopping just inches from my face. Then suddenly another shot sounded. This one a sharp crack, coming from a different direction.

"Who the fuck is shooting?"

"I don't know, but we'd better haul ass and get that RV out of here."

I've been afraid to move since those two disappeared. Clearly there's someone else out there shooting. I heard a light engine—maybe a motorcycle—not too long after. Not knowing who is all out there, it seemed safer to stay where I was but I can't tell if I've been here minutes or hours.

All I know is I'm cold, I'm thirsty but at the same time feel like puking, and I can't seem to keep my eyes open. I have to stay alert though, because as soon as night falls, I need to get out of here. My van can't be that far. If I can make it there, all I have to do is drive it down to the highway. Surely the roadhouse is still open and I can get help there.

I risk moving a little so I can dig for my keys in my pocket and blow a sigh of relief when my fist closes around them. It gives me some false sense of control. Something else to focus on so I can keep the panic at bay. Every time my chest tightens, I start counting backward from a random number until my breathing eases again.

It's quiet, other than the occasional faint sound of traffic from the highway, there's not much else. I catch myself dozing off, and each time I do I squeeze the keys in my hand a little tighter, hoping the sharp sting will keep me alert.

At some point I hear another engine, the heavier rumble of a truck or a big SUV. It almost sounds like it's coming right at me, and I hold my breath once again, listening closely. The slam of a door, the crunch of a few footsteps, and then they abruptly stop.

"Nella!"

At the sound of Fletch's voice, I inhale air so fast I

almost choke on it. I try to call out, but dissolve into a coughing fit instead.

"Nella!"

That wasn't Fletch. This voice is a little closer and, while still trying to clear my throat, I start shimmying out from under the tree.

"Here...I'm here." I do little more than rasp so I try again, this time louder. "I'm here!"

"Jesus Christ. Fletch! Over here!"

I recognize the service boots and sheriff's uniform pants as Ewing crouches down beside me. I try to push myself up but he immediately puts a hand on my shoulder, keeping me down.

"Don't move, honey. We're gonna get you some help first."

I almost smile at being called 'honey' by a man who undoubtedly was likely calling me a different name altogether less than twenty-four hours ago.

"Where is sh—Oh no, baby, no."

The sheriff is gone in a flash, replaced by Fletch, who immediately whips off his shirt and starts tying it around my leg. It should probably hurt but I'm numb, I don't feel a thing. With the sheriff talking to someone in the background about an ambulance and Fletch looking after me, I close my eyes and for a few moments give in to fatigue.

"Goddamit, Nella. You just had to push on, didn't you?"

His tone is sharp but I hear the concern behind it. Since it's clearly a rhetorical question, I wisely keep my mouth and my eyes shut. I figure I deserve his anger; I am pretty upset with myself.

"I'm of a mind to lock her up for obstructing an investigation."

Now, wait a damn minute...

My eyes snap open and find Ewing standing behind Fletch, but before I can voice a protest, the sound of approaching sirens has the sheriff disappearing from sight.

"Fletch..."

My voice is no more than a whisper. Why is talking so hard?

His hand squeezes mine.

"Hang in there, Babe. Medics are here."

Things are a blur after that and it's not until I'm about to be shoved in the back of an ambulance I realize I have to say something. I manage to grab Fletch's wrist at the last minute. Maybe it's because of what happened to Pippa, but I feel an urgent need to share what I know while I have the chance.

"Tell the sheriff to check behind the Mobilife building, Fletch."

"He's got a deputy over there already."

"I dropped my phone there; I think I broke it. Wanted to take pictures of the motorhome. It's there, Fletch, under a tarp."

"Ma'am, we need to get going."

I hear the EMT's words but my eyes are locked on Fletch.

"Wait..."

He leans forward and his lips brush my forehead.

"I'll be right behind you, Nella."

"But...I heard him say two names," I quickly blurt out as my grip on his wrist slips and the stretcher I've been strapped down on is slid into the ambulance. "Willy and Graham..."

I've lost sight of Fletch and hope he can still hear me when I add, "I recognized his voice."

Fletch

"I need you to head over to the rescue."

I just caught up with the ambulance and plan to stick to the bumper like glue while making a few necessary phone calls. I was briefly delayed by Ewing, who was peppering me with questions after I relayed what Nella mentioned. Unfortunately, I didn't have any answers for him and in the meantime the ambulance was disappearing from sight. I'm sure he wasn't too pleased with me when I finally simply walked off, got in my truck, and headed after Nella.

"What's going on?" Sully wants to know.

"Nella was shot in the leg, lost quite a bit of blood, and is on her way to the hospital. I'm right behind her."

"Jesus, brother, what happened?"

"I'll tell you later, but right now I need you to get to the rescue. You can tell Pippa about her sister, but you're gonna have to sit on her. There are a lot of fucking moving parts I don't know what to do with yet, so she'll be safer right where she is."

"She's in danger?"

"Not sure, but proceed as if she is."

"Gotcha. Nella gonna be okay?"

"Yeah. She should be."

She was going into shock by the time we found her and had lost a lot blood, but the injury itself looked pretty straightforward. Although, I'll admit I did breathe a sigh of relief when the medics showed.

"Good. I'll head out there now."

I've no sooner hung up when another call comes in. It's the sheriff.

"No phone, no motorhome," he says without any greeting. "We did find a large tarp and a pile of bedding, clothes, and other odds and ends. Sure looks like something got emptied out in a hurry. We found a bottle of blood pressure pills with the name of one of the victims we found near Troy."

Nella was right. It had been their Class A she saw.

"Kills me, Boone. This place was not even on my fucking radar. Been focusing on campgrounds and dealers, not repair shops."

"What about those names?" I prompt him.

"Hell, could be anyone. Haven't been able to get a hold of the owner so I'm driving out to Thompson Lake. Apparently, Clayton Brown likes to fish somewhere out there on his days off."

"Good luck finding him."

There's a whole chain of lakes running parallel to Highway 2 on the south side, among them Upper, Middle, and Lower Thompson Lakes. That's a lot of lake to search for one guy.

"I reckon I'll need that luck, even though Jethro suggested a few spots for me to check. Anyway, I just wanted to let you know one of my deputy's will be waitin' at the hospital. I need him to talk to Nella soon's she gets there. I've gotta know who she was referring to."

The medic had slammed the ambulance doors shut before I could ask Nella whose voice it was she recognized.

"I'd like to know that too." It's easier to know who the hell you're up against. "And by the way, I've got Sully going over to cover the sister, just in case."

"Probably not a bad idea. Okay, I'm at the lake. Lemme go look for the guy. I'll be in touch."

I place a quick call to Bo to ask him to meet me at the ambulance bay at the hospital. He can park my truck while I follow Nella inside, because I don't plan to take my eyes off her again. Then the rest of the drive I'm talking to Jonas, filling him in on what's transpired so far.

She's pale, even against the white sheet covering her up to her chin as they pull the gurney from the back of the rig.

"Sir, you can't leave your—"

Hospital security at the door tries to stop me and I'm about to let him know how unappreciative I am of his hand on my chest, when Bo comes jogging up.

"I've got this."

He snatches the keys from my hand and throws the guard a look. I don't wait around and rush after Nella, just catching up with her down the hall.

ER staff does their best to stop me from coming in, but it's Nella's own insistence I stay with her that finally has them backing off. They relegate me to a stool by the head of the bed. As they start examining her, Ewing's deputy shows up.

"May as well let him in too," she suggests with a sigh. "I'd like to get this over with."

"You have two minutes," the ER doctor warns the deputy who nods.

"Ms. Freling, Sheriff Ewing asked me—"

"I recognized the truck first," Nella interrupts him and gets right to it. "Two-tone blue and silver Chevy pickup, not sure of the model, but it looked older, maybe nineties. Good condition. Last time I saw the truck it was parked outside the Sandman Motel."

I'm about to jump to my feet, but a squeeze of her hand in mine keeps me in place.

Then she continues, "I never actually saw him, but I recognized his voice."

"Whose voice, ma'am?"

"Martha Crandall's son. Wyatt Crandall."

Twenty-Four

Nella

"Wait. Where are we going?"

I look over my shoulder as we continue right past the driveway to Hart's Horse Rescue. When I turn back to Fletch, he's staring straight ahead.

"Fletch?"

With his eyes on the road and his full beard covering half his face, it's difficult to gauge his expression.

"High Meadow," he finally shares.

"Why? I want to go home and see my sister."

"Not a good idea. Not with Crandall still out there. Doubtful anyone knows your sister is at the rescue unless you point them in that direction. Better not make it easy for them."

"You're saying she's still in danger."

"Yeah. I figure you both are. Safer not to have you in the same place."

"Who's going to be looking after her then?"

"Sully and Bo are keeping an eye out."

I still can't wrap my head around the fact that nice young man, who seemed so helpful and friendly, turns out to be involved in this. I'd like to believe he was somehow forced or coerced, but he sure sounded in charge when he was yelling and shooting at me.

He freaking shot me.

The real pain didn't hit until later last night. After the lights were turned low in the hospital room they kept me in, and Fletch had stepped out to let me sleep. Except I hadn't been sleeping, my eyes were closed but behind them the events kept playing through my mind on a continuous loop.

I didn't sleep much and I'm pretty sure Fletch didn't sleep at all. He never went any farther than the chair he'd set up in the hallway outside. When I'd asked him why he didn't just stay in the room, he said he'd be more alert out there.

I took that to mean I was too much of a distraction. I was determined to find a compliment in there somewhere.

Yesterday morning I was still pondering if I should risk letting him in again, but the moment I heard his voice calling my name the decision was made. I'd be a fool to question the intentions of a man who dropped everything to come and find me. Since meeting him, he's been right there at my back whenever I was in trouble.

So I'm done questioning him. If he says it's safer this way, it's because it is. I may be book-smart, but there is no way that can compete with the wisdom gained from his decades of experience.

"Okay," I concede, closing my eyes and leaning back against the headrest.

I can feel him scrutinizing me, but he doesn't comment and the rest of the drive is silent.

When we pull up to his cabin, I notice the sheriff's cruiser parked outside the ranch house.

"Think he has news?" I ask.

"Could be. Although he may be talking to Jonas about a search he needs help with. Wouldn't be the first time."

I keep my eye on the porch from where the two men seem to be observing us, while Fletch rounds the front of the truck. He opens my door but when it looks like he plans to carry me inside I stop him. Hell, like any warm-blooded woman, I wouldn't mind some strapping man carrying me around like I weigh no more than a feather, but I'd rather not have an audience for that. I still have a little pride left.

"Appreciate it but I've got crutches. I can walk," I tell him gently, hoping I don't offend him.

He glances over his shoulder at the ranch house before returning his gaze to me.

"Sure thing. I'll just give you a hand down."

I manage to make my way inside the cabin and am just carefully lowering myself on the couch when there's a knock on the door. Fletch opens it to Sheriff Ewing.

"For fuck's sake, Wayne. She hasn't even had a chance to put her goddamn feet up."

"Wouldn't bother her if it wasn't important."

"It's fine, Fletch," I intervene.

To be honest, I'm just relieved the sheriff's department is finally interested in what I might have to say.

Ewing sits in a chair on the other side of the small coffee table, while Fletch goes into the kitchen and comes back with a glass of water and two of the pills he picked up at the hospital pharmacy for me. He hovers until I swallow them and takes the empty glass from my hands. Then he perches on the armrest beside me, and slides a cool hand under my hair at the back of my neck.

"Spoke with Martha Crandall last night and again this morning. Her son never came home and she doesn't know where he might've gone to. She was, however, able to confirm he works at Mobilife, but she is convinced this is all one big misunderstanding."

"The fucking hole in Nella's leg says otherwise," Fletch grumbles.

"Hey, I don't disagree with you, but give the woman a little leeway; she's just found out her son may have been involved in a double murder. That can't be easy for a mother to learn."

Fletch huffs and I put a hand on his knee, which is apparently enough to distract him. His hand immediately covers mine and he glances at me from the corner of his eye.

"So you're saying you haven't located Wyatt yet," I prompt the sheriff.

"Or Willy," he says, giving Fletch a look. "Do you remember the two punks you caught hunting out of season a few weeks ago?"

"You said the one who took off was called Willy Stubble-something. Same Willy?"

"Stubblefeld. One and the same," Ewing confirms. "Turns out Willy and Wyatt are related. Cousins. I found that out from the owner of Mobilife who, by the way, swears upside down he doesn't know anything about anything. He admits Wyatt works for him but also occasionally does custom interior work on RVs on the side, and apparently Willy helps him with that. Brown allows them to use the shop for that on Sundays and Mondays when Mobilife is closed."

"How convenient," Fletch comments.

"Quite, although he was rather convincing. He even suggested a few places where those two might be hiding. A couple of hunting camps he overheard Wyatt talking about.”

“That’s why you were talking to Jonas.”

“Exactly,” Ewing concurs. “The camps are in rough terrain and I need the team to lead a search. But the reason I wanted to talk to you, Nella,” he directs at me, “is that nobody seems to know a Graham. Not Martha, not the Stubblefelds, and not Clayton Brown. Are you sure that’s the name you heard?”

I thought it was, but now I’m starting to wonder. After all, I was hurt and scared out of my mind yesterday. Could they have said something else?

“It sounded like Graham, but maybe it could’ve been Grant?”

I don’t say it out loud, but the slight drawl I’ve noticed among the locals might’ve made one sound like the other.

“*Grant*,” Ewing echoes as he nods. “That’d make more sense.” Suddenly he’s on his feet. “Appreciate your time. You’ve been very helpful.”

I’m still picking my jaw up off the floor when he walks out.

“Wow,” I react, looking at Fletch who is closing the door. “Was that a compliment?”

His mouth twitches.

“May have been. Hard to tell. Ewing isn’t known for being agreeable.”

∼

Fletch

. . .

I listen with half an ear to the phone call between Nella and her sister.

I'm starting to rethink keeping the two of them in separate locations. I haven't heard from Jonas yet, but if the team is going to lead the search as Ewing suggested, we might have a problem. We won't have the manpower to cover the search, Lucy's place, *and* the ranch. Maybe the sheriff can spare a deputy, but I don't really trust anyone other than myself or one of my teammates with either Nella or Pippa.

When I hear her end the call, I scoop some of the chili Ama must've left simmering on my stove in a bowl and walk it over to the couch.

"Here, eat something."

A knock sounds at the door before I can make it back to the kitchen to grab a bowl of my own. It's Jonas, who asks Nella how she's doing before turning his attention on me.

"Briefing, my office in fifteen."

"Make it the porch and I'll be there."

I'll be able to keep an eye on my cabin from the porch. Jonas nods his understanding before he turns back out the door.

"What was that about?" Nella wants to know.

"Probably logistics on the search. I shouldn't be too long. I'll have my eye on you the whole time," I promise, thinking she might feel unsafe.

"Let me know what's going on before you disappear?"

There's something vulnerable in the way she says that, but I suspect it has little to do with any risk of physical harm and everything to do with her emotional vulnerability.

I stop in front of her and bend down until I'm at eye level.

"Done disappearing on you, Babe. Not even if you ask."

I aim to live up to that commitment, even if it means defying orders and missing out on an opportunity to chase down those fucking degenerate punks and maybe get a few good licks in.

"I should be okay," she mumbles, her gaze dropping to my mouth.

"I'll make sure of it," I promise, my own eyes focusing on her plump one.

I haven't had a taste of her in far too long. When she bites her teeth down on the swell of her bottom lip, it's all the invitation I need.

Leaning in, I lick the imprint her bite left behind before slipping my tongue in her mouth. *Damn*, the spice from Ama's chili cranks up the heat that welcomes me.

I wish I could sink my hands into her hair, but as it is, they are firmly braced against the back of the couch to prevent me from doing a face plant on her lap. Not that I'd mind in the least, but she was just released from the hospital with a hole in her leg.

It doesn't stop Nella from sliding one of her hands in my hair, curling around the longer strands at my neck. The slight sting zips along my nerve ends and has me groan against her lips.

"*Shit*," she mutters suddenly, and I lift my head.

Forgot about the bowl of chili she'd still been holding in her free hand and half the contents spilled on the scrubs the hospital provided her with to wear home.

"Don't move," I say, taking the bowl from her hand and setting it on the coffee table. "I'll grab something clean."

By the time I return with a pair of sweats, she's already working on getting off the dirty scrubs.

"Hang on."

I brush her hands aside and help her change into the

clean pants. Then, for good measure, I take her mouth again, but briefly this time. Don't want to keep the team waiting.

"I gotta go. I know there's still some ground to cover," I start. "But for now, are we good here?"

Her hazel eyes blink lazily.

"I'm feeling fine. I think those meds are hitting me."

I bet she's feeling fine on those heavy-duty painkillers.

"Have a nap. I won't be long."

Her eyes are already drifting shut when I brush a kiss to her forehead. Then I hustle out the door.

Everyone but Sully is already on the porch, lining up for a coffeepot and mugs—courtesy of Ama I'm sure—sitting on the table under the window. I grab my own and pick a spot on the steps from where I can easily keep an eye on the cabin.

"Wayne Ewing was by earlier, asking for our help huntin' down Wyatt Crandall and Willy Stubblefeld," Jonas starts, leaning against a pillar. "The two idiots who shot Nella. They're suspects in the murder of that couple up near Troy and vehicle theft. Unfortunately, they're armed idiots, which makes it extra dangerous." He looks around and makes eye contact with each of us before continuing, "To make matters more complicated, we can't leave the ranch or the rescue without some kind of security. Nella and her sister might still be targets."

"Bring the sister here," Thomas says as he walks up the path to the porch. "Set both of them up in the house. I'm here, we've got a top-of-the-line security system, and my gun is always loaded."

"Jesus, Dad, don't fucking remind me."

Bo chuckles and I duck my head to hide my own smile. Jonas's father is a character.

The old man has challenged each of us at some point to a 'shoot-out' to see who could hit more cans off the top rail of the fence. Even though his enthusiasm hasn't waned—in younger years he apparently won his share of accuracy competitions—his aim is no longer what it was, as is evident from the bullet hole in the fender of the new ranch truck.

Jonas had been livid and threatened to take the gun away from him but Thomas announced he'd have to take it from his cold, dead hand which, according to his son, was always a possibility. It had been a public and highly entertaining exchange that required Alex to step in to calm the waters. Something she's good at.

The old man's point had merit though; it would take less manpower to keep an eye on both women here. Jonas thought so too and ends up calling Sully, instructing him to bring Pippa here.

Then he turns to me. "I need you to stay here." He meets my angry glare head-on and I swallow my objections. "Your anger is more useful keeping the girls safe than it will be in the field. I think it's obvious those two punks aren't the masterminds behind whatever operation they've got going on, but we need them in one piece to find out who else might be involved."

I can't argue his logic. I want to, but he's right; I can't guarantee I won't shoot them on sight for what they put Nella through. Plus, I have high stakes in keeping her safe.

The sharp nod I direct at Jonas conveys I'm on board.

The next twenty minutes are spent strategizing a plan of action and by the time Sully drives up with a mutinous Pippa by his side, the team is almost ready to move out.

They plan to wait until sundown and use the cover of night. It'll give the team an advantage with their night-vision equipment. In the meantime, Sully can fly his drone to do some surveillance on the hunting camps Ewing mentioned. If we can get confirmation on one single location, it'll be easier to coordinate a plan of attack.

"Where's my sister?"

Pippa's sharp inquiry is directed at me. She's still slight, but I can see her strength and personality are returning in spades.

"I'll go get her in a minute. She's safe."

The woman's eyes take in every member of the team before they come to rest on me again.

"What is going on?" She cocks a thumb over her shoulder when Sully hovers, his head bent. "This guard dog won't tell me anything."

Thomas has a hearty laugh at that, which earns him a scathing glance from both Pippa and the man she insulted.

"Ms. Freling," Jonas intervenes. "Meet my father, Thomas Harvey. Why don't you let him show you around while we finish up things out here? Fletch can get your sister when we're done and they'll be able to fill you in."

"The doc's gonna need to up my meds, I don't think my heart can take more pretty ladies," Thomas flirts, stepping up and holding out his arm for Pippa, who takes it with a smile.

We could all learn a thing or two from the old charmer.

Twenty-Five

Nella

I suck in a sharp breath when I try to move my legs, and my eyes snap open.

It takes me a second to process where I am. Seems like I've slept in so many different beds these past few weeks, it's hard to keep track. The heavy beams overhead and scent of fresh coffee and bacon filtering in tell me I'm at the ranch. Ama walking in with a glass of water and a bottle of pills in her hands confirms it.

"Fletch made me promise to give this to you before you tried to get up," she announces. "He's out front, dealing with a feed store delivery."

"Thank you," I mumble, grateful for the shirt Fletch lent me.

I take the glass and the pill she shakes from the bottle.

"Your sister is out and about, but I made fresh coffee and have saved you some breakfast when you're ready. Although it's technically brunch by now."

She exits the room before I have a chance to thank her.

Brunch? Guess I slept in.

I was so happy to see Pippa yesterday. It went a long way to soothing my irritation at having a bunch of men making decisions about me without giving me the courtesy of any input. Not that I let Fletch off scot-free, as soon as I had him to myself for a moment, I made sure he understood my displeasure. Even more annoying was how much it made me sound like a whiny bitch when he calmly and rationally explained the reasoning behind it.

I'm not proud to admit I may have pouted last night, making a point to ignore Fletch in favor of my sister, Alex, and Thomas, who is very entertaining. Still, I was a bit disappointed when it was Alex who showed Pippa and me to a guest room we were apparently sharing. But while Pippa had been in the bathroom, doing her thing, Fletch walked in carrying one of his shirts for me, and planted a hard kiss on my lips. Then he told me he'd be downstairs on the couch if I needed him, bid me a good night, and was gone again. To my surprise I slept like a log, apparently well into the day.

It must've done me good because I'm feeling a little better, a bit more myself. That was sweet of Fletch to make sure I'd take my pills right away, especially after I was a brat last night. It would appear I don't make a very good patient; I'll have to do better today.

I'm not supposed to have a shower yet, but I make do with a washcloth at the bathroom sink. Pippa brought over a few of my things last night so I had a clean shirt to wear, but I opted for Fletch's sweatpants again instead of my jeans. I'm sore enough to want comfort over looks.

"Any news?" I ask Ama, who just comes walking from the front office as I gingerly slide down the stairs on my butt.

"Here, let me give you a hand," she says, hurrying up to take my crutches from me. "Now you can use both hands. And no, we haven't heard anything but that's not saying much when they're out on a search."

It's much easier with two hands, I can keep any pressure off my bad leg this way. When I reach the bottom, Ama hands me my crutches back.

"Hungry?" she asks over her shoulder as she leads the way into the kitchen.

There's no sign of my sister or Thomas, but Ama catches me looking.

"The old man took Pippa to see the horses. I think they're out by the corral. It's a nice day, I'm sure they won't mind you getting a little fresh air out there if you want. As long as you stay under the cover of the porch, no one will even be able to see you. I can put a few pillows on that rocking chair out there so it's not so hard. You won't feel so cooped up."

That sounds perfect. The view from the large windows at the rear of the house is stunning, but from the front porch it'll at least feel I'm part of the activity. It'll also give me a great vantage point to keep an eye on Fletch.

"I'd love to."

Installed in the rocking chair with a large mug of coffee in my hand, I watch Dan—one of the ranch hands —work with a beautiful, spirited horse in the corral. My sister is watching as well as she sits on top of the fence, Thomas standing beside her. The ranch dog, Max, is roaming around the barn and I see Fletch carting something inside with a wheelbarrow. Somehow his eyes find me easily and even at this distance I can feel the heat of his gaze on me.

Ama walks out on the porch, carrying a tray she places

on my lap. It makes me feel spoiled. A feeling I'm not really used to.

"This is decadent," I comment, taking in the breakfast spread she put together.

Toast, scrambled eggs, bacon, hash browns, slices of honeydew melon, strawberries, and fresh huckleberries. It's way too much food for me. I pop a huckleberry in my mouth and the slightly tart flavor explodes on my tongue.

"These are delicious."

"I have a small patch at home. My daughter picked some this morning, she was trying to butter me up."

I look up at Ama, who is leaning on the railing.

"Butter you up?"

"Trying to. Una's my youngest, just turned seventeen last month, and thinks she can bribe me into letting her go to a concert in Helena with her boyfriend the weekend after next."

"Oh, dear." I grin around my bite of fluffy scrambled eggs.

"Exactly. Oh, dear. If James gets wind of it, he *will* chain her up inside the house."

Ama goes on to tell me a little about her family. Her daughter, Uma, who is in too much of a hurry to grow up and her son, JD, who is away at college. I'm a little envious when she speaks of her parents, her sister with whom she's close, and her family at large, which appears to include everyone here at High Meadow.

I've never had a large family. Even when Mom and Dad were still alive it was only the four of us. After that it was only Pippa and me, but with recent events I'm starting to wonder if I still have all of my sister.

While Ama talks, I actually manage to empty my plate.

"That was so good. Really hit the spot," I tell her when she removes the tray from my lap.

"Good. I'm glad. I have a confession to make though, when it comes to buttering up, the apple doesn't fall far from the tree." She grins. "I was hoping I could persuade you to show me how to make that flapper pie. I think my family would love it."

"We'll need lots of eggs, vanilla bean, graham crackers, and a few standard staples," I tell her as I get out of the rocker.

"I didn't mean right now," she says, shocked. "When you feel a little better."

"You can do all the work; I'll just be sitting down giving directions."

"Well, if you're sure." She shrugs and heads inside.

I follow a little slower, casting one last glance at the corral. When I walk into the kitchen, Ama is already pulling stuff from the pantry and the fridge. I take a seat at the island and recite the necessary ingredients for the crust.

In no time she has the milk, butter, and sugar for the custard coming to a boil on the stove, the egg whites and yolks are separated and resting in their respective bowls, and the heavy-duty food processor is loud as I watch Ama feed in one graham cracker after the other.

So loud, I don't realize someone is right behind me until I feel warm breath brush my cheek.

Fletch

"Whoa, easy."

I barely manage to grab the crutch coming at my face.

"Jesus, Fletcher," Ama scolds me over her shoulder. "She almost bashed your face in."

She's not kidding. I bent down to give Nella a kiss when she reacted and swung that crutch blindly over her head. She would've broken my nose too if I hadn't been just a fraction faster.

Clearly neither of them heard me come in, which isn't really a surprise given the racket Ama was making with that machine.

"Didn't mean to startle you."

She whips around in her seat, her pretty eyes round like saucers. Then they narrow to little glimmering pinpricks.

"Startle me? You scared the ever-living crap out of me!"

I'm having a hard time keeping a straight face so to hide it I tag her behind her neck, bend my head, and kiss the anger off her lips. Her mouth is tight and unyielding for a few seconds and then she gives in to the kiss, allowing me to slip my tongue in her mouth.

"Well, I'll be damned, son. Didn't think you had it in you."

I feel Nella seize up and lift my head, looking her in the eyes for a moment before turning my head to find a grinning Thomas and equally pleased Pippa stand side by side. Ama on the other side of the kitchen wears the same look on her face.

"I didn't either, old man," Ama seconds.

"Well, I'm not surprised," Pippa contributes with a smirk. "Irresistibility runs in the family."

Nella groans and I allow myself a chuckle.

"I assume you're all looking for lunch, but you're gonna have to get your own," Ama announces as she turns back to the counter. "I'm busy baking."

Then she flips the switch and turns that god-awful racket back on.

~

"We're O for two."

Sully looks glum as he hands me his horse's reins.

I'd just wolfed down a quick sandwich when I heard the trucks roll in. The team was back.

Jonas didn't say much before he disappeared to the house, except to instruct Dan and me to make sure the horses are fed and stabled. Apparently, the search has netted nothing so far.

"What about the third location?"

There were three hunting spots the owner of the RV repair place had suggested.

"It's all the fucking way up near the Canadian border. The horses need rest and we need some food and a couple of hours of sleep before we head up there."

"Go get some grub then. We've got the horses."

We, being Dan and me, but it doesn't take long to get them sorted.

The guys stay until after dinner before we load the horses back in the trailers for the team's trek north. Once again, they are going in under cover of night and I hope this time they find the bastards so we can get back to some normalcy and a bit of fucking privacy.

Nerves will only get more frayed the longer it takes, and already this afternoon I almost lost my temper with Thomas. Which is why I keep as busy as I can outside the house.

When the old man and the sisters settle in front of the TV, I escape to the porch to clean and oil my tack, something I haven't done in a long time. That's where Nella eventually finds me.

"Are you avoiding us?" she asks, lowering herself in the rocking chair.

"Not you," I correct her. "But yeah, in a crowd I'm only good for a short time before I get edgy."

One side of her mouth tilts up. "I can leave if you prefer."

"Don't." I reach out and put a hand on her knee. "The only thing better than being alone is being alone with you."

The slight tilt spreads into a bright smile that reaches all the way to her eyes and hits me square in the solar plexus.

"In that case, Thomas and Pippa just went to bed...you can be alone with me inside."

I'm receiving her invite loud and clear, but I can't take her up on it. The woman got shot just days ago. That said, I may not feel right about fucking her but there's nothing wrong with feeling her up a little.

I toss the rag on the saddle, stand up, and hold out my hand for her. She allows me to pull her to her feet, but squeals when I bend down and lift her in my arms, her crutches clattering to the porch.

"No one watching now."

Her arms go around my neck, her head drops on my shoulder, and I carry her inside.

I take her straight to the living room where someone—probably Thomas—had already turned off the lights. The room is cast in shadows with only a faint glow coming from the kitchen where the LED strips under the cupboards were left on.

Max, who is lying in his bed between the dining area and the living room, briefly lifts his big head to check who is coming in. I guess we pass muster because he lays his big head back on his paws and dozes back off.

I stayed down here last night. The couch—a massive sectional—was comfortable enough, even though I only dozed. I place Nella in a corner so she can stretch her legs along the short side, keeping her injured one elevated. Then I walk to the secondary panel by the sliding doors in the kitchen and set the alarm.

"Can I get you anything? Drink?" I ask turning toward her.

She shakes her head. "I'm fine."

"Take your meds?"

I want to make sure before her mouth and the feel of my hands on her curves make me forget. My body is already moving toward her.

She rolls her eyes.

"Yes. Anything else you need to know before you sit down?"

God, she's something else. Once she decides what she wants the mousy librarian becomes a demanding vixen, and I fucking love it. It's like a goddamn fantasy come alive.

"No," I growl when I stop right in front of her.

I fish my gun from the belt clip at the small of my back and drop it on the coffee table. Then I brace my hands on the backrest at either side of her, lean down, and drop a brief kiss on her lips.

"Sit," she orders when I straighten up.

I comply, perched on the edge as she reaches for one of my hands, studying it, her fingers tracing the ink on my knuckles. My hands are rough and broad—workman's hands. Hers are slender and elegant in contrast.

"Did you get these to hide the scars?"

"No, to remind myself how I got them," I answer truthfully.

The ink runs all the way up my arm and down one side of my back. Funny, she never asked about it before. She never commented on my scars before either, only acknowledged them after I brought them up. It's like she accepted both as part of me, like you would the color of someone's hair.

Even now, at my words, she simply nods like they are enough for her to understand the depth behind them. Maybe she does. Maybe I'm not the enigma I sometimes imagine myself to be. At least not to her.

I wait for the fear that usually accompanies this kind of exposure to hit, but there's nothing. Not even the overwhelming emotions I feel looking down at her scare me anymore.

This woman—this understated, undisguised, and honest woman—makes me want to step out of the shadows of my past. She's the promise of something I'd long ago given up on.

"Don't go," tumbles out of my mouth.

She looks confused.

"Where would I go? I'm right here."

"Home. Canada. Babe, I don't want you to leave."

"Fletcher..."

Her lips stretch in a sweet smile, but I suddenly need her answer.

"I put an offer on a place. Next door to the rescue."

"Fletch..." she murmurs.

"Fuck, I don't even know what I'm asking. All I know is I want you to stick around."

"I plan to, at least while I try to figure out what comes next."

I guess it's all I can ask after knowing each other for only a couple of weeks.

"I can show you what's next ..."

I go down on my knees in front of her and reach for the waistband of the sweats she's wearing. Then I pull them down along with her panties and lift her good leg to the other side of the couch so she is on display before me. This is what I had in mind when I sat her down in this corner. I just hope her sister or Thomas don't pick now to come downstairs, but I should hear them.

Her eyes darken as I place a hand low on her belly and use my thumb and forefinger to expose her clit. The moment my mouth closes over that hard pearl, one hand claws at the back of my head. With the other she grabs a throw pillow, covers her mouth with it, and gyrates her hips against me.

Goddamn. I could come from just eating this woman. She keeps no holds barred as she gives herself over to her body's needs and wants. Absolutely fucking perfect as she reaches for her climax unapologetically.

I'm lost in her taste and scent and hum against her slick core. Her legs start to tremble as she clamps her thighs against my ears and I double up on my efforts. I hear a soft growl and my eyes lift to her face a moment before her body jerks in the throes of her orgasm.

Then it registers she only now releases the pillow which was pressed against her mouth, yet I still hear the growling.

I surge to my feet and turn to where the dog is halfway out of his bed, crouching low with his head aimed at the front of the house, his teeth exposed.

"Get dressed," I whisper over my shoulder. "And get down behind the couch."

Not waiting for her confirmation, I grab my gun off the

table and start moving toward Max when he suddenly leaps forward, barking loudly, and heads for the front of the house.

I reach into the office doorway to snag the rifle we keep mounted on the other side of the doorframe for easy access. Then I cautiously walk up to the front door, where the dog is making a racket. A strange glow is visible when I press my eye against the peephole and I instantly know what I'm looking at.

Yanking open the door I don't bother disarming the alarm, I want it to go off.

I'm gonna need all the help I can get.

Twenty-Six

NELLA

I'm still scrambling to get back into my pants when the alarm goes off.

Immediately, I hear movement above me. I assume if anyone slept through Max's midnight serenade, this high-pitched beeping would've penetrated for sure. It's the kind of noise that puts you on edge if you weren't already there.

My body is still recovering from that delicious orgasm, but now my heart is racing with the added surge of adrenaline and my mind is already bouncing around like a pinball.

I know Fletch told me to get down behind the couch, but there's no way I can without at least knowing what is going on. Sticking to the shadows, I inch along the wall toward the hallway.

I'm almost there when I hear footsteps come down the stairs. I poke my head around the corner to see Thomas flipping open the alarm panel by the front door, which is wide open. Beyond him I see a red glow coming from the direction of the barn and I suck in a sharp breath.

"Dad gum it, girl! Y'all scared the livin' poop outta me," he complains as he quickly punches in a code.

The sudden silence is as startling as the alarm was, but then I hear a sound that has my entire body break out in goosebumps.

"Is that—" I begin to ask when Thomas steps out on the porch.

"Oh, dear Lord..." the old man mutters as he hurries down the steps as fast as his legs will allow.

I walk outside and the sounds are louder here. The barn is engulfed in flames and what I'm hearing are the frightened squeals of horses.

"Nella, call 911, make sure the fire department is coming fully loaded! And the vet, number is on the tack board in the office," Alex barks in passing as she sprints past me.

For a moment I'm frozen by the spectacle when suddenly my sister brushes right by me too and heads in the same direction.

"Now, Nella!" she yells.

My legs come unglued and I stumble inside the house to the first door on the left.

I locate the portable phone and almost drop it when it starts ringing.

"Hello?"

"Nella? This is Wayne Ewing, everything all right there?"

I'm guessing he gets some kind of notification when the alarm goes off.

"No. The barn is on fire. Oh, my God...the horses. I have to call the fire department. Fletch and Thomas are out there. And my sister. Oh, Jesus...Pippa."

My teeth chatter with the violent shakes overtaking my body.

"Nella? Where are you?"

"I'm in the office. I need to call the vet." A high-pitched whinny can be heard clear as day. "Can you hear the horses? I have to go help."

I'm already walking out of the office, barely aware of the tears streaming down my face as I listen to Ewing's calming voice.

"Listen to me. I'm on my way, so is the fire department, and I'll call the vet. What I need you to do is take the phone and lock yourself into the downstairs bathroom, okay?"

"Okay," I lie.

No way in hell can I cower inside and listen to this, knowing the people I care most about in this world are out there, doing the right thing.

"Hang in there," I hear the sheriff say as I step outside.

Fletch

Flames lick down from the hayloft and it's raining burning embers on my shoulders as I wield the ax at the door.

The fire must've started in the tack room. I found the entire front of the barn engulfed and inaccessible. I directed the old man and Alex to the rear barn doors to release the horses from there, but King's stall is nearer to the side door leading to the manure pile. My horse is cut off from the barn doors on both sides.

I can hear him inside—the terrified sounds he makes, the stuff of nightmares—and I swing the ax again. I keep telling myself as long as I can still hear him, he's alive. Someone must've thrown the heavy-duty latch on the inside and I've tried kicking it down without success. When the hole is big enough for me to reach through, I ignore the falling embers burning my skin and I rock the latch back and forth until it finally slides free.

Smoke billows out the moment the door is open, and I quickly pull my shirt over the bottom half of my face. Visibility is zero and it's only by feel and memory I find the latch to King's stall, but nothing happens when I throw open the door. I'm not thinking of my own safety when I reach a hand in front of me and step into the pen. Some of the straw in the stall is smoldering which is likely why he's cowering against the far wall.

"Let's go, King," I rasp against the thick smoke. "Come on, boy."

My fingers encounter quivering flesh and a hot puff of air. His nose. Instinctively my hand grabs onto his halter and he follows me without hesitation.

It's an amazing bond between horse and man, one built solely on mutual trust. I know I can close my eyes and trust King to navigate me down the steepest cliffs, just as he trusts me to lead him from danger, even if what I'm asking of him is against every instinct he has.

I lead King away from the barn and straight to the corral, where a small group—Thomas, Pippa, and Alex—is keeping the other horses calm. Six of them in total. King is almost vibrating beside me when Alex, who is ready with the hose, douses both my horse and me before aiming it back at the others.

Smart of her to focus on the horses instead of the barn. It would've been a futile attempt, I'm afraid. The hay became fuel to the fire and before I even got outside, it had spread along the entire length of the loft. I can hear sirens coming closer but I don't think the fire department is going to do much more than make sure the fire doesn't jump.

I glance around at the horses to gauge their injuries but it's difficult to tell, even though someone thought to flick on the floodlight next to the corral.

"We sure this is all of them?" I ask.

"Yup."

This from Thomas. Pippa is standing beside him and looks to have a very nervous Missy in hand.

"Don't start with me," Nella's sister snaps when she catches me looking. "I wasn't going to sit around."

No, I imagine she wasn't, then again, I didn't expect her sister to either. Or Dan, for that matter. My gaze automatically goes to the house where I see the sheriff's cruiser parked. There is no sign of him though, which seems odd. The front door is wide open and an icy sliver of unease makes my breath catch in my throat.

I let go of King and start walking to the gate, my eyes never leaving the porch.

"What's wrong?" Thomas is the first to ask.

"I don't know," I answer truthfully.

Two fire engines are coming up the driveway, and I wave them over to the barn. Then I continue toward the house, taking the porch steps two at a time. I'm about to walk in when Ewing appears at the end of the hallway, an inscrutable expression on his face.

When you've been in the field for decades, body language becomes an almost more effective mode of communication than words. And the sheriff's body language is conveying nothing good.

Something is horribly wrong.

"Nella?"

I can barely get her name out, still have her fucking taste on my lips.

"Was talking to her as I was pulling onto the highway. Found the phone lying on the porch when I got here. I can't find her, Boone."

Storming through the house like a man possessed, I throw open doors, check behind and under furniture, and call her name in hopes perhaps she did as I asked and hid. *Nothing.* She's not here.

I fucking left her here. Ran out like an idiot to rescue a bunch of horses and a goddamn barn, and left the woman I was supposed to protect alone.

A frustrated howl rips from my chest as I grab my head with both hands and bend over.

Life can't be this cruel.

"Where the hell is my sister?"

Pippa barrels through the door and stops in front of me, planting her hands on her hips. She juts her chin defiantly, despite the abject fear on her face.

"I'll find her," I promise.

"What happened?" she demands to know.

"I think I know."

A woman's voice I can't immediately place comes from behind Pippa, who instantly steps aside.

"Gemma, what are you doing here?" I rush to the frail woman's side.

Gemma is Dan's mother, who has advanced metastatic colorectal cancer. Gemma and Dan moved into one of the cabins before the summer, when Jonas discovered the farmhand was struggling to look after his mother while also maintaining an income they could live off.

"Dan went after them."

"Who is them?" Ewing inquires.

"I never saw them, but he said there were two men and a woman. Dan was on his way to help at the barn when he spotted them." Then Gemma turns to me. "I'm sorry. He told me to call the house and I tried but no one answered, so I walked here instead."

She sways on her feet and I slip a careful arm around her. The woman is so slight, I'm afraid I'll break her.

"Do you know where they went?" the sheriff pushes.

"My boy thought they might be heading for the old logging road along the river."

That road is more like a trail by now. It would be fastest to get to on horseback. Otherwise, we'd have to drive out to the highway, head south for half a mile and hit that overgrown cutoff right before the bridge. Problem is, the only tack that didn't perish in the fire is mine. It's still out there on the porch. I can't take King, he's injured, but maybe one of the other horses is in better shape.

"Look after her," I instruct Pippa, handing Gemma to her before I tear out of the house.

"Hold up," Ewing says when I collect my saddle and bridle and make my way down the steps. "Where are you headin'?"

"Logging road. It's a good fifteen, twenty-minute walk if they cut straight through the woods. I may be able to catch them on horseback, but my guess is they'll have a vehicle waiting. If you access the road from the highway, we may be able to block them in."

I'm already rushing down the steps when his next words stop me in my tracks.

"We may be too late either way."

He's not wrong, it's not like the thought hadn't crossed my mind that whatever they intended to do to Nella was already done. In all the chaos here, a gunshot could've gone undetected. But I'm not ready to consider that possibility. Not yet.

"We're gonna find her," I insist, just as Pippa comes bounding down the porch stairs.

"I'm coming," she announces.

"Like hell you are," Ewing counters.

I don't have time for this shit.

With long strides I make my way over to the corral and snatch Buttercup. She's an old biddy, but still has some fire in the tank and pretty much unflappable. While I quickly saddle her, I fill in Alex and Thomas and let them know Gemma is up at the house by herself.

Then I swing onto the mare and dig my heels in.

The sheriff's cruiser is just pulling out as I head around to the other side of the house. I'm not surprised when I get a glimpse of Pippa in the passenger seat. The Freling women are not easily deterred.

I guide Buttercup past my cabin and into the woods. It's dark, especially under the tree cover, but every so often the moon will peek out, giving me a bit more visibility. I wish I had my night-vision gear but I don't, nor do I have my compass. I'm going purely on gut here, and I hope to God it steers me right. Normally I'd be looking for tracks, signs someone passed through, but that's not an option now. Speed is imperative or they will get away, and my instinct is all I've got.

Every now and then I stop Buttercup, long enough to listen for any sounds of movement. I'd imagine three people stumbling through the woods in the middle of the night would make some noise.

Through the trees I can see an occasional silver ripple—a reflection of moonlight—and I know I'm getting close to the river. The growth is less dense. I pull back on the reins so

I can dismount and walk the rest of the way. Buttercup makes too much noise and I don't want them to hear me coming.

I've walked maybe twenty feet when a hand shoots out from behind a tree, clamping on to my arm.

"Fletch..."

Twenty-Seven

"Move, you miserable cunt."

The guy with the stringy blond hair—I guess that must be Willy—yanks on the rope tied to my bound arms and I almost do a face plant. My leg is in bad shape and I'm having a hard time keeping up with these yahoos. Wyatt is behind me with the gun. He actually scares me more than the foul-mouthed Willy.

I'd give them both a piece of my mind, but unfortunately the first thing they did after shoving the barrel of a gun in my face was slap a piece of duct tape over my mouth. They tied my arms in front of me and whisked me off the porch. The whole thing took no more than a handful of seconds.

I couldn't scream, unfortunately, but I could listen...and listen I did.

From what I was able to piece together they were supposed to get both me and Pippa, but hadn't counted on my sister beelining it out of the house right behind everyone else to help rescue the horses. Willy, the mouthy one, said something about Graham who would be pissed if they showed up with just one of us. I'd wondered why they hadn't just shot me—finished the job—but I realized then the plan was to take me to this...Graham, whoever he is.

Still, I'm not so sure Wyatt would hesitate to put a bullet in my back if I tried to take off. Not that I'd get far on this leg.

Despite the brisk night air, sweat is pouring down my face and stinging my eyes. I'm not sure how far I can keep trudging through these woods when I notice a break in the trees up ahead. Is that water? I remember Fletch mentioned Fisher River bordering the south and east side of the ranch when we were out on our ride. Did they sneak in by boat? I guess it would be smart, it's much harder to track someone on water. Also, from what I remember of the maps of the area, Fisher River hooks up with the much larger Kootenay River, which could take us anywhere. Heck, if you followed it all the way north of the border, it would take you to within half an hour of my apartment building in Cranbrook.

Stumbling through the trees with a gun at my back, I've never felt farther removed from my life there. I feel like an entirely different person, barely recognizing the woman I was then. So much has happened, it feels like a lifetime ago. When every day is the same as the one before—safe and predictable—you don't feel the passage of time so clearly, but since coming here I've been swept along on this continuously changing adventure and it feels like months have passed.

Even that horseback ride Fletch took me on feels like it

was weeks ago and not just days. A pang of hot grief penetrates the cold fear at the thought of him.

Am I ever going to see him again?

Does he even know I'm gone?

I want to believe it. I want to believe he is somewhere behind us, coming to find me, but I'm afraid to. More afraid of being disappointed when he doesn't show, than of facing whatever these guys have in store for me by myself.

Another yank on my arms snaps me back to the present as Willy pulls me out of the cover of the trees onto a dirt trail along the river. I'm trying to slow down as much as he'll let me as we walk parallel to the water. I can't even feel my leg anymore at this point. It feels like I've been walking forever.

"There she is," he says, pointing ahead at a pickup with a large RV hooked up to it.

So many thoughts are going through my head as the two lead me toward the camper. What are they planning to do with me? Is their boss waiting in there?

I go even slower, but am immediately poked in the back with a barrel.

"Keep going."

This time it's Wyatt prompting me when up ahead the door to the trailer swings open.

"Where's the other one?"

Not even the gun shoved between my ribs can get my feet to move when I hear that voice.

"Jesus, you two are more useless than tits on a bull, ain't ya?"

"She was never alone," Willy protests, but the woman won't hear of it.

"Wanna get anything done you gotta damn well do it yourself," she mumbles. "Well, get the girl off the road already, would ya?"

Willy jerks on the rope and I stumble forward. I really don't want to go inside that trailer but Willy shoves me up the steps.

Recognizing Wyatt had shocked me to the core—he'd been such a nice, helpful guy before—but being fooled twice like this has me terrified.

The moment I step inside the trailer it becomes clear how much trouble I'm in.

"Gonna make this fast," she says, her own gun pointed at my head. "Finish what my dang boys started. Can't trust the young generation to do anything right anymore, can ya? First, they let your sister get away, although I've gotta say, I was sure shocked she survived. Stubborn girl, but I guess that runs in the family, don't it? You don't give up lightly either. Your moxie surprised me, but it's too bad that stubborn streak landed you here." She motions to the floor with the gun. "Need you to get down on your knees, girl."

Like hell I'm going down on my knees. If she plans to kill me, I'm not about to make it easier for her. The woman is batshit crazy. Unfortunately, retreat is not an option because Twiddle Dee and Twiddle Dum are blocking the door. But that also potentially puts them in her line of fire, which is probably why she wanted me on my knees.

A flash of light shines in through the window. Looks like headlights.

"Grab her, Wyatt," the woman barks. "You two take her in the bedroom and stay quiet."

I bang into furniture as I'm roughly hustled to the rear of the trailer. There I'm shoved facedown onto a bed where I'm joined by one of them. I assume Wyatt, since he was holding the gun, which is currently being pressed against the back of my head.

"I will shoot you if you make a sound," he hisses, and if I

wasn't so damn scared, I'd laugh. I thought the plan was to shoot me either way.

Outside I can hear a door slam, then nothing for a bit before there's a crunch of footsteps coming toward the trailer. If that is Fletch, I hope to God he's careful. I don't think this woman would think twice about putting a bullet in him.

The loud rap on the door is unexpected. I startle as Wyatt jumps off the bed.

"What the hell is she doin'?"

"Shut the fuck up, Willy," his cousin mutters.

A second knock sounds at the door, followed by a voice.

"Sheriff's office! I need to talk to you about parking here. Can you open the door?"

I recognize Sheriff Ewing and for a moment relief floods me, but it doesn't last.

"Hold yer horses!" she calls back. "I'm just gettin' my clothes on!"

No she's not and suddenly I'm worried for the sheriff.

My wrists are still tied in front of me and currently tucked under my body, but I quietly roll over and bring my hands up to my mouth. In one fast move, I rip the duct tape off. It hurts like hell. I blink furiously against the sudden tears burning my eyes as I suck in a lungful of air.

"She's got a gun!"

Fletch

"I followed them for a little while and guessed they were heading toward the river. Nella's not moving too well so they're going pretty slow, so I circled around them to get ahead. I was hoping maybe I could find some way to intercept them, when I saw the trailer."

Dan and I are crouched down behind a large tree stump on the edge of the logging trail. A thirty-or thirty-two-foot camper hitched to a late model Chevy Silverado is parked on the other side, right along the river.

"There's someone inside," I observe as I watch a shadow move behind the blinds.

That's got to be the elusive Graham, or Grant, whatever his name is. I wonder if this is one of the stolen RVs. Ewing should be able to tell once he gets here.

Suddenly Dan grabs onto my arm and I hear the movement too. It's coming from our left. The sound of footfalls on dry dirt.

"There she is."

The voice belongs to a young punk, about Dan's age. He's holding a goddamn rope tied to Nella, who is limping badly behind him, followed by the other motherfucker. Relief at seeing her alive is quickly replaced with rage surging through my body. I must've made a sound or something because Dan digs his fingers into my forearm in warning. That's when I notice the second guy jab a gun in the small of Nella's back.

I move now and she's dead.

We watch as the door opens and a small figure is outlined against the light flowing from the trailer. There is something about the woman's voice that nags at me, but I can't place it. I clench my jaw when I have to watch those two fuckers manhandle Nella into the trailer, but I have to keep a cool head.

As soon as the door closes, I'm on my feet and pull my

cell from my pocket. Ewing is going to roll up any time now and he needs to know what he's going to run into.

"Coming up the logging road now. Did you find them?"

"Got Dan here. Three of them plus Nella in a trailer on the side of the river. At least one of them is armed, maybe more."

I can see the shine of headlights through the trees on my right.

"Shit, I can see your lights."

It takes us less than a minute to come up with a plan. It's not much but it'll have to do. Not like there are that many options.

I hand Dan the rifle I had slung over my shoulder and keep my sidearm for myself.

"Stay here. Shoot only if you have to," I tell him before crouching low and stepping out of the tree line, my gun in hand.

When the sheriff's cruiser pulls up alongside the pickup, I use the distraction to make my way across the road unseen. I duck behind the RV and peek around the corner to see Ewing standing beside his cruiser. He seems to be talking to someone but I can't see Pippa in the passenger seat. I hope he told her to get the hell down and stay there.

The moment he starts walking toward the trailer, I look up for a way in. There's a window to what has to be the bedroom. It's tough for me to see inside with the window so high off the ground but on the other side of the window is a ladder. I don't waste a second, when I hear Ewing pounding on the door, and climb up the first few steps. Then I wait to make sure any noise I made was covered by the sheriff's racket, while peeking in the window.

Nella is facedown on the bed right underneath the window. I can't see much more but hear a muted exchange from inside the room. Two voices, both male. Leaning over a little farther, I catch sight of those two punks huddled by the door, their backs turned to the window.

On the other side of the trailer the sheriff starts pounding again, but this time he announces himself as the sheriff's office. The woman I heard before responds, with some nonsense about getting dressed.

Then I watch as Nella moves in the bed, rolling to her side, and ripping a strip of duct tape from her mouth.

"She's got a gun!"

Every single hair on my body stands on end at the sound of her frantic scream, which is followed closely by the first gunshot.

Then all hell breaks loose on the other side of the trailer.

In the bedroom I watch the punk with the gun swing it around at Nella, and I don't hesitate to aim and shoot before he can. Instead of shattering the window, my bullet formed a small hole at the center of a dense spiderweb of cracks obscuring my view. I don't even fucking know if I hit my target.

Barely hanging on to the ladder with my left hand and leg, I swing out and aim my other foot at the damaged, tempered glass as hard as I can. It takes three solid kicks before the glass crumbles and without hesitation or thought, I propel myself through the window.

I land on the bed, on top of a body, and I immediately roll off when I hear a grunt. One glance tells me it's not Nella though. It's the guy with the gun, he's facedown, but I don't fucking see Nella.

Darting a quick look at the wide-open bedroom door I see no sign of the second punk either. Did he grab her? A loud crash sounds from the front, making the entire trailer shake. I dive off the bed and crouch low, about to peek around the doorway to get the lay of the land when a volley of gunshots has me duck down.

A woman's pained cry is followed immediately by the sheriff's voice.

"On your knees! Hands on top of your head. Do it *now*!"

"Nella!" I call out as I scramble to my feet.

Stepping out of the bedroom, I search the scene in front of me. The front end of the trailer is caved in and a large section of the trailer's metal shell is peeled up like a can. I can just see one of the sheriff cruiser's headlights through the hole in the wall. The woman I saw earlier is partially pinned under the debris. The second kid is on his knees by the door, hands folded on top of his head, Ewing towering over him. But I don't see her.

"Fletch?"

The soft voice comes from behind me, from the bedroom.

I find her wedged in the narrow space between the wall and the mattress on the other side of the bed, where she is partially obscured by the punk on the mattress. I not so gently roll him out of the way to pull Nella free.

Then I wrap her in my arms, and clutch her to me, as I sink to my ass on the floor and bury my face in her neck.

"Jesus Christ, Babe. Cut ten years off my life."

Twenty-Eight

"Their grandmother?"

Alex is visibly shocked.

"Betsy Waters. Sick, isn't it?" Pippa observes and I can't say I disagree. "And here's the kicker…" She pauses briefly for effect. "I knew! Well, clearly I'd forgotten I knew, but something clicked when I saw that trailer and it all came back."

It's after four in the morning and we got back to the ranch maybe half an hour ago. All the lights were on and Alex had been waiting up for us. I'd called earlier to give her an update and she'd mentioned alerting the team, who are on their way home. Thomas was wiped and had gone off to bed, but the rest of us didn't feel like sleeping. The adrenaline is still draining and the fresh pot of coffee Alex made helps to keep us alert as we wait for the team to get home and the sheriff to pick up his ride.

The three of us drove home in his cruiser. His idea. He

told Pippa, since she'd already appropriated his vehicle to ram the trailer when the shooting started, she might as well drive it to the ranch. Luckily it was still drivable, despite the substantial front-end damage.

By the time we got here the fire trucks were gone and the big barn was nothing but a pile of blackened rubble. I'd sent Dan back earlier with Buttercup and, apparently, he helped Alex deal with the horses after Doc Evans checked them out. Four of them are now out in the field behind the breeding barn but King and Missy, who were injured, are stabled inside.

There's little else to do right now but debrief, and there's a lot of stuff to cover. Especially coming from Pippa. They say trauma can be the cause of memory loss, but apparently trauma can also be the trigger to its recovery.

All the pieces appear to be flooding back and her mouth almost can't keep up with the flow. Clearly, she needs to share what she remembers and there is a lot to sort through.

Nella, who is tucked under my arm, seems a little shell-shocked as she quietly absorbs and processes all the missing information her sister is providing.

It was the two cousins, Wyatt and Willy, she saw snooping around her rig when she returned from a hike. She'd seen Willy before, visiting Betsy Waters, the same campground neighbor who'd recommended she boondock out on Scenery Mountain in the first place. She remembers the punk had called the old woman, "Gram."

It wasn't a *Graham* or a *Grant* we should've been looking for.

Instead of keeping her distance, Pippa shares how she approached them yelling, hoping to chase them off, but instead of running Wyatt pulled a gun on her. They backed her up to the edge of the cliff before shoving her over the edge. She remembers falling, but nothing after until she came to and founds herself hanging in a tree, without any idea how she got there or where she was.

Interesting that it wasn't Willy—the punk I'd seen hunting illegally weeks ago and was known to the sheriff—who was waving the gun in any of these scenarios. It had been Wyatt—the polite one, the 'good' kid—who apparently was the aggressor.

It's the quiet ones that can be most dangerous. Willy is a punk, a criminal for sure, but mostly a follower. His cousin, on the other hand, is more disturbing. Wyatt apparently never got into any trouble with law enforcement or even pinged their radar. Yet he'd been the one inciting the violence, which makes me wonder if perhaps he developed a taste for blood after the encounter with Pippa, and killed that couple near Troy.

I don't think there was any physical violence involved in the robberies prior to Pippa. Or maybe there was and there are cases we don't know about yet. People get lost all the time, and occasionally human remains are found in the mountains that can't be identified. But for every bone found, I'm sure there are twenty more that will stay lost forever.

"I'm hungry," Pippa announces, interrupting my macabre train of thought.

She's suddenly like an Energizer Bunny, fired up and restless, as she follows Alex to the kitchen.

"She's back," Nella mumbles, snuggling up closer.

"Pippa?"

"Yeah. This is how she is supposed to be, a spark plug; vibrant, eyes wide open, and always in tune with herself and the world around her."

I detect a note of wistfulness. Or maybe it's just fatigue

coming through in the tone of her voice. Either way, I tuck her in a little tighter.

"I've always envied her that," she confesses on a whisper, almost as an afterthought.

I could remind her of what we were doing last night in the exact same spot on the couch where we're sitting now. Nella was the spark plug then. The live wire I couldn't wait to get my hands on. The woman who left no doubt what she wanted and how she wanted it.

Even underneath those layers of perceived respectability and false modesty she's cultivated, the core of her personality is as real, as fearless, and as aware as her sister is.

But she's been through a lot, she has to be hurting, and she's got a ton of stuff to process. Maybe this isn't the right time to remind her of that.

So I tell her something else instead.

"Been scared plenty of times before, but never as scared as I was last night. Wasn't kidding when I said it cut ten years off my life."

She tilts her head back so she can look up at me with those warm eyes.

"I'm sorry."

"Nothing for you to be sorry about, but it made me realize how deep I already have you under my skin."

I brush a finger along her lush bottom lip as she slowly smiles.

"Yeah?"

Tracing the arch of her eyebrow with the same digit, I follow her nose down to its tip, and end up right back at her mouth.

"Yeah. So it's too soon, and it may well send you running back to Canada—although I'll hunt you down—

but I don't wanna chance you never knowing I love you, Nella."

Her eyes gloss over and her nostrils flare as she sucks in a sharp breath, and she's about to say something when someone else beats her to it.

"Awww...that's so cute."

My head snaps up to find Pippa standing ten feet away, a big goofy smile on her face. Alex is right behind her, grabbing her arm.

Max barks twice, jumps up from his bed, and rushes toward the front door.

"All my fault," Alex apologizes as she pulls Pippa back to the kitchen with her. "I told her to see what you wanted for breakfast."

Then Jonas's voice comes booming down the hall.

"Bacon and eggs for days, Sweets!"

Nella

I'm in Fletch's bed, in his cabin, wide awake.

I can't seem to stop the film reel that's been on an almost continuous loop since last night. Of course, it doesn't help I've had to go over the entire ordeal a few times.

I'm so tired, I can't fall asleep. I hate when that happens. My eyes won't stay open but at the same time my brain won't shut up.

Sheriff Ewing finally showed up mid-afternoon. He'd just come back from the hospital where both Wyatt and Betsy were taken. Betsy, who'd started firing at the sheriff out the window, was injured when Pippa rammed the RV with the cruiser. Wyatt was not so lucky, because Fletch's bullet hit him in the shoulder and he needed surgery. Ewing returned to the hospital so he could talk to Wyatt as soon as he woke up after he'd already questioned Willy in jail.

Talk about a dysfunctional family, with harmless-looking senior, Betsy Waters, firmly at the helm. Or maybe not so firmly, since apparently first Willy, and later Wyatt, were quick to point their finger at Gram as their ringleader. Not a surprise, since Betsy was busy pointing fingers at both of her grandsons.

I still can't wrap my head around that fact. Ewing told us both Betsy's sons were out of the picture. One was killed in a hunting accident many years ago and the younger one, Willy's father, has been in prison even longer. With her own sons gone, she groomed those boys to see her through her retirement. From what I gather, without their mothers' support.

Hell, the woman turned them into criminals, only to sell them out in the end to save her own old, wrinkly ass. God knows, maybe she sold out her son too. Who does that? What kind of mother or grandmother would sacrifice their own flesh and blood to save their own?

And this is what keeps me awake when my body needs rest desperately.

Fletch tucked me in, kissed me goodnight, and mentioned stopping in at the barn to check on King. He's been worried about the injured horse hurting himself. The vet already had to come back once today to give King another sedative because he was agitated.

Alex mentioned it would take time and quite a bit of work for the horse to get over the trauma. Apparently, that's something she does, working with traumatized horses. A horse whisperer, or equine therapist, which I guess is the official title.

She seems to really love what she does. Lucy is the same way, and I know my sister has always followed her heart. I always considered that a luxury, one I myself couldn't afford, but now with my entire future open maybe it's my chance to choose with my heart instead of my head.

"I can almost hear you thinking."

I turn my head to where Fletch is leaning against the doorway.

"I didn't hear you come in."

"I was quiet, 'cause you're supposed to be sleeping."

He pushes away from the doorpost and walks to the bed. I move to make room so he can sit on the edge. Then he reaches to brush some hair off my forehead.

"Pain?"

"No, it's not my leg. My mind is churning."

Right now it's stuck on the words he shared with me—and inadvertently Pippa and Alex—in the early morning hours, but I don't tell him that.

"Wanna talk it through?"

"I'm mostly still processing stuff."

I know I'm avoiding, but what is in my heart are words I've only ever shared with my parents and my sister. They've always been special, like the silver cutlery that spends the whole year wrapped in blue paper in a drawer, only to come out for Christmas dinner. I have to work out in my head what it means I want to share them with him—the ripple effect once the words are spoken.

I'm a planner.

He leans down and brushes a kiss to my cheek.

"You're thinking too hard, Babe. Give me five minutes to get ready for bed and I'll empty that busy mind of yours."

The promise of his words is apparently enough to shut my brain down and jump-start my libido, and the next few minutes all I can focus on are the faint sounds coming from the bathroom. The anticipation is so strong, I hold my breath when the water turns off and the door opens.

He's naked and I push myself up to sitting. I haven't really had a chance to see him so I take the opportunity to study him in the glow of the nightstand lamp. He doesn't seem to mind and indulgently allows me a slow perusal.

His body looks as tough as his personality appeared at first. The hard planes earned through honest physical labor, the scars and imperfections showing a harsh passage of years, and the slacking lines and softening of contours bearing witness to middle age. The only thing showing no signs of aging or softening is the proud rise of his cock.

I've never studied a man so closely, so honestly. It feels more intimate than roaming hands in the dark. Suddenly I feel the need to allow him the same.

I can feel him watching me as I flip back the covers on the bed and pull his shirt I've repurposed as sleepwear over my head, dropping it on the floor. Then I shimmy a little inelegantly out of my panties and toss them on top.

"You're hurt."

His voice sounds strangled as his eyes seem to drink me in.

"You'll be careful." I give him my trust.

Then his knee is on the mattress next to my hip, his hand fists in the hair at the base of my skull, and his tongue plunges between my lips.

Yesss.

This is what I need. This hunger, this insatiable craving that aches to be satisfied. The grunts, the nips, the skin that heats and grows slick under my exploring touch. The give and take of desire without reservation or apology. Lips tugging at nipples, fingers seeking out wet silk.

His hips ease between my legs as he lowers himself carefully, lifting my good leg wide to allow him room. Then I feel the flushed head of his cock slicking itself along my folds before he plants himself deep.

Skin to skin, soul to soul, without any barriers. *Vulnerable.*

This is honesty. This is trust.

This is love.

As he stills to allow my body to adjust to him, I lift my hands and cup his face. His dark eyes on me smolder like hot coal. It's only us in this moment, nothing and no one else.

"I love you, Fletcher Boone."

I watch as his eyes close and he slowly lowers his lips to mine for an infinitely tender kiss before he mumbles against my mouth.

"I'm a happy man."

Twenty-Nine

FLETCH

"A few more loads should do it."

I'm covered in soot, head to toe, but so is everyone else helping to tear down and clean up what is left of the barn. We've got a contractor coming in next week to dig a new foundation. Jonas is not fucking around as he keeps us going. We've been at it all day and look like fucking chimney sweeps.

Aside from the injuries and trauma to the horses and the loss of the contents of the tack room as a result of the fire, Jonas hadn't seemed too heartbroken to see the barn gone. As it turned out, after a very profitable stud season with the addition of Blitz—our Arabian stallion—to the stable, he'd already been in the process of having drawings made up for expanded facilities.

He showed us the plans a few days ago. The new, larger barn would have a section with three foaling stalls segregated from the main barn and with its own separate entrance. Each stall is supposed to be outfitted with an electronic monitoring system and can double as an infirmary as needed.

Changes are coming to the breeding barn as well with the addition of a few larger stalls there for the studs, an updated cooler system, and a few other improvements in the workspace.

Ironically those two idiots provided an opportunity and most of the funding for the project by burning down the barn. With an arson report and the sheriff's statements in hand, and Jonas's attorney on standby just in case, it didn't appear the insurance adjuster who came out a few days ago would deny the claim.

What's going to be a pain is working around construction with horses that are still jumpy from the fire itself. Alex already suggested maybe moving Missy and King over to the rescue where she has room in the barn for them to recover and it's quiet.

I fit one more charred board in the wheelbarrow and haul this load to the container they dropped off yesterday afternoon. It's heavy work and I'm feeling the effects. I'm not as spry as I used to be, so my leg muscles are burning and my arms feel like they're full of lead. I doubt I could lift them over my head at this point.

What keeps me going is the cold beer and the first taste of that bighorn I bagged I promised myself waiting back at the cabin. The only thing better would be if Nella were there waiting for me as well, but after the first couple of nights she and her sister went back to the rescue.

She said it was for Pippa's sake, so she could continue to work with Lucy, who is apparently branching out into equine therapy, and Pippa is her first patient.

After the words she gave me last week, Nella explained she wasn't entirely clear on what she wanted her future to look like, but she wanted me to be part of it. I don't question that. Hell, I'm not quite sure what it looks like for me, but as of a few days ago I'm the proud new owner of a single-level ranch-style house, a big-ass barn, and about ten acres of pretty land.

A place I'm hoping won't only be home for me, but for Nella as well. She does things at her own pace though, and I'm trying hard to honor that. I had to swallow down a long list of objections that came to mind when she called yesterday to tell me she and her sister had to head back to Canada to deal with a couple of things.

I heard from Wayne Ewing that with the testimony from the two cousins, and the help of law enforcement in Idaho, they were able to recover a total of twelve RVs stolen from Lincoln County. It included Pippa's rig, which she got back earlier this week, and the Freling sisters plan to drive that thing back across the border.

"You don't look too happy, brother," Bo points out as he passes me a fresh bottle of water. "Trouble in paradise?"

Part of me wants to tell him to fuck off, but for once he sounds genuinely interested instead of looking to yank my chain, which is his custom.

"Nella and her sister are heading home to Cranbrook today."

"I heard. Sully says they'll be back though."

"I know. Still sucks."

"Mm-hmm," he sympathizes before changing the subject. "When are you supposed to be heading to your new place?"

He picks up one end of a heavy beam and indicates for

me to pick up the other end. Together we start carrying it over to the roll-off dumpster.

"First of the month is coming up so Esther is moving out this next weekend," I answer. "I figure any time after, but I want get a bit of work done first."

"Like what?"

"Bit of paint here and there, put in a new counter and upgrade the appliances in the kitchen. I'll eventually reno the bathroom, but the big stuff can wait."

Bo chuckles. "Good call. Women like to be involved in big decisions."

I snort. "And since when are you an expert on the subject?"

The cocky son of a bitch smirks.

"Women are my specialty."

"Oh yeah? Then how come you've been striking out left, right, and center with Lucy?" I tease him.

It's impossible not to notice he lays on the charm thick with her, but she is having none of it. Mind you, getting to know Lucy, I wonder if it's just Bo who isn't working for her, or if she's simply not in the market, period. I have a suspicion it may be the latter.

I heave my side of the beam into the dumpster and Bo tips in his end. He doesn't look amused anymore and is silent when we return to the remaining pile of rubble. Maybe his interest in her is more than another notch on his belt.

"Listen, I'm—" I start but he immediately brings up his hand to stop me.

"It's all good. Let's just finish getting this shit cleaned up."

He wants it dropped so I will.

We work side by side for another ten minutes and by then it's nearing on five o'clock so Jonas calls it a day. I'm about ready for a shower and those beers I have chilling in the fridge and head to my cabin.

Damp but clean, I just sit down on the small porch with a cold one when my phone rings. It's Nella.

"Your timing is impeccable," I tell her.

"Good to know."

I can hear the smile in her face.

"How's Canada?"

"The same. Beautiful." There's a brief silence before she adds. "I saw Jeanine and Phil Hicks today."

I remember that's how Nella got my name in the first place.

"Yeah?"

"I hope you don't mind I invited them to come visit us some time."

Now it's my turn to take a moment while I let that sink in.

Fuck me. I'm part of an us.

"They're welcome any time."

Nella

"God, this is beautiful."

Pippa knew a gorgeous dispersed camping spot on Mineral Lake, just twenty minutes south of Cranbrook.

We had to find an alternative because we couldn't stay at my apartment in town. It was no longer mine.

We've been here a week now. It's amazing the amount of work it is to pull up stakes. The to-do list had been a long one. Canceling subscriptions and memberships, closing out utility accounts, and notifying dentists' and doctors' offices. In addition, we also met with an immigration lawyer to get a better idea of what would be required to actually build a life south of the border.

In the meantime, I took out extra travel insurance to make sure I'd be covered for the next six months because that's as long as I can stay in the US as a visitor. It'll give me time to figure out what steps to take next. The last thing I had to do in person was pick up my medical records yesterday and sign the paperwork to transfer all my balances and assets to the bank account I opened in Libby last week.

It had been a frantic few days when we first arrived. I immediately went to the building manager's office to give them my notice. There I discovered that the manager has a waiting list and if I could empty out my place by the weekend, I could avoid paying for an additional month. Seeing as I'm not sure how far and long my money has to stretch, I jumped all over that.

That first night I called Jeanine to let her know I was back in town for a bit and see if she'd have time to meet up. My plan had been to tell her what happened in Montana over coffee, but she dragged it out of me and—after expressing her shock and imparting words of caution at my plans—she offered to come help pack the next day like the good friend she is. Her husband, Phil, showed up after his shift and hauled some stuff to the dump for me.

Before Pippa took off on her trip, she'd rented a storage unit to hold the stuff she didn't want to get rid of but couldn't bring. We were able to fit the things I want to hold on to—mostly stuff my parents had given me plus a few remaining heirlooms—in the unit to be dealt with later, and a lot of the small stuff is packed in the RV.

"Here," Pippa says, walking up behind me and handing me a steaming coffee mug over my shoulder. Then she takes the camp chair beside me.

It's pretty chilly out this early in the morning, so I pulled Fletch's sweats I stole and a flannel shirt on over my pajamas. To finish my ensemble, I have my hands shoved in a pair of socks and tucked my hair under a slouchy knit beanie I found in the motorhome.

I don't even look like myself and I love it.

Pippa's attire looks similar to mine. We make a fine pair of hobos.

"Yours?"

Pippa plucks at the sweats.

"Stole them from Fletch."

I grin and turn my head at the same time she does. She's smiling as well.

"You rebel, you."

She's got that right. I'm feeling pretty reckless after dismantling the predictable existence I'd created for myself.

Reaching out I tap her mug with mine.

"Are you ready?" I ask her.

We're heading back to Montana today.

The plan is to stay at the rescue—Lucy is expecting us—at least for now. I like the idea of doing things in stages, giving myself a chance to adjust to the changes in my life. I'm still learning to draw outside the lines and enjoying the freedom of choice. That's the plan anyway. In reality, I have a feeling my ass will be in Fletch's bed before too long. I'm ready to see him.

"I am, but I've been thinking," Pippa muses. "I'd like to do some more equine therapy with Lucy, try and rebuild some of that confidence I had when I first left for my travels. But then I might want to take a month or two on the road."

She glances over and reaches for my hand, giving it a gentle squeeze.

"Don't get me wrong, I have my plan, but I want to be sure I'm ready to take it on."

I know she's looking to start up a business for herself. She was very interested when the immigration lawyer talked about ways to fast-track a work visa or green card. Opening a business would be one such way, provided you had a certain amount to invest. Money talks and it just so happens my sister has a bit socked away.

She's not lacking in funds; she's lacking in confidence.

I return her squeeze.

"I already know you are, but I understand you need to believe that yourself."

"You always were good at pep talks," she observes with a smile. "Making me feel like I could do anything. Reach for the stars."

"Because you could," I confirm. "And you can."

"Yeah." She shifts sideways in her seat and looks at me intently. "So why couldn't you do the same?"

I feel the sting of impending tears in my nose and swallow hard.

I don't tell her I willingly stayed in the background to provide the stability she needed to soar. I own that choice, and the weight of it doesn't belong on her shoulders.

Instead I tell her, "I'm reaching for stars now."

"And I can't tell you how happy that makes me." Her eyes shimmer as she smiles at me, but then she abruptly surges to her feet. "All right. All this mushy stuff makes me hungry. Scrambled eggs?"

"Perfect. I'll get the toast going."

Two-and-a-half hours later we're all packed up and ready to go when I climb into the passenger seat and look over at Pippa.

"Let's do this."

Thirty

FLETCH

I haven't heard a thing from her in a couple of days and she hasn't returned any of my texts.

She was camping somewhere with her sister where they didn't have the best reception, but I know they had to go into town regularly, surely, she could've gotten in touch then.

The house has provided some distraction. With Bo's help I have most of the kitchen dismantled and we're in the process of painting the cabinets, replacing the hardware and doors, and building a new island around an old sideboard I found sitting out in the barn.

My first major project was supposed to be building a deck, but once I started tinkering in the kitchen, it kind of snowballed.

The large open concept space is a bit of a mess. My TV and couch—the only living room furniture I brought over —is covered in heavy duty plastic to protect it from paint and dust. Doors are off their hinges, two walls are only half painted, and instead of fixing either of those, I'm sitting here on the kitchen floor, sanding this old piece of furniture so I can convert it into a kitchen island because I thought Nella might like it.

So yeah, I'm pissed and about ready to hop in my truck and drive to Canada myself, when I hear a vehicle coming up the driveway.

I drop the sandpaper and get to my feet, brushing my dusty hands on the seat of my jeans as I make my way to the front door. I open it and barely have a chance to register the motorhome parked in my driveway when I'm nearly knocked on my ass by the woman running at me full tilt.

"It's beautiful!"

Her smile is wide and unrestrained as she lifts her face to me. A little over a month ago, when I met her, I had trouble seeing how pretty she was. Now, it's impossible to miss the sheer beauty that seems to radiate from her pores.

"This place," she prompts when I don't respond. "I'd seen it from the road but never had a close look. I had no idea the yard was so pretty, and those views coming down that driveway! The house is nice too. I love the porch, and—"

I swallow the rest of her ramble when I take her mouth.

Funny, I was pretty ticked off with her and had every intention of making her aware of it. It all seems pretty unimportant now. She's here, she looks great, sounds happy, she feels fucking amazing in my arms, and tastes even better.

"Hey, honey. I'm home," she jokes when I finally let her up for air.

"Good. Was about to come find you," I grumble, but only for show.

324

She combs her fingers through my beard, giving it a light tug.

"I missed you too, Fletch."

I'm clearly not fooling her for a second.

Right, a change of subject is in order.

"Where's your sister?"

I glance over her shoulder at the RV.

"She's at the rescue, next door." She grins up at me. "We're gonna be neighbors."

"I'd hoped we'd be a little more than fucking neighbors."

She bumps me with her shoulder. "I'm talking about us and the rescue."

There it is again—*us*.

I fucking love it. Who'd have thought?

"I meant eventually, of course," she adds.

Eventually, my ass.

"That why you brought the motorhome? You plan to camp out in my driveway?" I tease.

Her mouth tenses and she takes a step back. Clearly not enjoying the teasing.

"No. Lucy says I'll always have a bed *next door* waiting for me," she snaps.

Like that's going to happen.

"You have a bed here."

"Actually...I'm pretty sure we dropped off my bed at the dump just outside Cranbook last week."

I tug at her hair. "You're being a smart-ass."

"Maybe. And maybe you should try actually asking. You know, actual communication of intent could prevent so much misunderstanding."

I cup her face in my hands and press my smile against her lips.

"Babe...this place—including the big new bed I set up in the master—was meant to have you in it. Stay?"

"Oh, all right." She rolls those gorgeous hazel eyes, and I stifle a snort. "I'll stay."

"So why the motorhome?"

"Aside from a few big pieces that didn't fit, everything I own is packed in there."

Then she pushes past me into the house, aiming straight for the old sideboard I was working on.

Wow.

This is happening.

Part of me is waiting for the urge to run to hit me, but there's nothing. No panic, no anxiety, no second thoughts, just...happy.

"This is gorgeous!" she calls out, running her hands over the aged wood as she sits down beside it. "Where did you get this?"

She turns her head and beams that smile at me.

Nella, sitting on the floor of the kitchen I'm trying to make sure has enough room for my cooking and her baking, looking like there's nowhere else she wants to be.

Yeah, *very* fucking happy.

Nella

"Oh, sweet Jesus."

I literally see stars as his body collapses on me.

Fletch woke me up with his mouth. Best wake-up routine I've ever been introduced to. Better even than sipping coffee while watching the spectacular sunrise over Mineral Lake.

How we ended up in the bathroom, my body bent over the vanity with Fletch's weight pressing down on me, I have no idea. All I know is my limbs are like Jell-O and I don't think my heart will ever return to its normal rhythm.

"Morning, Babe," he mumbles in my neck.

"Hmh…" I barely manage to grunt and he starts to chuckle, his body shaking on top of me.

"That good, huh?"

I keep my eyes closed and don't react. It's not like he needs the boost to his ego, it's sizable enough.

I feel him push off me, his lips pressing a kiss between my shoulder blades before his weight disappears completely. Next, I hear the water in the shower turn on and Fletch's voice call out.

"Come on, Nella. Get your butt in here."

Groaning, I lift my face off the counter and stumble into the shower where I collide with his solid back. I instantly wrap my arms around him, pressing my cheek against his skin.

"You foiled my plan," I mumble.

"What plan was that?"

"I was gonna wake *you* up this morning. I had the whole thing planned. You were supposed to be the one left feeling boneless and relaxed on your birthday."

I feel his body shake when he chuckles.

"Are you complaining?"

I snuggle in a little closer.

"Well, no. But you wouldn't let me buy you anything so that was gonna be your birthday gift. Happy birthday, honey."

He removes my arms from around his waist and turns around to face me.

"Babe, waking up with my cock in your mouth would've been a fine start to my birthday, but nothing beats your taste on my lips." He brushes the wet hair off my face as he pulls up one eyebrow. "That said, nothing says happy birthday like a blowjob in the shower."

Fletch turns forty-eight today. I wouldn't have known if Bo hadn't mentioned it a few days ago when he came to work on the kitchen. Fletch brushed it off like it was nothing important and I gather he wasn't in the habit of celebrating, but this is the first birthday we've been together and I want to make it special.

Unfortunately, with our kitchen still in disarray I wasn't able to do any baking here. Alex was kind enough to let me use the big kitchen at the ranch yesterday. A few of the guys—including Fletch—had been off to Billings for a few days with a trailer full of young horses for a Livestock Commission horse sale—so the house was relatively quiet. Ama let me do my thing in the kitchen, but Thomas stuck close by for quality control. His idea, not mine.

We're supposed to head over to High Meadow to look at the six-year-old buckskin mare Fletch brought back from Billings. I have a sneaky suspicion he got her for me, thus stealing my thunder on his own birthday, but I have a few surprises up my sleeve as well.

One is the lunch I know Ama and Alex are putting together in honor of his birthday and the other is the massive Black Forest cake taking up the entire bottom shelf in the ranch fridge. Both involve food and his ranch family so I'm sure he'll enjoy those.

There is one more surprise I'm hoping to spring on him

at some point, but I'm not as confident about his reaction to that one so I'll play it by ear.

~

"You should turn this into a business. You can't get shit like this in Libby."

Bo shoves the other half of his Black Forest cake in his mouth.

"Fucking delicious," he mutters around the massive bite.

We never made it out to the barn.

We barely made it out of the truck when we pulled up to the ranch. Thomas was already out on the porch and announced it was *about fucking time* we got there because Ama had been slapping his hands away from the food all morning.

Fletch tried to throw me a dirty look when we walked inside to find my sister and Lucy, along with the entire team, assembled in the kitchen but he wasn't quite able to hide the upward tilt of his mouth underneath the beard.

The spread was amazing, Ama had apparently made Fletch's favorite things and I made mental notes what they were. It's only been a couple of weeks since I got back from Cranbrook and we're still in the process of figuring each other out, learning likes and dislikes.

My cake was a success, as evidenced by Bo wolfing down his second helping.

"Eventually I'd like to," I admit. "But it might be a while before I can actually work here. It's a lengthy process."

Bo raises an eyebrow before looking for Fletch, who is talking with Jonas over by the window.

"Yo, Fletch! Get your head outta your ass and marry her,

brother. Solves her problem and we can have cake like this all the time. It's not brain surgery."

Fletch's eyes come straight for me. I guess he's checking to see if I said anything to prompt this, but I just throw up my hands.

"Wasn't me."

Still, he heads over, stopping right in front of me so I'm forced to look up.

"You saying you don't want to?"

Wait. How did he come up with that idea?

"I never said that," I quickly protest.

A triumphant smirk pulls at his lips and subdued chuckles go up around me.

"Good. That's settled then," he says decisively. "We can get your blood test done in town tomorrow and pick up a marriage license at the county clerk's office."

I'm not sure what's happening, it feels like I just got the wind knocked out of me, and it takes me a moment to process what he says.

"Blood test?"

It's Ama who answers, a grin splitting her face.

"Women need to undergo a blood test in Montana. Only state in the country where that's still a requirement."

"Just women?"

She shrugs. "Honey, that's Montana for ya."

"That's barbaric," is Pippa's heartfelt contribution.

Over the next twenty minutes I let shared indignation at the archaic and misogynistic laws of this beautiful state distract me from what I fear may have been the closest I'll get to a wedding proposal.

Then the impromptu celebration breaks up, and Fletch pulls me toward a small paddock behind the breeding barn.

"She's beautiful."

I hold out my hand for the mare to sniff. She lets out a small snort before nuzzling my palm with her soft lips.

"What's her name?"

"Willow," Fletch answers.

"That's a pretty name for a very pretty girl," I mumble as I lift my other hand to rub her forehead. Something she lets me do without complaint.

"You like her?"

"She's really beautiful."

"Then she's yours."

Yup. As I suspected, he's stealing my thunder.

"Need I remind you this is your birthday and not mine?" I snip, giving him a look that does not seem to impress him much.

He's leaning with a hip against the fencepost and his arms crossed over his chest, looking relaxed and mildly amused.

"So?"

"So maybe you can save your surprises for when there's reason to celebrate me."

"Every day is reason to celebrate the woman I love."

Dammit.

That's a really good comeback.

"With a blood test and a run to the county clerk's office?"

He shrugs. "That's what's required for a marriage."

"So is the agreement of both parties, yet I didn't hear a question and I'm pretty sure I didn't give an answer." I cock my thumb over my shoulder in the direction of the ranch house. "Unless of course that back there in the kitchen was your idea of a proposal and you took my shocked silence as agreement."

Understanding lights his eyes and he pushes away from the fence to take a step toward me.

"It's important to you."

I roll my eyes, but it's mostly in an attempt not to show my emotions that suddenly wash over me.

"Seeing as it's the only proposal I'm likely to get in this lifetime; yeah."

He takes my hands in his and brings them to his mouth, kissing my knuckles.

"Gonna be honest with you, Nella. Married, not married. It doesn't make a lick of difference to me or the way I feel about you. I didn't realize it was that important to you or I would've handled that differently."

"I don't think it would be, normally, but—"

I'm about to share my last surprise with him when Willow suddenly neighs. I turn around to see she apparently caught sight of a few other horses in a neighboring field and is trotting along the fence line toward them. Fletch steps up behind me, folds his arms around my front, and rests his chin on my head as we watch her go.

"I'm sorry," he mumbles against my hair.

"Don't be. I'm just being...hormonal."

Not a word of a lie. I actually went to the clinic a few days ago to see if maybe I was perimenopausal. I'm forty-three, it would be well within the realm of possibilities. It wasn't until I was actually asked if there was a chance I could be pregnant—started saying no and caught myself—that was even on my radar.

Once it was, all the pieces started clicking together.

I take his hands and place them low on my belly. It takes him a couple of seconds, but then I feel him freeze behind me.

I hold my breath; I have no idea how he's going to react.

It's a lot. All of this is a lot and becoming more complicated by the minute.

I know it, though, I can't look at this any other way than as a gift. No matter how he will react.

Fletch's large hands slowly spread and relax on my stomach. His large body curves around me and he tucks his face in my neck, his lips brushing my ear.

"I'm holding perfection."

THE END

Keep reading for a sample of the next book in the series:

High Ground

High Ground

COMING AUGUST 8, 2022

Not much has gone according to plan for mechanic, Pippa Freling, recently. With lots of bridges burned behind her, she decides to stick close to her sister and give Montana a try. Things are looking up when she joins a local group of animal activists, buys an auto shop for a steal, and even tries her luck with the opposite sex. But it doesn't take long before her hopeful new future is derailed once again.
This time permanently.

Maintaining tight control is the stronghold in Sully Eckhart's life. It served him well during his years in special forces and has kept him out of trouble since. But his self-restraint stretches only so far whenever he finds himself faced with the one woman who has the ability to shake his determination. A woman he's tried to avoid for months—since the first time she shook his resolve—but who now finds herself in the middle of a serial murder case.

However, when she not only ends up a person of interest to the

FBI, but firmly in the crosshairs of a killer, he has no other option but to stick close.
And give up all control.

～

SULLY

"I've got something."

I circle the drone around, dipping a little lower to get a better view.

The red ball cap caught my eye on the first flyover. I can't recall one mentioned in the description of missing hunter, John Harper, but that doesn't necessarily mean anything. The bright splash of color in the rock gully below is definitely out of place and warrants closer investigation.

"Where?"

Jonas leans over my shoulder to see the small screen on the drone's controller.

"Give me a sec, I'm just swinging back over the spot. It'll be the left side of the screen on the rocks at the edge of the creek."

I maneuver the drone even lower between the trees.

"There he is. Fuck," Jonas mumbles.

Now I can make out the figure of a man in hunting camo, facedown in the water maybe six feet from where I spotted the ball cap.

Looks like it's going to be a recovery instead of a rescue.

The missing man has family back in Wyoming. He's here a few days before the opening of the bear season, in April every year, to get camp ready before his buddies show up. When they arrived two days ago, they found his belongings at camp but Harper was missing.

The start of the spring hunt is always chaotic so the game warden, with his hands full, bounced the call to the sheriff, who contacted us this morning.

High Mountain Trackers—our search and rescue team—often gets called in for missing individuals and we frequently work together with law enforcement. We search on horseback, which is a bonus in these mountains and often hard-to-access terrain. A bit old-style, but we also utilize technology in the form of the Matrice, my drone. Well, not mine technically, but I operate it. It's a great tool to get the lay of the land before we go in with the horses.

Sometimes we get lucky—like today—and find what we're looking for on the drone's video feed.

"Even if we could get a chopper out here, there's no way they'd be able to get him out. Good thing we brought Hazel," Jonas observes.

Hazel is our new mule. She came to us through Hart Horse Rescue which belongs to my boss Jonas's spouse, Alexandra Hart. The team's mounts are all sturdy quarter drafts, which can handle a bit, but adding an extra body to their load when they already have to carry us through often rough terrain is asking a lot.

The mule comes in handy, and even though she's ornery and doesn't particularly like people, she gets along well with the horses and she doesn't spook. Perfect for transport. The modified saddle Jonas picked up has a fully adjustable backrest and straps to secure even an injured or unconscious individual. Previously we'd have to double up on one of the horses, often slowing us down and sometimes causing more injury.

"I'll catch up with you," I tell the guys.

I still have to bring the drone back and pack it up, which won't take me long but it doesn't make sense for the others to wait. My horse, Cisko, won't have any trouble catching up to Jonas and Bo.

There's only three of us today. My other teammates, James and Fletch, left for Helena this morning with one of our prize studs, Phantom. Aside from High Mountain Trackers, Jonas also owns High Meadow Ranch. It's a fairly small stud and breeding facility where we all work when we're not out on a search.

Up until recently, Fletch and I were neighbors in staff cabins on the ranch, but last fall Fletch bought a neighboring property where he lives with his new wife, Nella. Bo has always lived in Libby, twenty minutes up the highway, and James and his family live just south of here.

I like my cabin so I don't plan on going anywhere. I've got no family of my own, am close to work, and like the convenience of having my meals cooked for me by either Ama—James's wife—or Alex. I occasionally enjoy shooting the shit with Jonas's dad, Thomas, over a glass of good bourbon and a rare Cuban cigar on the porch, and other than that I don't need much.

Sure-footed Cisko closes the distance to the others before they reach the bottom of the gully. Bo dismounts first and crouches down beside Harper, who is partially submersed.

He reaches out to feel for a pulse but immediately veers back. "What the fuck?"

"What's wrong?" Jonas voices.

"If that's Harper, I'll fucking eat my hat," Bo announces. "Whoever that is has been gone a while longer."

Both Jonas and I get down for a better look.

Now I can see he's definitely been here for some time. From what is left of his head, this guy looks to have cropped gray hair, whereas Harper's was supposed to be dark.

"Doesn't look like he tripped and fell," I point out.

I can't tell for sure, but it looks to me like he was shot. A high-velocity rifle bullet to the back of the head would leave that kind of damage. Doesn't exactly appear accidental either. More like an execution.

"No, it doesn't," Jonas agrees. "Hands off, Bo. We're gonna have to get the sheriff in here."

He gets on the radio right away and relays the information to Ama back at the ranch, who promises to get Sheriff Ewing on the horn.

"I spotted a clear-cut just south of here," I volunteer. "There's gotta be a trail leading to it. That may be easier access for the sheriff's department. I can go check it out."

"Sounds like a plan. Whatever we can do to cut down waiting time, because we still have a missing hunter to find," Jonas points out.

Good point. This clearly isn't Harper so he's still out here somewhere. Hopefully just lost and not in similar condition to this guy.

I swing back into the saddle and guide Cisko across the shallow creek and up the south end of the gully. I noticed the clearing on the other side of a ridge. We left the vehicles and trailers up where Harper and his friends usually set up base camp, which is north of here, and made our way down on horseback. It took us close to two hours to find the body so it would be good if I could find a faster alternate route for the sheriff to take.

This side isn't as steep and it takes me less than fifteen minutes to get to the edge of the clearing.

I didn't expect to see the motorhome tucked in under the trees on the opposite side, but I'm completely thrown when a familiar figure steps out of the door.

*****

Pippa

Hell, no.

Last person I want to run into up here—or anywhere else for that matter—is heading straight toward me.

"Once wasn't enough?" he says, the customary friendly expression gone from his face.

I know exactly what he's referring to.

"Are you suggesting I should let fear rule me?" I snap back.

Last year, when I first camped near Libby, I'd fallen victim to a family of thieves stealing recreational vehicles. I was hurt in the process and ended up with a brain injury and memory loss, but I survived and came out stronger. It's how I first met Sully, actually. My sister and her now husband were the ones who found me, but he's the one who transported me out of the woods on his horse. I owe them my life, Sully included, but that doesn't mean they get to rule it. I'm not about to let what happened keep me from enjoying what I love to do most; seeking out nature and solitude.

There's something about being entirely on your own and self-sufficient—a simpler way of being—which feels both empowering and humbling at the same time. My experience last year has only made that feeling stronger.

Sully swings out of the saddle and turns his body toward me.

"No, but at least be a bit more cautious. Stick closer to town, to other people."

"That would kinda defeat the purpose now, wouldn't it?"

I know I'm not being very nice, but his sudden concern for me is coming out of left field. A far cry from the cold asshole he turned out to be last time I saw him. That was a huge mistake I unfortunately can add to a long list of them and will definitely not be repeated.

"Pippa—"

"No, Sully. I'm a big girl. I don't need you—of all people—looking out for me. I'm perfectly safe here."

I watch the nostrils of his patrician nose flare as his blue eyes narrow on me. He's annoyed, which is too fucking bad.

But then he takes the wind out of my self-righteous sails.

"There's a dead man with a hole the size of a fist in the back of his head in a gully less than a mile from here. You may want to reconsider that."

My exit wasn't exactly graceful.

Never mind that I was already packing up to head back to town for an appointment, but after he dropped that bombshell, I was in a real hurry to get out of there. Especially after he mentioned law enforcement being on the way. I hustled, I'm not stupid. Aside from the fact I'm seriously freaked out right now, I know what will happen when the sheriff arrives and I don't want to be stuck here for hours when I have somewhere to be.

Without another word for Sully, I hopped in my rig and carefully worked my way back down the logging trail.

"Hey, you're back," Marcie answers her phone.

"On my way back to town now. I just picked up a signal."

"How was it?"

"Great, I got a few good hikes in. Nothing else to report though."

The last spot I was at was a little farther up the mountain, north from here. It's where I discovered a couple of baiting barrels on one of my hikes. I immediately packed up and left that spot, calling my friend, Marcie, on my way out to alert the group. That was four days ago but I hadn't been ready to head back to civilization yet, which is why I decided to set up camp down here.

Apparently, a stone's throw from a corpse.

I don't know what it is about me that seems to be in the wrong place at the wrong time a lot. Maybe it is true that I attract trouble. It's something my ex used to say. Of course, he was more trouble than anything else.

I wasn't even aware baiting bears was a thing until I bumped into a pair of hunters in November of last year when I was boondocking on the east side of Libby, not far from the Kootenay River. They were hauling buckets of what smelled like rotting fish and bags of stinky garbage down the trail.

Marcie and I met at rehab in the hospital last fall—she'd been in a car accident—and had struck up a friendship. She's a local real estate agent, an avid outdoorswoman, and also an animal activist. Something I can identify with. When I mentioned my encounter with the hunters appearing to carry garbage into the wilderness, she explained about baiting bear, which is apparently legal in other states but not Montana. A contentious point for many local hunters and guides.

The basic premise is they leave food in a particular spot, starting late winter. Then when the bears wake up from hibernation, half-starved, the stench of rotting food draws them to these spots. They gorge themselves and keep returning for an easy meal. At the start of hunting season, all the hunters have to do is sit in a blind and bide their time. It's like shooting fish in a barrel.

I don't care if it's legal in other states, I find the whole thing reprehensible. I'm not at all against hunting, but let it at least be equal.

Through Marcie I got involved with Fair Game Alliance, a group of passionate individuals who monitor for that kind of illegal activity. All Fair Game does is keep an eye out and when they see anything suspicious, they alert the Lincoln County game warden to intervene. Here in the Libby area, the game warden has his hands full and can't be everywhere this time of year, which is why volunteers like me keep our eyes open.

It gives me a sense of purpose. Something I'm craving after a good year of floundering.

Oh, it was fun at first, going where the wind blew me, making a bit of money here and there putting my mechanic's license to good use with some RV repair services. But I started craving steady roots and was on my way back home when I ran into trouble here in Montana last fall. Since then my sister, Nella, has moved here and is making a life for herself. Married a local guy, started baking for some local businesses, and now even has a little one on the way. She's all the family I have, and there's no way I want to go back to Canada now.

There's nothing left for me there. Any dreams I may have had for my future have burned to the ground. The marriage, the business I built from scratch, the family we were supposed to have, those are all gone. My ex saw to that. All I ended up with was a whack of money he had to pay me to buy me out of the business that used to be mine. I bought the Jayco motorhome, stuck the rest of the money in mutual funds, and took off to find myself again.

And I did. Right here in Libby, Montana.

I'm trying to put down roots here. Last month I bought the closed-up auto repair shop on the south side of town I passed regularly. Marcie was able to get me a great deal. Unfortunately, as a Canadian, I can buy a business, but I can't actually work in it. Not without a green card or at the very least a work visa, which I already applied for, but even a visa can take months.

In the meantime I wait, I volunteer, and I try to stay out of trouble.

Which is why I need to avoid Sully Eckhart like the plague. The man is like salted caramel; one taste just makes you want more.

I should know.

ABSOLVING BLUE

REVEALING ANNIE

DISSECTING MEREDITH

WATCHING TRIN

Rock Point Series:

KEEPING 6

CABIN 12

HWY 550

10-CODE

Northern Lights Collection:

A CHANGE OF TIDE

A CHANGE OF VIEW

A CHANGE OF PACE

SnapShot Series:

SHUTTER SPEED

FREEZE FRAME

IDEAL IMAGE

Portland, ME, Series:

FROM DUST

CRUEL WATER

THROUGH FIRE

STILL AIR

LuLLaY (a Christmas novella)

About the Author

USA Today bestselling author Freya Barker loves writing about ordinary people with extraordinary stories.

Driven to make her books about 'real' people; she creates characters who are perhaps less than perfect, each struggling to find their own slice of happy, but just as deserving of romance, thrills and chills in their lives.

Recipient of the ReadFREE.ly 2019 Best Book We've Read All Year Award for "Covering Ollie, the 2015 RomCon "Reader's Choice" Award for Best First Book, "Slim To None", Finalist for the 2017 Kindle Book Award with "From Dust", and Finalist for the 2020 Kindle Book Award with "When Hope Ends", Freya spins story after story with an endless supply of bruised and dented characters, vying for attention!

www.freyabarker.com

www.ingramcontent.com/pod-product-compliance
Lightning Source LLC
Chambersburg PA
CBHW060853210726